BAND OF BACHELORS: LUCAS

SEAL BROTHERHOOD

SHARON HAMILTON

AUTHOR'S NOTE

One of the important things about writing romantic suspense is that the stories have to be believable, to be compelling drama. And because it's romance, we add the elements of the romantic relationship that is every bit as important as the suspense. I don't pretend to guess what the proper formula is. For me I guess I weigh heavier on the romance. My justification is that falling in love is every bit the mystery as anything else, and highly suspenseful too as the chemistry brings two strangers together in ways they never could have imagined.

I've had some famous mystery and suspense authors say they can't write romance.

Well, love is the biggest mystery of all, isn't it? The chemistry that joins two people from that first kiss to the blending of the hearts and minds until that soulful connection is matched on the inside, as it is on the outside.

I take liberties with facts. I take liberties with news accounts. But if you were to ask me if something like what happened in this story could happen in the U.S. today, I would tell you that it probably is happening.

I am grateful to the men and women who protect us at home and abroad, for without them, we are not truly free.

And I'd be out of a job.

Sharon
Sonoma County, California
September 11, 2015

SEAL BROTHERHOOD SERIES
Accidental SEAL (Book 1)
Fallen SEAL Legacy (Book 2)
SEAL Under Covers (Book 3)
SEAL The Deal (Book 4)
Cruisin' For A SEAL (Book 5)
SEAL My Destiny (Book 6)
SEAL Of My Heart (Book 7)

BAD BOYS OF SEAL TEAM 3
SEAL's Promise (Book 1)
SEAL My Home (Book 2)
SEAL's Code (Book 3)

BAND OF BACHELORS
Lucas (Book 1)
Alex (Book 2)

TRUE BLUE SEALS
True Navy Blue (prequel to Zak)
Zak (Book 1)

NOVELLAS
SEAL Encounter
SEAL Endeavor
True Navy Blue (prequel to Zak)
Fredo's Secret
Nashville SEAL

DEDICATION

I always dedicate my SEAL Brotherhood books to the brave men and women who defend our shores and keep us safe. Without their sacrifice, and that of their families—because a warrior's fight always includes his or her family—I wouldn't have the freedom and opportunity to make a living writing these stories. They sometimes pay the ultimate price so we can debate, argue, go have coffee with friends, raise our children and see them have children of their own.

One of my favorite tributes to warriors resides on many memorials, including one I saw honoring the fallen of WWII on an island in the Pacific:

"When you go home
Tell them of us, and say
For your tomorrow,
We gave our today."

These are my stories created out of my own imagination. Anything that is inaccurately portrayed is either my mistake, or done intentionally to disguise something I might have overheard over a beer or in the corner of one of the hangouts along the Coronado Strand.

Wounded Warriors is the one charity I give to on a regular basis. I encourage you to get involved and tell them thank you:

support.woundedwarriorproject.org

CHAPTER 1

Lucas woke up with the sun slicing daggers of light into his eyes.

Fuck me.

He rolled over to shield his face from the bright morning and fell off the couch, right onto his tailbone.

Goddamit. The sharp pain added to the bruise he'd already created from previous sleepless nights. His ass had made divots between the second and third cushions of the sectional, which was as equally uncomfortable to sit on. The couch's grey scratchy fabric was Scotchguarded, making his back and balls itch. His buddies on SEAL Team 3 had picked up this wonderful piece of *loungery* for two hundred bucks four months back. The San Diego Goodwill had been so happy to get rid of it, they gave the team the matching loveseat without charging a penny extra.

From the floor, Lucas stared eye-level at the hunk of junk he'd battled with all night long and knew it would still go up like a torch regardless of the Scotchguard. As he pulled his body up, the matching loveseat veering off to the right gaped at him, its bent footrests looking like huge gumless jaws. The thing was laughing at him.

It was nothing like his king-size bed with the Egyptian cotton sheets at home—the home he'd been kicked out of a month prior. He hadn't expected to have to sleep on his buddies' couch this long. When he'd first been shown the door, he hadn't been too worried, convinced Connie would soon change her mind and invite him back.

He'd envisioned that 'welcome home' party every day and night, in spite of the fact that his last vision of her was of her screaming at the top of her lungs, those delicious blue veins at the sides of her neck protruding like they were fat, blue birthday candles. His sobbing three-year-old daughter stood next to her mother, burying her face in Connie's thigh as the toddler screamed in her arms. It broke Lucas' heart to see his wife clutch the baby, his horror-filled expression showing fear and confusion.

That was one shitty day, but he knew in his heart of hearts that at any time, she'd soften and he'd be back home, in their bed, sliding against her smooth thighs and kissing the place between her legs, making her scream his name. Oh, he was the candy man, all right. His dick got hard just thinking about it. She'd never had a man go down on her before they got together. She'd been a good Catholic girl, and the nuns had filled her head with stories of how the germs from his hot tongue would poison her womb.

As if they knew.

His arousal meant only one thing: he'd have to finish it in the shower or he wouldn't be able to get his jeans on without pain.

Someone swung open one of the four bedroom doors with enough force they nearly ripped it off its hinges. "What the fuck just happened?" asked Jake, his mop of black hair sticking straight up like an unclipped Mohawk. "We just have an earthquake, Lucas?"

Lucas grimaced. "No, that would be my ass hitting the ground."

"Would you quit that? You'll wake up the whole fuckin' household."

Lucas stood in his shorts, bare-chested and barefoot. He inclined his head to the side, arms outstretched, palms up as if listening for the complaints—which didn't materialize—from the other three rooms. "And your point is?" Lucas asked, after a few seconds of silence.

"Geez, Lucas, would you put your fire hose away. I've seen it, remember?" Jake pointed to Lucas' groin.

Standing at full attention, Lucas' *unit* had found freedom from the hole in his American flag shorts and was ready to par-tay. He quickly tucked it back in, but it popped out again. That time, he turned his back to Jake, properly stowed his cannon, then whipped around to find that Jake had disappeared back into his room.

Only two of the bedrooms had their own private bath with a shower, since the guest bath only contained a toilet with a cracked seat and a sink. Lucas didn't want to wake anyone else up, so he headed for the half bath, looking forward to perhaps working on his aim while studying the raunchy posters pinned up all around the little room. They didn't have to worry about entertaining females in the men's club of a house, since most of the SEALs who lived there had sworn off any women, except professionals who would definitely not be looking at the posters.

He washed his hands twice, feeling more relaxed, then padded into the kitchen to make some coffee. He covered the coffee grinder with a towel to muffle the sound and inhaled the only luxury the boys allowed themselves: fresh ground coffee.

He paused his musing to glare at the coffee pot, performing its death gurgle. He surveyed his temporary 'home sweet home'. The garbage can was overflowing—even the recycle side—with beer bottles, pizza boxes, and half-gallon plastic orange juice containers. A wet bath sheet and t-shirt hung over an old, paint-splattered folding chair, one of four, surrounding a square card table with coffee rings stained into it. Their big-screen TV sat on top of two pallets they'd hauled from the dumpster. The light beige rug was mostly *dark* beige from oil, food, and coffee stains, and one plate-sized red stain from someone's Hawaiian Punch spilled a week back. They'd been trying to clean up each little accident, until the punch mishap. After that, they understood that when they deployed, they'd not get their deposit back on the house. Ryan said they might even owe the landlord something.

Look at me...already considering myself part of this sorry band of bachelors.

Lucas chastised himself for even considering this to be the case. He'd be out of there so fast it would take them a couple of days to miss him.

Sorry-assed sailors. Unlike his Connie, the bachelor frogs had only themselves to blame for their poor choices. Jake had children littered all over the world, just like their old pal, Gunny, who used to own the gym they all trained at. He wasn't exactly sure how many he'd fathered, but knew it would take two hands to count.

The coffee pot began to shut down, as he took stock of his friends.

Cory Brown was a preacher's son, way too trusting, and had started dating girls from his father's church after high school, until several parents complained he was deflowering the future generation of Sunday school teachers. And then he knocked one up, and that was it. Reverend Brown made sure the right thing happened. That marriage didn't last more than a month after the baby was born, and then Cory was being sued for child support that would take over half his pay, including his SEAL bonus.

Ryan and Alex got married in a double ceremony in Las Vegas, and had similar stories of woe.

No, none of them had spent much time finding a fine, quality girl like Connie. Yes, she was a bit hotheaded, but Lucas kind of liked it when she got steamed up, as long as it was something he could wiggle his way out of. The unfortunate bachelor party in Vegas was the last straw, though. And the stripper he'd had his photograph taken with turned out to be a transvestite, not that it made any difference to Connie. Lucas had been hoping it would.

But all that would be over soon.

He turned off the coffee maker, poured himself a cup, added a shot glass full of real Half and Half and walked out onto the deck overlooking the valley below and Coronado Island in the distance. He considered getting the boys up because a Specialist from Virginia was coming to do some training with them, even though it was Saturday. The military didn't observe weekends if the upcoming mission was urgent. This one apparently was.

Below him in the parking lot, a sweet brunette in an impossibly tight, short skirt stepped out of a cherry-red VW convertible. She looked up at him, shielding her eyes with one hand and slinging her large bag over her shoulder with the other. Lucas straightened himself up and sucked in his gut, smiling as her gaze found him and gave him an appreciative perusal.

He told himself it wasn't really a bad thing. One thing to look, another to, well, partake. He didn't want to blow his chances of sliding back into Connie's expensive silk sheets, or being buried deep inside her sweet little jellyroll. But looking was okay. He'd just not chat her up. So he waved.

Her grin was fine. She looked like the kind of girl who had all manner of dirty little thoughts. She licked her lips, straightened her upper torso and smoothed over her tummy and hips with those palms of hers. One wrist had a charm bracelet that tinkled in the distance. Without an invitation, she headed straight for the entrance to the upper floors, right below him.

Holy hotness. Did she think I invited her up?

Inside, he found Ryan, Alex and Cory up and showered, making a barefoot line in the kitchen like old men at a rescue mission.

"I say strawberry waffles before we head over to the base," said Cory as he poured his coffee.

"Ask them to leave the whipped cream can this time," said Ryan.

Jake exited from his bedroom, followed by a cloud of steam, matching the shirtless wonders in the kitchen.

Cory nearly spit out his mug of Joe. "Dayum, Shipley. Good thing we're not shooting this morning. I'm going to be shaking for a week," barked Cory.

"Use more cream," was Lucas' answer. "Hey, guys, you know anything about this Thom guy? He's some kind of security expert?"

"Something to do with a little pod of terrorists they encountered over in Mosul." Alex sat down on the floor, back straight against the wall, his feet out in front of him. Ryan soon joined him.

"Kyle said they've got information the group plans to do something here in California. A retaliation," added Jake.

"Helluva thing to do on a Saturday, haul us in there," said Cory.

"What the fuck difference does it make?" Jake wrinkled his nose and forehead. "Not like I've got a date."

Lucas snorted. "Oh, so you call those hookups 'dates' now? You really go on dates, Jake? Man, I must be rubbing off on you."

"You should talk." Alex and Ryan were punching each other in the arm, which escalated into a coffee fight. Alex continued, caramel-colored liquid dripping off his chin. "Don't see you dating anytime soon, shitface."

Lucas hated the fact that his last name had taken the ugly moniker ever since the unfortunate bachelor party he didn't remember.

"Geez. I hang around you guys too much and I might stop believing in true love."

Lucas was pelted with coffee, one of the SEALs throwing the ceramic mug itself, which hit him at bicep level.

"Okay, okay. I get it. It's just that I'm not ready to give up on my marriage like you guys. I may not have as many kids as you do, Jake, and I may only have known her a little bit longer than you two knew your wives, Groves and Nowicki, but I *definitely* know how to fuckin' use a condom, Cory—*especially* if I'm gonna screw a girl in the back of my father's sanctuary."

"Hallelujah, praise the Lord," someone shouted.

"A fuckin' religious experience, I call it," Jake said as he high-fived Cory.

"See, that's where you guys go wrong. You don't treat women with respect."

No one said a word. Then the unofficial spokesman for the group, Jake, inserted his opinion. "So, if you feel like you don't fit in, why don't you fuckin' leave?"

The silence that followed made Lucas nervous. He could sense more than a couple of his buddies felt he'd crossed the line. There were some hurt feelings they often didn't verbalize, but he sure could feel it. He knew he had to be careful.

"You don't know a damned thing until you've really walked around in another man's shoes. Or, in Cory's case, his high heels." Lucas delivered it straight and for just one second he thought he'd made thing worse.

But then the catcalls began, which was a signal things were returning to normal. Lucas relaxed enough to apologize and make it sound like he meant it. And he did. The doorbell buzzed.

"You know," said Jake, who walked over to Lucas and fist-bumped him, "you're probably right. You're the one who's gonna make it in this relationship game. For us assholes, well, I think we're pretty much fucked."

All of them laughed.

The doorbell buzzed again twice this time, and Cory jogged over and opened it. Lucas couldn't hear anything but a sweet voice asking if she could talk to Lucas. He didn't know how, but he just knew it belonged to the lady in the red VW. *She knows my name?* He was flattered, until he remembered his situation, and Connie.

"Sure, come right in, ma'am," Cory offered, showing her the way with his arm.

Her bright red lips were the same color as the VW. She had the whole ladybug thing going on—with her black skirt, the black and white polka-dot blouse that was a bit sheer, showing him she wore bright white, lacy underthings—his personal favorite. She kept her knees together as she carefully stepped over their dirty carpet, her spiked heels making her balance a little difficult. She extended her hand with the charm bracelet softly clinking, and he extended his.

"Holy crap, Shipley, you've been holding out on us," someone said. The team separated and gave Lucas and the girl space like a drop of oil in water.

"So, you're Lucas Shipley," she said sweetly, and then gave him a devilish smile that made his shorts erupt.

He nodded nervously as she shifted her bag, which had fallen off her shoulder.

"Excuse me," she said as she extracted her hand and unzipped her purse. Bringing out a large white envelope, she didn't give him time to stop admiring her shapely form.

"You've been served."

CHAPTER 2

Marcy Gelland looked over at the woman who was ending her marriage of five years. Connie Shipley was initialing and signing where the little orange arrows indicated. It wasn't easy, Marcy knew, to just wash your hands of a marriage, especially a marriage with property and children. She saw how resolute Connie was, how firmly she pressed, signing her name with a big script flourish like she was autographing a bestseller in front of a crowd of people. The baby was trying to grab her pen, then her hair, the top of her dress, her earrings, but still Connie persisted, gently peeling back his chubby hands. Her young daughter was coloring with felt-tipped pens on the dark blue carpet at her feet.

She knew there would come a time during the process when Connie would wonder if she was doing the right thing. That was always the risk in taking on real estate listings where the couple was divorcing. One moment they hated each other, then the next they were doing the hot and dirty on the kitchen floor. She'd worked with couples who started out being adversaries, requiring her to take a neutral stance. But if one of them wanted to keep the marriage together, it was a fifty-fifty chance that party would prevail, and then suddenly representing them became impossible. Harder still were the cases when the house had already sold, and the buyers were looking forward to moving in.

But as she watched Connie with the paperwork and discussed the numbers with her, Marcy had the impression the woman was completely sure of her decision.

"So, when can I get Lucas' signature?" Marcy asked the attractive blonde Navy wife as she bounced her baby on her knee.

"Sorry. That's your job, Marcy. I'm hoping he'll cooperate, but I'm not sure."

"So you are the one forcing this, then?"

The baby was fussing. Connie drew a bottle from the large satchel under the table and unceremoniously stuffed the nipple in the baby's mouth. "Excuse me. What did you ask?" She frowned, bouncing the youngster.

"It was *your* decision to sell everything off, then? Did you try to work it out, go to counseling?"

Connie gave her a look she knew quite well. Her half-lidded eyes told her she was tired of trying to explain it, even to herself. "Not sure whose great idea it was to post the pictures of the SEAL bachelor party online, but it was irrefutable evidence."

"Ah." Marcy studied her. She decided to let it go without asking for further clarification. "But he won't be surprised, I guess."

Mrs. Shipley laughed, tossing back her head. The baby's arm had traveled down Connie's shirt, between her breasts, while his other hand fisted his blond curls at the temples. That's when Marcy saw an anchor tat on Connie's right breast, and underneath the anchor was the name *Lucas*, written in fancy script. She wondered what Connie would do to cover up or alter that message.

"I'm pretty sure he expected to be invited back. But I don't think it was me he wanted. Just my bed." Connie followed the comment by raising her right eyebrow and giving Marcy a sultry look.

Marcy sensed it was not a good idea to pry any further, but she did need some help getting the listing contract signed.

Connie put the empty bottle back in the diaper bag and put the baby over her shoulder. Marcy thought she handled the little one with callused indifference, as she lifted him up and down against her shoulder and chest until they heard a gargantuan burp followed by sounds of spillage.

"Dammit," Connie said as she stood up, handed the baby to Marcy, and then retrieved a cotton cloth from the bag, wiping her neck and shoulder, her front, and her back. Then she wiped down the chair and dabbed the carpet.

Marcy had never held a baby before, so she continued to grip him under his armpits as the blue-eyed cherub stared back, then promptly spit-up clotted milk, which dripped down his chin and soaked into his cotton t-shirt.

Connie came to her side, taking away the baby before the smelly liquid fell on Marcy. "Did he get you wet? Oh, Marcy, I'm so sorry," she said, holding out her cloth.

"He's got a bunch of stuff—," but before Marcy could complete her sentence, Connie had eliminated the evidence.

"Look, next is going to be a huge explosion," Connie said as she patted the baby's underside, "and you don't want to be around for that one. So I've got about two minutes." She fished out a card and handed it to Marcy. "Here's his cell phone, but the email no longer works. He's getting something else set up, since he no longer lives at the house."

"Gotcha. So I should call him?"

"Yes. Now, let me just tell you a couple of quick things and then—" Connie sniffed in the baby's diaper area—"so far so good. I feel like I should warn you: do not believe a word the man says. He's a sweet talker, and he might even come onto you, you know, try to seduce you so you'll go easy on him?"

"Oh, not to worry, Connie. Besides, I have a boyfriend," Marcy lied.

"Well, that doesn't matter one whit to him. I could tell you stories. I got tired of being all alone and scared to death while he was overseas. And then when he came home, he either wanted to screw day and night or he wouldn't want to do anything. He'd just watch TV. The kids would be screaming, and he'd be near comatose. I needed a big fuckin' break. I'd been stuck with them for months sometimes and here he couldn't help out, lift a finger."

Marcy was filled with compassion for the woman who felt abandoned, tied down with kids she was responsible for raising nearly on her own. Whatever glue had held this marriage together was gone.

"Then there was the staying out late, drinking with the guys—Marcy, he was hanging out more with them than with me. If he didn't have some bar thing to go to, some fuckin' *Macho Brotherhood* thing to do, he was in bed." She wiped a tear from her cheek. "Those guys are always getting married, divorced, their ladies leaving them. It's all just one excuse to Par-Tay. And he's got these loser friends who have messed up their marriages, too. They're a bad influence on him."

Marcy had gotten the picture minutes ago, but Connie seemed hell-bent on smashing her points in with a dull knife. "What about counseling?" she asked.

"Counseling? Those guys don't do that. Deathly afraid someone will label them as unstable and they'll lose their precious Trident. He didn't like to talk about feelings, especially *my* feelings. He was like, 'So, join a gym, or why not take up a hobby, like quilting or gardening.'" Connie rolled her eyes. "I mean, really? I'm trying to raise two kids all by myself, and he was streaking out there clear across the world from me, and doing who knows what that he couldn't talk about. Marcy, it was all just too much."

Like it was an exclamation mark to Connie's speech, they both heard the explosion in the baby's diaper. Those big blue eyes looked to Marcy as if she had an answer for him.

Marcy wrinkled her nose at the smell. "What do you need?"

"I need to get my life back. I need a nanny."

After Connie left, Marcy gave the SEAL a call. She heard loud music in the background, some whistles and "Oh yeah, yeah, baby." Marcy knew Lucas Shipley was at some sort of strip club.

"Hallo?" The husky, inebriated voice boomed in her ear.

"Is this Lucas Shipley?" she asked timidly.

"Who the fuck wants to know? You drive a red Volkswagen?"

"Pardon?"

"It's a simple question," he slurred. "Do you fuckin' drive a red Volkswagen? Inquiring minds want to know, darlin'. You might as well jump on in with the good news. Everyone else has."

"No."

A loud cheer went up as she heard a female voice in the background. The bump and grind music was so loud, the phone was beginning to cut out.

"Hello, baby. You have a fine ass." His sexy whisper was barely audible.

"Excuse me?" Marcy's back straightened as she felt the jolt travel down her spine.

"Ah, fuck, honey. I'm hanging up the phone right now." He whispered to Marcy, "'Excuse me, it's been nice, but I gotta go." She heard him shout out to the stripper, "No! Baby, don't go!"

The line went dead.

Marcy nearly threw her phone against the wall. It was all the evidence she needed to be totally convinced Connie Shipley was indeed doing the right thing for herself and her young family. She could completely understand why she wanted to separate from this scumbag of a husband.

Marcy was going to help her make him pay.

CHAPTER 3

The morning began just like it always did. Lucas fell off the couch. Behind Jake's closed door, Lucas heard, "Fuck!" Climbing back onto the scratchy couch, he tried to bury his head under his pillow as Jake let loose a string of invectives. That started another SEAL yelling at him, and then Cory swung open his door and came running out so fast, Lucas thought he was going to get thrown over the balcony.

"Would you fuckin' quit this shit, Lucas? We gotta tie you to the sofa?"

"Maybe I should get a rollaway?"

Alex appeared right behind Cory with his eyes narrowing. "I think you need to get yourself another crash pad, Lucas. It's clear this is a more permanent arrangement—and you're becoming a pain in the ass. Around here, sleeping in on Sunday mornings is sacred. *Sacred!* You need to find yourself another king-sized bed somewhere, and fast."

Lucas thought about the night before. They'd dropped Thom off at his hotel, but the SEAL from Virginia Beach couldn't walk, so they'd had to carry him into the room. It had fallen to Lucas to fish the room key out of the man's pants, and that wasn't pleasant at all.

He vaguely remembered Thom's wife calling. *Wait a minute.*

"Did Connie call?" he asked, sure someone's wife called. Or girlfriend. His mind was totally fuzzy.

He was about to ask the little crowd gathered again when the sound of the coffee grinder jolted him harder than if he'd been hit in the eye socket with a dull spear. Holding his ears with his palms did nothing to stop the pain.

Lucas collapsed again and waited for silence.

"Check your phone, asshole," Jake barked. "Now, in addition to having you over here at no rent, out of the goodness of our hearts, you want us to be your answering service, as well?"

"Okay, fair enough," Lucas said as he checked his cell. "I don't recognize this number." He hesitated and decided to hit redial later. "So, on that other point, I'm willing to share in the rent. I can pay in advance, up front. Question is where do I sleep?"

The unanimous answer was, "Not in my room."

Jake stepped up to deliver the final ultimatum. "I think you're shit out of luck, sailor. You need to find some place permanent."

"I really think she's gonna change her mind. Something tells me she's just bluffing." Lucas thought about all those deployments he came home and all he wanted to do was stay in bed and screw. Connie wanted relief from the kids. Why didn't he see that? But Lucas was so damned happy to be alive, to be home, to be in his bed again with the woman who made him feel terrific, when she was into it, he thought she'd be just as into him. Wasn't that what she missed all the time he was away? He couldn't figure her out. He was, after doing it for Connie, for all the people in this wonderful country. Why couldn't she get that?

"Seriously? You really think she'd go to all the trouble and expense of filing for divorce—that had to cost her at least a grand—*and* have it served, and you're still thinking she's gonna take you back?" Alex was shaking his head, his mouth puckered like he'd just taken a spoonful of motor oil.

"What fuckin' planet are you on, man?" Ryan asked.

Connie had accused him of being insensitive. But he *was* being sensitive. He was going out with his buds, not leaving them alone. Some of them had gotten home to find their wives with other men, even pregnant by other men. Other fuckin *regular Navy* guys and that was just tight. Nothing good about that. They were all responsible for each other. He wouldn't expect they'd abandon him, so why shouldn't he support them? It wasn't about the drinking or the strippers, it was about the community, and the healing that occurred when they all hung out together. Everyone returning home whole meant fixing stuff on the way back, as well as the adjustment to being home.

He could see now this would never be good enough for Connie. She had to be the center of attention, even ahead of the kids, and that bothered him. She just didn't get it. And she never would. She was like a clock that had been over sprung and would never again purr like that kitten he liked in bed, the lady who drove him wild with fantasies all during his time overseas.

"Redial, my man. Then I'm going back to bed," Jake added.

Lucas punched the red arrow on his phone, and the call was connected.

'This is Marcy Gelland from the Coronado Bay Realty. I'm either on the other line or assisting clients. If you would leave your name and number and the reason for your call, I'll get back to you as soon as I'm free. Thanks, and make it a great day!'

Lucas hung up. "Realtor," he said sheepishly. The day was suddenly turning dark.

Jake started to laugh. "You son of a gun, Lucas. Don't you have a clue what's happening to you? Your wife is trying to sell the house right out from under you."

"I'll just give my tenants notice and move into it. Mom left it to me when she passed. I can't afford both houses anyway," Lucas answered. "She's stupid to sell it. Don't know how she'll afford to get another place since she's not working."

Ryan leaned in, handing Lucas a fresh mug of coffee with the usual dosage of cream. "She doesn't have to work, my man. *You* do."

Marcy sounded a bit frosty on the phone, Lucas thought. She insisted on a meeting, requesting he come down to her real estate office.

"Couldn't we meet at the house? Haven't seen the kids for a week, and you'll need Connie's signature anyway."

"Already got it, and I don't think she wants to see you."

It pissed him off that she would have such an opinion about the details of his marriage, since she'd only been hired to sell the property.

"Lucas, I can't find the information I need on the home at Linda Lane, and the property in Sonoma County. Do you have mortgages on those?"

Lucas fisted his right hand and nearly cracked the cell with his left. "Wait a minute. My mother left that house on Linda Lane to me. That's *my* house."

"Did you ever get the transfer done after your mother's death?"

"You're not hearing me. I'm not selling that house. I'm keeping it. I need some place to live."

"I'll require the rent rolls and how much the taxes are. Is there a mortgage? Connie thought it was given to you free and clear."

"You know, I'm talking and you're not hearing me. That was *my* house left to me by *my* mother."

"Except you were married at the time."

"So?"

"So, half of it belongs to Connie. You know California's a community property state. I'm no attorney, Lucas, but I think maybe you should get one and right away. Connie intends to sell this property, and the house up in Sonoma County, too."

"That fuckin hunting cabin has been in my family for a hundred years." His voice cracked like a teenager. "No way is that going to Connie."

"Look, go get an attorney. In fact, I insist you do so."

The cold bitch didn't sound like she had an ounce of compassion.

"I could give you three names as recommendations. But in the meantime, you can't stop Connie from putting the house, the house you two lived in together, on the market. She can't *sell* it without your permission, but she can encumber her half. And if she goes to court, the judge will order it."

He felt her voice soften just a touch, but she was still all business and still too pushy.

"Maybe if she gets the house sold, and she gets some money, she'll ease up on the other properties. Maybe not. But you need to get an attorney right away, and you need to meet with me to get this paperwork signed."

"I need time to digest all this. I just got served with papers yesterday."

"Oh." He heard the hesitation in Marcy's voice. "So, this was a surprise, then?"

"Yeah, it was pretty much a surprise."

"Can we compromise?"

He could hear some sweetness, but he didn't trust his ears yet.

"I won't have you give me any signatures on the Linda property and the cabin in Cloverdale, but can we at least do the paperwork on the house so I can get it on the market Monday morning?"

He'd agreed because he didn't know what else to do. He'd trained for everything under the sun, every eventuality, but he'd not been prepared for the attack coming from the one person in the world he always thought would be there for him.

Connie was taking the house they'd picked out together as newlyweds, with money for the down payment that came from his SEAL signing bonus. She could try to take what his mother had left him, as well as the cabin up in the woods, but she could *not* take his dignity. That, no woman would ever have that, *especially* not Connie.

CHAPTER 4

Marcy didn't expect the tall SEAL to arrive so soon. She'd been involved in checking the new listings and had begun to upload some of the Shipley house information to the multiple listing service. She was waiting for his signature before she hit send.

The pink stucco home was on one of San Diego's nicer streets. The picture she'd taken that morning didn't do it justice. It had a rounded doorway like many of the bungalows in the area, with a red-tiled roof and iron grates over the tiny windows on the whole front side of the building, including the front door. Built just after the Depression, every house in town of that vintage was nearly identical, except for some interior remodeling and reversal of floor plan. The living room was always on the right or left and the kitchen was opposite, on the other side of the dining area. The homes had been built for younger families, but younger families could barely afford them anymore without help from outside.

She was admiring the pleasant picture on the screen when she heard his deep voice behind her.

"You're Marcy Gelland?"

When she turned, his dark hair and deep blue eyes threw her off-balance for a bit. He was stuffed into jeans that were baggy at the calves and knees, but well filled out in the butt and groin area. And he'd caught her checking him out.

His eyes smiled while his lips didn't move except for a tiny muscle on his left, which was a good thing. The resulting dimple at the left side of his mouth was giving her palpitations.

Well, of course he's handsome, Marcy. What did you expect?

He smelled of fresh soap, wore a white button-down shirt with rolled-up long sleeves, showing his corded muscles and multiple forearm tats, including a string of frog prints going from his wrist to the crook in his arm. She was glad she'd decided to wear her dark blue suit, her power suit. She needed the strength and resolve it gave her.

Standing, she extended her hand and felt him give her a full-contact handshake ending with a little squeeze. He returned her palm in an altered state. Her heart was pounding so hard she was sure her little dangle earrings were shaking.

Picking up her file, she asked him to follow her to the conference room. She could easily imagine him gazing at the movement of her hips under her skirt, so she attempted to walk completely without swagger, so as not to encourage him further. His mannerism wasn't at all what she expected when he pulled out a chair for her. She was forced to say thank you, and then felt his fingertips glide across the top of her shoulders as he returned to his side of the table, sat with his fingers folded on the tabletop in front of him.

Marcy recalled what Connie had told her. He could be a charmer, and no doubt he was on his best behavior right that moment. If he expected any special favors, he was sorely mistaken. She inhaled, elongated her neck, settled her jaw and applied her professional mask as she met his stare.

He was stoic, seemingly unaffected by her in the slightest, leaning back against the padding in the office chair, breathing shallowly, but drilling her with his gaze. She could tell he was checking her out elsewhere, with his peripheral vision, but was skilled enough to hide it.

In spite of herself, she was dying to know if she'd measured up.

Get hold of yourself. He's a predator, after all. Good at sizing up people, assessing his odds and calculating weaknesses. "So, Mr. Shipley—"

"Lucas. You can call me Lucas if you're going to rob me. No need to be all formal about it."

"I'm not robbing you—"

He put one paw on her hand, the one clutching the legal-sized manila folder with the listing information in it. The action made her jump and immediately pull away.

"Marcy, may I call you Marcy?" He didn't wait for an answer. "Let's cut the crap. I've given it some thought for, oh," he pulled out his cell phone and checked the time, "about thirty minutes. She can have the house. She can keep it, sell it, give it away to a homeless shelter for all I care about it. That's no longer a place I want to have anything to do with," he said, pointing to the folder.

"Mr. Shipley—"

"I said call me Lucas," he interrupted.

"Mr. Shipley, this hasn't been negotiated and until you get yourself an attorney, you shouldn't be offering anything like that to me. I'm supposed to be an impartial neutral party to this transaction, representing both of you—"

"Sure you are." His arms were crossed and his left eye squinted, pulling up the left side of his lip.

"Well, you're certainly not making it very easy for me."

"What freakin' rule says I'm supposed to make it easy for *you*? You think this is freakin' easy for *me*?"

"No. But I'm here to get your signature on the listing contract for the house. *Only* the house. I'm going to tell your wife—"

"Soon-to-be ex-wife."

Marcy nodded and stared back at his oversized fingers. She saw cut marks on the inside of his bent and misshapen forefinger and a scar running up from the knuckle of his middle digit to above his wrist. The scar was nearly covered by a patch of dark body hair. He was missing the last joint on his fourth and little fingers. The vision distracted her until she saw him dip his head down, looking up and across to her side of the table, expecting an answer.

"You were saying something about my ex-wife?"

She took a deep inhale. "Mr. Shipley, I was offering a peace pipe, of sorts. We can do this contract, and I can get the house on MLS tonight or first thing in the morning. I'll tell her you wouldn't agree to the other two houses. Perhaps, with your cooperation here, this afternoon, I can convince her not to pursue the other two homes."

He leaned back in the chair, hiding his hands underneath the table. His chest fully rose as he gulped in air, and then his shoulders dropped as he exhaled. The scent of his body laced with what smelled like menthol shaving soap hit her in the face like a blast furnace and, in spite of herself, made her panties wet.

"And just why would you do that?"

She didn't really have an answer, because it had just come to her as a strategy and she had no idea from where. "Just...I don't know." She shrugged, seeking words to describe what she couldn't. Her insides were a jumbled mess. "I guess I feel like we should take this in little bites. The whole enchilada is probably hard to swallow at this point in time, Mr. Shipley."

Oh, no. There it is again, looking at me that way. The edge of his upper lip curled in amusement. If they were familiar, if they were a – W*hat in the devil are you doing, Marcy?* By the arch of his dark brow, she could tell he was tempted to say something dirty about the size of her mouth and the whole enchilada, and she worked very hard to put it out of her mind.

She closed her eyes so as not to watch him, putting her forehead into her palm, trying to seize back control of the conversation. It was no use, when she opened her eyes, and regarded the hunky SEAL sitting in front of her, with that sexy way he objected to everything she was trying to do, even the favor she was trying to bestow on him, the butterflies in her stomach instantly multiplied. Connie was right. He was a charmer of the professional class. A sheer force of nature. Her heart was beating like she'd just run a marathon.

Normally, the calmest person during a negotiation, but today, right then, she was losing it, big time. She'd never before met someone who affected her so. Was she excited for the challenge, or was it something else?

God help me.

CHAPTER 5

Thom Grande was waiting in the warehouse where the rest of Kyle's squad assembled. The SEAL from DEVGRU in Virginia studied each man carefully, as Lucas knew he'd been trained to do. Lucas had deployed with the Varsity Group, as Team 6 was known, two summers before, although not during the deployment that took out BinLaden. It was a special operation of four weeks, which gave him a nice signing bonus—enough for the down payment on the house Connie now wanted to sell.

When Thom's blue eyes met Lucas', he winked, acknowledging the antics of the night before at the strip club. Lucas wished he could remember more of it. He hoped he hadn't blown his chances to do a rotation with them, or perhaps join Team 6 in the future. Since he didn't have anyone around to hold him back, doing the most dangerous tours overseas was suddenly looking like the cure he needed. Way better than waiting for legal papers and the inside of courtrooms. He'd be crying, the kids would be crying, and sure as shit, Connie would drill him with a look that would send him straight to Hell.

Thom walked over to him, and they shook hands.

"How's your head, Shitface?"

Lucas turned to Jake, who snickered.

"I'm fine," Lucas mumbled. To Ryan and Jake, he whispered, "You fuckin' told him?"

"It slipped," Ryan whispered back. "But it was kind of obvious."

Jeffrey and Danny entered the room, and Kyle called the meeting. "Okay, gents, yesterday was the briefing on that terrorist Jihadi John and what Thom and his boys have been dancing with. We have some late-breaking intel we were waiting for before we gave you the whole story."

They waited. Thom stepped forward and stood next to Kyle.

"So, I've got some bad news, gents," Kyle said.

Lucas could taste the juicy deployment he knew was coming up. Wouldn't that make his soon-to-be ex shit her pants? Turf the little hottie realtor, although he wouldn't mind hanging out with her again. He'd enjoyed the sparring the previous afternoon. He hadn't been able to sleep much that night, thinking about all the things he could do with her, all the positions...

"You think something's funny, son?" Kyle said.

Lucas saw bodies turn in his direction. His shit-eating grin and pleasant fantasy went right out the window as he realized they were waiting for him to respond.

"Yeah, asshole, I'm talking to you." Kyle had his hands on his hips and a mean scowl on his face.

"Sorry, sir. Was thinking about something else for a second."

Kyle's jaw clenched. "You see what I'm talking about? You guys do that over there and you'll get your brains splashed over all your buddies. Focus, goddammit. We're not in high school." Kyle sighed and continued with the monologue, but gave Lucas a nasty glare. Thom was standing half a body width behind Kyle, with his palm to his lips, having a hard time keeping a straight face, so the SEAL looked down.

Alex rubbed his dick against Lucas' left butt cheek, messing with Lucas' concentration, so he whipped around and tried to pop him.

"You wanna just sit this one out, Shipley?" Kyle barked.

Lucas knew if he told on Alex, he'd lose the respect of the team. He had to take it on by himself. "Chief Lansdowne, I got the runs. Got them last night. I was going to make a dash for the head, but I suddenly got control."

He knew they were all busting a gut inside. Thom broke out in a full smile that Kyle couldn't see.

"You want to go to the little girl's room, then, Shipley? Or are we good now? Can we go on with our meeting?"

"Yes, Chief Petty Officer Lansdowne. I'm good."

Kyle took one step back, folding his hands at his waist behind his back. "This here is SO Thom Grande, and he's going to tell us what we just learned today."

"Thanks, Chief Petty Officer Lansdowne," Thom Grande said in a soft voice.

His smirk was subtle. Lucas could see his affable nature made him a natural-born leader. He couldn't remember everything that was said the night before, but he remembered SO Grande had confided he'd had his share of difficulty with an ex-wife himself.

"We spent about four months last year on deployment, jumping in and out of Mosul, trying to rescue sensitive information and looking for one mean motherfucker, Jihadi John. I'm glad to say drone strikes have nearly wiped out the network he created and grew. But we don't really know anything further since that region is off limits to us now, as you know, or at least officially."

Thom paced in front of the thirty-man squad, walking a nearly straight line right down the middle of one crack between two poured slabs of concrete flooring, like the precision footwork was enjoyable to him.

"The nature of the enemy—of any enemy, for that matter—is to adapt to their environment and to stop doing what's not working and expand what is. This cell is no different. The drone strikes and night raids we used to do a couple of years ago were eating into the propaganda value of their campaign. They went quiet after we captured the cluster of leaders at the top, and those bastards are now housed in Kurdish prisons, guarded by men who would rather kill them than guard them."

Lucas waited for the first shoe to drop. He was salivating, the mantra *deployment* ringing in his ears.

"And when they went quiet, we thought perhaps they'd had a change of heart, or that the younger generation didn't have the stomach for war. We considered it a good sign."

Thom stood within two feet of the front line of SEALs from Alpha squad. "I was sent here because we received some intel we think is credible, and it involves Teams 3 and 5. Today, it was confirmed, and that confirmation was what I was waiting for before I could level with you all, completely." He locked gazes with everyone in the front row. Then he paced back the way he came, gaining eye contact with every man in the second.

Kyle watched them all, as well. Thom completed his analysis of what was to be their future. Lucas couldn't wait to hear the words, *We'll be deploying within the week.*

"We have reason to believe there was a death squad sent specifically to go after members of Teams 3 and 5, as retaliation."

He let it sink in a bit. No one said a word.

"Somehow, they got it that Team 3 and Team 5 were the ones who rounded up their leaders. They intend to bring some of you boys back home with them as hostages. To return the favor, so to speak. To show that it can be done—"

Lucas was hearing things he never thought possible, things so far from his imagination he had a hard time understanding the actual words. It was as if Grande was speaking Pashtu.

"—that terrorists could come here on U.S. soil, could kidnap a bunch of Navy SEALs and bring them back to Iraq. Their own twisted version of a snatch and grab."

The squad erupted in a string of expletives, each mumbling their favorite words of disgust.

Jake was the first to speak coherently. "You have to be shittin' me. That's the dumbest idea I've ever heard."

Thom smiled, even though his gaze remained hard. "I agree. It sounds farfetched." He looked right at Lucas as he continued, "But *if* they could, and that's a pretty big *if,* the propaganda factor would be huge. Even if they halfway carried some part of it off, their mission would make headlines all over the world."

Kyle took one long step, coming to sharp attention as he joined Grande. "Unlike our side, those bastards don't care about the loss of life. They're looking for sensational things they can do to swell the ranks with new recruits. Trust me, gents, something like this would be huge for them, even if they fail. And make no doubt about it—they *will* fail."

Lucas still had one last hope for deployment. "So, what is it we do, exactly? Like when do we leave and get these assholes before they try to come over here and attempt their suicide mission?"

"You boys aren't going anywhere overseas; not yet, anyways. You're not due to deploy for another five months, at least. You get to stay here while the other teams are out. Team 5 will deploy in thirty days, as planned. But you guys—you? You get to hang around Coronado and become bait."

Lucas was getting sick to his stomach.

Alex rolled his shoulder and growled, "SO Grande? Could you answer a question that's bugging me?"

"Sure. Go ahead. I'm here for your questions. All of them," answered the Varsity SEAL.

"Why don't we just meet them in combat over there, like Lucas here just said?"

It was Kyle's turn. Sucking in air, his back erect, he answered, "Because, Nowicki, they're already here."

CHAPTER 6

Marcy was uploading the rest of her listing, sending out the reverse match emails to agents who were looking for property in this price range and location, when her cell phone rang. It was Connie.

"Hi, there. Just uploading your listing right now, Connie."

"Thank God. Do you have to inspect the other two houses, Marcy? I found keys for both of them."

"Well, Connie, I was going to talk to you about that." Marcy was trying to dart between the divorcing couple, noticing how anxious Connie was to untie their bond of marriage. "Why don't we just take it one step at a time? I think Lucas has shown some cooperation. Maybe we can get a great offer on your house right off the bat, and that would take some of the financial pressure off you both for a bit until you get settled. We can always handle those other two listings later. We could perhaps offer to be reasonable if he cooperates, which would be much better for you."

"And why would I do that?" Connie's cold tone sent Marcy a chill.

"Well, I think it's in your best interest to have his full cooperation on the sale of the house, Connie, don't you?"

"I don't care about getting cooperation. I want to make him pay."

"But Connie, don't you want to walk away with the most amount of money?"

"You mean, would I rather walk away with a ton of money or the satisfaction of screwing him six ways to Sunday? If you have to ask that question, Marcy, you don't know me very well."

The baby started crying in the background, and Connie went to retrieve him. Marcy really didn't know Connie as well as she was going to, but she did know this wasn't headed anywhere good.

Connie picked up the phone again and continued, "If you're coming out here today to put the lockbox on, I can give you both keys. I have no idea if either of them are occupied—"

"He told me the house on Linda Lane had a tenant in it."

"See? I told you he'd cooperate. That's more than he's told me. He hides that rent money, spends it on God knows what. Gambling. Girls. Drugs—"

"Drugs?" Marcy's hackles raised a bit. The suggestion seemed to be completely out of character, even for Lucas. He was, after all, an elite Navy man.

"Sure, why not? I mean, he does everything else. The man's a fuckin' human tornado. He and those boys of his are wreaking havoc wherever they drop their pants—"

"Look, Connie, I don't want to—"

"Maaaaar Seee. Did that asshole try to charm his way into your pants? He can, you know. I told you he can."

The dance Marcy had started became very tedious and she began to wonder if she had the skill to stay out of the frying pan, or avoid getting hit by it as it went flying past her head. "Look, Connie, can we just keep it simple? I don't think he wants any trouble, he just—"

"That sweet-talkin' dickwad."

Marcy was walking on quicksand. These two were going to be a real piece of work. Suddenly, she wasn't so confident she'd be able to keep them in their own corners and avoid killing each other. "You have to give the tenant notice for those kinds of things. I don't even have any way to contact them."

"Then I'll go. I'll just fuckin' walk right up to the house, knock on the door, put little Jack on my boob, and ask to fuckin' walk around the house that I half-own. I can take pictures, right?"

"Connie, you're not hearing me."

"I'll tell them if they want to stay, they'd better cooperate with open houses, tours coming through, people walking through at all times of the day and night."

"All things you'll put up with on your house, is that correct?"

"*Hell, no.*"

Jack started to fuss. Again.

"Look, you've talked with him about it. He didn't react."

"He most certainly *did* react. He strongly objected. Only way I could get him to sign the contract for your house was by telling him we'd do it one step at a time. Same as I'm telling you now, Connie. Seriously, this is in your best interest."

"Why don't you just fill out the paperwork, and I'll sign those two new contracts today. He can sign when he realizes I'm serious. Oh. And how much equity is in both?"

Marcy was beginning to see why they were divorcing. Connie was every bit the piece of work he was. "He didn't tell me about the mortgages or taxes, but I did ask him."

"That jerkoff."

"I don't think he would have signed the listing agreement on your house if I held him up for all three listings, Connie." How many times did she have to repeat that fact before it sunk in?

She could hear Connie telling something to their daughter. "I have to go, Marcy. What time will you be here?"

"I can get there within an hour. After I finish a couple of things, I'll be right over."

Connie hung up without saying another word.

On the way over to Connie's, Marcy couldn't understand how two people could make babies together and still act like children themselves. And how he could go through the grueling training to become a Navy SEAL, have all the stamina—mental stamina—to do that job and not be able to reel in his emotions. That was her first thought.

Her second thought was about how completely *unboring* the guy was. She imagined he would be a piece of work in the bedroom if he loved like he argued. He had skin in the game. Life mattered to him. *Things* mattered to him. Was it because he had to control his breathing, his fear, and his thoughts of impending death so many times in the battlefield he just let it all hang out in real life?

Yeah, that's probably it. Being a trained warrior, he was out of his element stateside, having to do things like be soft and gentle and worry about someone else's feelings. He'd married someone else who also had a hair-trigger and needed the intense relationship a guy like him could bring. That not only wasn't in his training, but he'd probably been trained to funnel everything emotional away from the job as a stress-coping mechanism.

And so the wife and family received the brunt of his inability to connect. The family got what was left over after his deployments, not his best side, either.

Still, she wondered what they'd been like when they first married. She imagined they'd exploded like rockets lighting up the sky. Those two were probably incapable of doing anything halfway.

She allowed herself a smile. Maybe she was going about it wrong. Maybe she should just sit back and enjoy the show. At least they weren't turning on her.

Not yet.

She rang the doorbell, and Connie's disembodied voice told her to come in. She laid her paperwork down on the dining room table, including the folder with his signature on the contracts and disclosure statements, and then sat and waited. She needed Connie's John Hancock on the disclosures.

Connie wafted into the room wearing the tightest pair of jeans Marcy had seen, along with a push-up, low-cut cotton top that revealed her ample cleavage.

"He filled out the Transfer Disclosure, Connie. I gotta have you review what he put down, initial and sign these."

The SEAL wife sneered at the stack of papers. "Wow. He musta been there for hours and hours. The guy can't read, you know. He covers it up well, but the Neanderthal doesn't read anything. He likes graphic novels and—"

"Connie, he reads just fine. It didn't take long. I helped him with some of it, but he filled it all out."

Connie crossed her arms over her chest, sending her boobs north. "Sure you did." Connie's look was a challenge.

"What does that mean?"

She huffed and leaned over Marcy's shoulder, grabbing a pen. "Just sayin'. Okay, where do I sign?"

Marcy indicated where she was to initial and then sign beneath his signature. "Fuckin' jerk signed in my spot."

"Makes no difference—"

"So, you don't think it makes a difference who's on top?" She wiggled her eyebrows.

Marcy looked away and felt heat creep across her cheeks.

Connie laughed. "I'll bet this is the last divorcing SEAL you'll ever represent, huh?"

"No. It isn't the first, and it most certainly won't be my last, either."

"Well, if you can keep the cows in the barn and keep his pants on, you might get paid. One of my best friends is a realtor, and she wouldn't touch this with a ten-foot pole."

"I'll bet," Marcy said under her breath, slipping the contracts into the folder. So much for feeling lucky about winning the listing from the agents she'd had to battle it out with. Unless that was a lie, too. Sensing Connie's unfriendly stare on the top of her head, she pulled out the blue lockbox and held it up. "This goes on a water pipe or, if there is none, the front door, but it scratches the wood. It has to be on something that won't go anywhere."

"Put it on his fuckin' flagpole. And I'm not talking about his dick."

The woman's cursing was beginning to wear on every last one of her nerves. She'd never have guessed wives cursed like sailors, too. Marcy fought for composure. "So, that's where, exactly?"

"Oh, that's right. His huge honker of an American flag isn't on it. Some days, when the breeze picks up, I'd have to battle that damned thing so I could get out the front door. He likes 'em big, like everything, except his women. He likes them with huge tits in fancy white lace, likes skinny waists and loves to talk dirty in bed."

Marcy felt heat begin to crawl up her neck, but managed to will away the blush. She wondered how the Lucas she'd met could have hooked up with this woman, and though it wasn't really her business, for her own sake, she needed to know. A slight worry for the health of the children began to grow as well.

Connie gave her a little wink and a half-smile.

"Gonna miss that part of things a bit. But I'm working hard to find me a replacement—quick."

CHAPTER 7

After the meeting, Thom Grande came up to Lucas, the rest of the team barely within earshot. "Understand you're having trouble with the missus."

"That's fuckin' putting it mildly."

"So that explains your behavior last night. Not that I minded tagging along."

"You forget yourself, Grande. I think you forgot the part about us helping you walk and plopping your sorry ass on the bed at your motel. Or don't you remember that?"

Thom nodded and grinned at his cowboy boots. They looked expensive to Lucas, but then Lucas, being a California kid, didn't know anything about boots.

The SEAL peered up at Lucas and gave him that knowing look. "Been there, done that."

"What, the going to strip clubs or the domestic wars?"

"Guilty on both counts. But that kind of action at clubs and bars and shit, Lucas, there's nothing there except a fake good time. It's all fake, man. Save your marriage if you can."

Lucas started to chuckle. "Well, it isn't up to me, Grande. The woman has her own ideas of where the boundary lines are, and I fuckin' crossed into enemy territory when I wasn't looking."

"And she won't forgive you?"

"Nothing to forgive. She thinks I did the thing with a transvestite who takes a really good picture. Not that the big guy wasn't attractive, just not my thing. I've never been unfaithful to Connie, but I can't convince her otherwise."

"So, you keep pushing the envelope, hoping some woman will just grab your balls and make you forget your wife? That's your plan? That what you're saying? You know how dangerous that is?"

"Look, man, this is all good here, but you're not my fuckin' psychiatrist. No offense intended. I got Kyle and the guys here watching out for me. I'm good. I'm just going through a rough patch. I got kids I won't be able to see, a wife who wants to have nothing to do with me for nothing I've done, and now she's taking me to the cleaners. I fucking re-upped for four years to get the down payment for this fuckin' house she's taking away from me. And now the bitch wants my granddad's hunting cabin and the house my mother left me."

Grande stepped back. "No worries. I feel you. Didn't mean to butt in, Shipley." He held his palms out to the sides as if demonstrating he didn't hold a weapon. "Just if there's any advice I can give you, the best advice I didn't get until it was too late, is to get a good divorce attorney."

"Fuck it. She can have it all."

"And she'll keep taking it until you fight her, my man," Alex said as he slapped Lucas on the back.

"Listen to him, Shitface. This guy has the scars to prove it," added Jake.

"Come on, assholes," Kyle called out. "Get the hell out of the building. I gotta lock up."

They met for beers at the Scupper. The usual parade of high school students and college party girls was in and around the bar, sliding up and down seats like they were working a pole at a club, the skirts shorter and tighter than Lucas remembered. They were looking younger and prettier the more beers he drank.

One of Kyle's old-timers, Calvin Cooper, sat down across the table. "You're gonna have to face your demons, Lucas, or you'll be no good to us. Being sober is no joke, my man."

Cooper's gentle rolling voice was soothing, but a warning nonetheless. His plain talk and even sharper stare made Lucas sit up. Coop's huge six-foot-four frame loomed over the table like he was the king at court.

"I can handle it."

"Oh, sure you can. Until you can't, and then you'll be balling one of those sixteen-year-olds with a fake I.D., and bam, you're off the teams. You gotta ask yourself what's really more important, being married or being a SEAL. 'Cause right now, you can't do both. It's eating you alive, man. You're hooked up with a woman who can't handle the heat. She's gone over the edge. She's bent. And you're in some la-la land, thinking you can turn her back into the little kitten she was when you married her."

"How many times you been married, Coop?" Lucas liked the big SEAL medic.

"Mentally? Lots of times. But nah, I tried out a lot for all those teams, but in the end, there was only one lady for me. Just once, man."

"So, how can you talk?"

"You forget I've been doing this over eleven years. I've seen it all. If Kyle doesn't toss you, I will. I'll give you a mental so fast you won't be able to find your dick. Just imagine how the Navy will put you to use with that in your folder."

As one of the team medics, Coop could easily end his career. He wouldn't want to, of course, but if it meant saving the life of the others on the team, weeding out someone who wasn't paying attention, it would be something he'd have to do for everyone's safety. And though Lucas would be off the teams, his obligation to the Navy would continue. He'd get stuck cleaning toilets on a ship or perhaps being a BUD/S instructor and dishing out his brand of hate on all the young, new recruits.

"One more piece of advice, and then I'm going to get these gentlemen to escort you home. Get yourself a fuckin' lawyer. Stop feeling sorry for yourself. Quit reacting and start making a plan. Either walk away or fight. Those are your only two choices."

The giant stood, threw down a twenty, even though he'd been drinking mineral water, and in a couple of long strides was out the doorway.

Minutes later, Lucas left as well. The night air was crisp and the stars were out. The warm, salty breeze was something Lucas loved more than just about anything.

Just about.

They had five days until they started training for hostage rescue and house-to-house searches. They'd all have to requalify on the range, and anything less than expert was not acceptable. Lucas decided he'd go visit the cabin, get in touch with his childhood and see what the ghosts of Northern California had to say to him.

Besides, it beat waiting for Connie to serve him with more papers. And the ghosts were a helluva lot kinder than Connie's mouth.

But his dick still got hard when he thought about what wonders she could do with that mouth.

CHAPTER 8

Marcy had a friend from college who lived in Sonoma County and sold real estate. And she happened to be married to an ex-SEAL. They had a small winery operation a lot of the San Diego crowd had invested in. She decided to call her.

"Hey, Devon. I've got a property I need to check out in Cloverdale. Was thinking maybe I'd drive up and see you and Nick for a day or two. What do you say?"

"That would be great. You want my help with the listing in any way?"

"I don't have the listing yet. Divorcing couple. He's a SEAL, and they don't exactly see eye to eye on everything yet."

Devon giggled. "They never do, unless *you* screw up, then they get reunited."

"In this case, I'd actually walk away. They have two beautiful kids. A shame, really."

"Not everyone can make it. Lots of divorces in the community. What day are you coming?"

"How about tomorrow?"

"Sure. My place is open. We just finished the guest cottage, and I don't have anyone renting it until the weekend. The place is yours."

"Thanks."

"Does Nick know him?"

"The SEAL? Name's Shipley, Lucas Shipley."

"I'll ask him. Safe journeys. Why don't you fly up? We got direct flights now, just like in the big city. I'll pick you up at the airport. Would save you a whole day each way, unless you want the drive to ease your mind."

"You know, I think I'll do that. But let me pick up a car at the airport. I'm going to need my own wheels."

"Yup, unless you want to drive one of our tractors."

Marcy drove from the Charles Schulz airport down the freeway into Santa Rosa, and then took the two-lane country road to Bennett Valley. A small shingle sign at the end of a crushed granite driveway marked the property as Sophie's Vineyard. The rows of lush green vines under a bright blue cloudless sky welcomed her. The rich black soil of Sonoma County provided stark contrast to the colors of the fresh crushed straw covering it. Something emotional was building inside, and she wasn't quite sure what was happening. She felt like there was a new adventure looming—something unexpected was about to happen. It would alter her path forever.

Devon and Nick's modern home was built on the site of Nick's sister's nursery grounds, a nursery that had failed as an enterprise, but succeeded in bringing together Nick and Devon, a couple who were living out their dreams in the wine country. Though Nick had retired from the teams without a pension, he was more than content running the day-to-day operations of the small winery. Devon made enough money for them to live on while the grapes were developing. It was a storybook romance from beginning to end.

Devon wrapped her arms around Marcy and gave her a squeeze. "So great to see you, Marcy. Wow. Things in San Diego must agree with you."

"Thanks." Marcy blushed. "I've been lucky, I guess."

Nick appeared at the doorway. He was as handsome as Marcy remembered—tall with wide shoulders, blond hair and green eyes. Wearing jeans with suspenders and a khaki long-sleeved shirt rolled up at the sleeves, he was wiping his hands on a rag.

"Hey there, Marcy," he said as he gave her a quick hug and kiss on the cheek.

"You're looking all farm boy-like, Nick. No body armor, guns, or tats covering half your body?"

"Oh, I got the tats," Nick said, showing her the line of frog prints extending from his wrist to inside his elbow joint, just like Lucas had.

"All the guys on Kyle's squad have them. Sort of a rite of passage. You're working for one of us?" Nick squinted and asked, tossing the rag onto the seat of a riding mower.

"Lucas Shipley. You know him?"

"Yeah, Devon asked me. Can't say that I do, but there were a bunch of guys at the end, coming on board. How long's he been with the teams?"

"All I know is he re-upped a couple of years ago. His bonus was what gave them the down payment on the house I'm selling."

She allowed her voice to trail off. This was part of her job she wasn't proud of.

"Ohhh, ouch. Well then, I probably knew him. Some of the guys do extra training, though. Languages, medic long course, details at Quantico, burn center in Texas. He could have been doing one of those."

"And you took a lot of time off, Nick, when Sophie—"

Marcy had been told the story of how Nick's sister had been poisoned with arsenic in her well water by a neighbor who was now serving time for her murder.

Devon frowned and then drew herself out of her private thought. "Well, I'm not being very hospitable leaving you out here. Nick, you want to get Marcy's bags?"

Marcy opened the truck as Nick picked up two overnight suitcases and slung her briefcase over his shoulder.

"I still get to do all the heavy lifting around here," he said as he widened his eyes and pretended to be overloaded.

Devon slipped an arm around Marcy's waist. "So, tell me about yourself. What's new? And I need to hear about all the hunks in San Diego you're dating."

As Marcy stepped into the doorway, she was stunned. Far from looking like a house, the place more aptly resembled a church. The living room was two stories tall, with a large glass garage door facing out to the hillside garden beyond. The carefully crafted rock walls and meandering garden paths she could see from the large window were stunning. Inside, the living and dining room contained eclectic things from all over the world, including a couple of flower boats from India and a carved sandalwood cabinet that looked like it came from a palace. She smelled fresh coffee and heard light jazz playing in the beautiful room.

"This is amazing. I guess I had a hard time visualizing it when I was up here for the wedding." She turned around a couple of revolutions. "It doesn't look like the same place."

"That was before we got all the furniture in the house. Was a great place for a wedding, though," Devon said.

Nick came back from the hallway and took his wife's hand. "I've set your things on the bed in there. You have a fireplace, but I'd keep it off. We're getting some heat these days. The pilot light keeps the room toasty, sometimes too warm."

"Thank you so much," Marcy said.

"You want something to drink? We were going to have an early supper."

"Wine. You have any wine?"

Nick walked over to a huge floor-to-ceiling wine refrigerator cabinet with double doors, housing more than a hundred bottles of wine. He turned to Marcy and said, "We got white. We got red. You get to pick."

"You have any that came from here? I'd love a red wine."

"Excellent choice." Nick presented the cool bottle to Marcy, where she read the label, *Sophie's Choice*.

CHAPTER 9

T he trip up the coast was always enjoyable. Except for a couple of areas of commuter congestion, the ride was uneventful and stress-free. Lucas used the time to listen to several audio books he'd not made time for in San Diego. The beautiful ride went by quickly, even with the three stops for gas. Like most men on SEAL Team 3, he owned a Hummer, something Connie had been bugging him to get rid of because of the expense. Today, he was glad he'd prevailed in this one thing.

Watching the landscape change from ocean to rocky shoreline in the Monterey area, back to farmland north to Silicon Valley, and then back out to the coast at Marin, all the way nearly to Bodega Bay, it was hard to envision the beautiful scenery as a war zone. But if Thom was right, that's exactly what it was. Stopping for oysters at Marshall's Cove, he drank a beer and watched the sun as it began dropping to the water's horizon. A local motorcycle club was loud and apparently staying nearby. Listening to their language, he pegged them for cops, not bandits.

It touched him as he watched the band of brothers play together, how the cops from the East Bay were trying so hard to have a normal life, just like he and his SEAL buddies did in Coronado. These men had seen the carnage left by society and chose to serve honorably, just like the SEALs. And just like the SEALs, in their off time, they didn't want to look anything like cops. They wore their red bandanas and black leathers. Beefy arms sported tats. And every one of them had all manner of ear piercings. Some of the bikers were alone, some with wives or girlfriends. The ladies were in all sizes, shapes, and ages.

Good for them.

The public had no idea what evils lay out there, even in the brown and green hills of the wine country of California. Evil was everywhere. Lucas knew it was his job to keep evil at bay. And now he'd be doing that at home, as well.

He knew from the talk and the reaction from the other guys that this was a hard thing to wrap their minds around. Danger at home. Sure, the cops were used to it, but SEALs? Having to watch their six at home, in the land of freedom? Where everything was apple pie, and it was easier to tell the good guys from the bad guys?

Forget politics. Leave it to a bunch of politicians to make treaties and agreements they knew no one would keep, and leave it all to the fighting men and women to enforce the unenforceable. Wasn't their fault they were losing the war, and now was it really coming over here? No one could win that kind of war. Even the zealots wouldn't win.

It was just like the cops, trying to deal with the complexities and political decisions of local laws. Up to them to enforce the unenforceable, too.

He finished his oysters as he mentally said goodbye to the guys acting like badasses down at the designated fire pits on the beach. He drove east, and then in an hour arrived in Cloverdale.

He'd forgotten how the sound of the crickets made him feel safe. As long as they were doing their two-toned chirp thing, it meant no strange animal or person was on their way. Just like frogs at the local frog pond he'd played at as a child. When the din stopped suddenly, that was when you paid attention to your surroundings. His grandfather had taught him that.

Lucas fished for the old brass key, slipped it into the lock and instantly he was taken back twenty years, even though it had only been less than ten since he'd been here. That was the summer Granddad had passed away, and his dad soon after that, as if the two were brothers, instead of a very close father and son.

He'd always envied his dad's relationship with his grandfather, probably forged because he'd been raised without a mother and there wasn't anyone to dilute their relationship.

Their whispers in every corner still haunted him as he examined the crude, knotty pine cupboards the three of them had made one summer. He opened the cabinet next to the sink and, sure as shit, there were the holes in the cabinet door where he'd had to re-drill for the screws attaching the hinges three times. His dad wanted him to do it, until he learned how to do it right. The puttied holes were testament to a lesson learned, and no one ever talked about it after it was accomplished. As he grew into a teen and came up to hunt with the two most important men in his life, he liked to look at that door just to remind himself of where he'd come from. It was like proof of his existence.

The cabin had only one bedroom. The old brass bed sported the quilt his mother had made, and when he checked out the spongy mattress that always squeaked when his father happened to take his mother up sometimes, a small cloud of dust rose. Lucas quickly removed the quilt and took it outside, shaking it furiously. He left the colorful patchwork quilt over the porch handrail to air out.

Lucas reset the refrigerator switch and plugged it in, hearing the familiar purring of the old turquoise Philco appliance, stowing the milk, eggs and beer he'd brought, along with some meat for a barbeque he was looking forward to the following night. He found rags and cleaning supplies and did a thorough scrub down of the whole cabin, working until well after midnight. It was a labor of love, homage to a time long past and perhaps never coming again. Just like the refrigerator, he felt his reset switch had been tripped. He was ready for the change.

The cold shower he took before bed was exhilarating after the twelve-hour drive. He found a flannel nightshirt of his father's in the bureau drawer, stowed his Sig Sauer under his pillow, brought the quilt from the porch inside and, draping it over the bed, crashed.

At first light, the birds began chirping, and Lucas found it impossible to sleep any further. He checked his gun, made his bed and unpacked the few things he'd brought with him. The tall highboy dresser with its cracked mirror stood faithfully to serve him, like a butler, showing a reflection of himself in the darkened glass.

He took another cold shower, this time not feeling so cold, considered shaving and decided against it. He put on his jeans, a new t-shirt, and then a sweater of his father's he'd found hanging in the closet.

He was going to make some coffee when he heard a car drive up. Quickly stowing his gun in the back waistband of his pants, covered by the sweater, he looked through the window to the driveway outside. Next to his burgundy Hummer, a white sedan was parking. Out stepped Marcy Gelland.

He opened the front door and leaned into the frame, arms crossed, until she looked up and saw him.

"Oh. It's you!"

"Yes, Miss Gelland. I do own this cabin—at least for a little while longer, anyway."

Her oversized satchel was slung over her shoulder. She had on a pair of forest green recycled ankle gardening boots, and a big white, silk shirt with a pocket stitched over one breast, covering long, tan slacks that were going to be way too warm in a couple of hours. She'd done her hair up in a clip, and she wore no makeup. He liked her better that way.

"You following me now?" he asked, not moving from the spot, daring her to try to gain entry into his private domain. "I told you I wasn't going to sell this place."

She turned around, glancing at the tree line before her eyes at last landed on the thatched roof of the cabin. Then she tilted her head and spoke to him. "Beautiful here. I don't blame you a bit."

"So, you've seen it. Now, you can go, Miss Gelland—or is it Mrs. Gelland?"

Her lips parted slightly, one side turned up, amused. "Marcy. You can call me Marcy. Unlike you, I've never been married."

"Touché." The sting in her comment hurt like a pinprick, but it sucked him back into his impending court battle with Connie. He dropped his arms at the sides, suddenly not knowing what to do with them. "Well, that's it. Show's over. I have nothing else left to offer, unless you like strong coffee and scrambled eggs."

"I love strong coffee and scrambled eggs. I'm afraid I can't make either one successfully."

He didn't know why he said it, but before he could take it back, found himself whispering, "Well, perhaps you're better at other things."

"I should hope so," she said timidly. "I guess, according to you, I rob people for a living."

"Ah, an honest woman who admits her vices. How refreshing. Do you ask for forgiveness before or after you fleece them?"

At first, she didn't smile, just stared back at him. She wasn't afraid, which was such a turn-on. "I solve problems. Most of my day is spent solving other people's mistakes and problems. And I'm damn good at it." She narrowed her eyes, as if taunting him to say something nasty.

Lucas was struck with the inability to fight with her. Whatever was going on, he couldn't dislike her, and he wanted to, perhaps needed to.

Marcy still didn't move an inch. There she was in the middle of the fuckin' forest, way far away from anyone who could hear her scream. He was trying to stand up to her, trying to hate her and everything she stood for. He wanted to blame her for what his life was going to become. She was a willing accomplice to his wife's selfish attitude.

She remained standing, as if waiting for instructions. Defiant, almost petulant, daring him to cave in and show his ungentlemanly side. She hugged her file folder and oversized purse, looking way more desirable than she probably knew. But when she broke a smile and stepped closer to his perch, she finally dropped the hand with the folder, catching it at the side of her hip, and giving him the view of her chest he'd wanted to see. Although he wasn't going to let her catch him at it, his peripheral vision took in the whole lovely sight of her.

She glanced up, recognizing something, and gave him a playful, narrowed look. "I think we got off to a bad start. I'm not here to cause you any pain, or to rob you. Mr.—"

"Lucas. If I'm calling you Marcy, you're calling me Lucas."

"Yessir," she said as she straightened her spine, her pert little lips doing that pouty thing.

What a blessing she was. What a fresh piece of something he'd never had and wanted desperately.

"Like I was saying, *Lucas*…"

Her large brown eyes smiled up at him, and his heart melted. He hadn't realized he was so starved for mature female attention, the kind that wasn't tipped or bought and paid for.

"I think you misunderstand my intentions. I'm not here to sell your cabin. As a matter of fact, I'm not sure I can, or that Connie has the right to order either of them sold. That will have to be worked out in a settlement agreement between the two of you."

He could see that the longer he watched her speak and focused on her lips, the more talkative she became. Words were nervously stringing together, and all he could think of was her light pink tongue darting out behind her white teeth, and the way she licked her lips and nervously bit her bottom one.

"You haven't taken my suggestion and gotten an attorney yet, have you?" she finished and took in a deep breath.

"That was only a little over a day ago, Marcy." He was thinking to himself that his perspective was changing by the minute. "But I'm all ears. Perhaps you can recommend someone for me."

The double meaning seemed to make her blink very slowly, considering what he'd said. She quickly looked downward toward her ridiculous boots.

"Where'd you get those?" he asked with a chuckle.

"Costco."

"No socks. Can't go into the woods without socks. You'll get ticks on your ankles, or worse, traveling up your pant legs."

Marcy cocked her head and frowned then gave him that full gaze that did him in. She forged her response. "You going to continue to defend the perimeter, or am I invited in for those scrambled eggs and strong coffee? Or have I said something to cause you to change your mind?"

There was an exchange between them without words. It fell to him to speak up first, perhaps acknowledge what was going on inside him, hopefully inside her, too. He knew when a woman liked what she saw, and she was definitely transmitting it. "On the contrary. But enter at your own risk."

He let his words linger there until she dropped her gaze again. Stepping aside, he turned and opened the door for her to walk into his life.

Once inside, she slowly took stock of the place, carefully examining the pictures on the walls, the cabinets, the hooked rug in front of the fireplace, the kitchen area, and the sparse furniture of the living room with one table lamp he'd made as a Boy Scout.

"It's lovely. I can see why it has special meaning to you. Lots of memories here. I can feel them, I think."

He'd been holding his breath. "Thank you." He stepped closer to her, and slowly brought his palm to her cheek and cupped it. Letting his fingers brush against her flawless skin, and then dropped his hand. He wanted to be careful, not push his boundaries, but the granite in his pants was making him very uncomfortable.

She turned once again, and he wanted to lace his fingers through her hair, take that damned clip out and muss it all up real good, before he gave her the kiss she so deserved. Hell, *he* deserved that kiss. It had been a long, insane dry spell.

She set her folder down on the table, placing her bag on top of it. "Can I help you with something?"

Oh, yeah, darlin'. You can help me heal that big wound in my soul. Get me feeling right about myself again, about the world. "Let's see. Can you crack eggs?" he asked as he brought out a carton from the refrigerator and set them next to a green bowl from the cupboard. "I even have the right implements." He drew out a wire whisk from one of the drawers.

Her fingers wrapped around the base of the whisk, and for a moment, their fingers touched. It would have been so easy to curl her into his chest, kiss the top of her head, and feel her blood pumping in her neck as he nibbled there. She smelled divine, and he was fairly sure her temperature had risen, since there were tiny beads of sweat on her upper lip.

He moved away from her to light the propane stove and pull out an iron skillet. As she cracked several eggs, he brushed behind her to get the butter. He felt her jump at his proximity, and it gladdened him. He would take the whole day cracking eggs and eating breakfast if she'd let him. Suddenly, he wasn't in a hurry to go anywhere or do anything.

He poured water from a gallon jug into a saucepan on the stove, and after boiling it and cooking the eggs, filled the coned coffee filter to the top and watched as it drained into a ceramic pitcher.

He added cheese and some spices to the eggs, made toast in the frying pan, poured their coffee, and put the cream on the table.

"Breakfast is served, Madame," he said with a bow, placing the two plates on the table across from each other.

"So how often did you come here growing up?" she asked.

"Some of the best times of my life. My grandfather and father used to bring me up every summer. Sometimes my mom, but only occasionally. Learned to hunt and fish. They told stories about being a man that scared this little boy to death."

Lucas worried he'd revealed something perhaps he shouldn't.

The silence was awkward and in need of filling. Marcy beat him to it. "Wow. These eggs are terrific—I think the best I've had."

"Not my best skill," he said, smiling into his coffee mug.

She answered him with a smile. "You want an update on the house?"

"I don't care about that right now, really."

"Okay."

"No offense."

"None taken," she said breathlessly. "Lucas, this property was yours before your marriage, from what I can see. Unless you encumbered it in some way." Her eyes were soft.

"The bank asked me to use it as additional collateral on the loan, because Connie had a couple late payments on her student loan."

"But you didn't borrow against it, right? Pull any money out of it?"

"No. Just used it as a kind of guarantee for the house loan."

"So, if *that's* paid off through escrow, then *this* house would be, what, free and clear?"

"Yes, ma'am."

"I'm no attorney, but I understand that if it was yours before you got married, it remains your sole and separate property. I don't think you can be forced to sell it."

"That's good news," he said, letting out a breath. "So, I have a question for you, Marcy, since we're talking about business sorts of things." He was about to risk a little more, feeling suddenly comfortable and intrigued.

"Shoot," she said as she finished her eggs and took a gulp of coffee.

"Why are you here?" Her eyes widened at first, and then she returned his honest gaze.

"Well, you'll probably have to submit a valuation for this place during your divorce proceedings, when they start. And, I don't know." She shrugged, brushing some crumbs from her lap. "I guess I was looking for something. Not sure what."

Those eyes again searched his face.

"Did you find what you were looking for?" he asked as he covered her hand with one of his.

She hesitated a bit, giving a jolt as their fingers wove together, and then he drew her hand to his face and kissed her palm.

She swallowed hard. "Yes. I think I did."

"Is this wise, Marcy? You're going to have to stop me, you know, because I can't."

She closed her eyes again, as if searching the back reaches of her mind. "I don't want you to stop," she said, her eyes still closed.

CHAPTER 10

Marcy quivered with anticipation as he took her by the hand and, without looking back, brought her to the little bedroom. In front of the patchwork quilt, he reached around her waist and drew her to him, holding her as her hands traveled up his arms. She arched back and they parted. He bent and kissed her. When his kiss went deep, she was lost.

This wasn't the smart thing to do. Somewhere, she knew this, but she'd been starved for this meal. She knew deep inside, she'd always regret it if she didn't just take a chance and let herself glide into something unwise and dangerous—with him.

I'm going to have to cancel the listing and give it to someone else in the office, she thought while he kissed her neck. He removed her hair clip, tossing it to the corner, his fingers lacing through her hair.

Other equally ridiculous thoughts flew past her when his fingers probed down her front as he slowly unbuttoned her shirt. She'd worn a lace bra. White. Exactly what Connie had said. The look on Lucas' face told her it wasn't a lie. *Lucas likes his women big-chested,* which Marcy was, *and in white lace,* which she also was.

"Lucas, wait a minute."

"No." He continued exploring her top, trying to get his tongue into the cup of white lace to taste her nipple, kissing her in other impossible places.

"If we do this—"

"Honey, we're doing this."

"Then I can't represent you."

"Ask me if I care," he whispered in her ear. "I need this. I think you do, too."

He was right, of course. But her job, her morals, every alarm and bell were sounding off the wall.

"I—I don't think this is a good idea."

"Same answer. Ask me if I care."

"I feel like I'm taking advantage of my position."

He continued kissing her neck and between her breasts. In spite of herself, she felt his hard ridge, and instead of backing away, she pressed into him.

"I intend to take full advantage of you taking advantage of me," he answered in a whisper.

"It isn't wise."

"No, it isn't."

"It isn't smart." She sighed as her lips told him something else.

"Not smart at all," he murmured before he completely covered her mouth.

When their lips parted, she was leaning in to him, holding on to him like he was her lifeline.

"But is it right, Marcy? Ask your soul. Is this something you should have, something you *deserve*?" He ducked his head a bit to gaze into her eyes. She could see he was giving her the choice.

"Is it, Marcy? Is it right for you, because it's sure right for me." His thumb brushed against her lips.

"Would you stop if I asked you?"

"Yes, after I kissed every inch of your body. After I made you come so many times, you didn't remember your name, baby. Yes, I'd stop. If you begged me."

Dayum. Dayum.

"I don't do this. I'm not that kind of girl."

"I know what kind of girl you are. The kind of girl you're showing me is just fine. I like your kind of girl very much," he said as he continued kissing her, his long fingers reaching into the top of her panties after his other hand unzipped her skirt, and it dropped to the floor. The heavy bulge in his jeans against her nearly nude sex was such a turn-on she sparked a fever.

She crossed her arms behind his neck, pulling his head down to hers. "I'm lost, Lucas. Help me."

His long groan had her bud pulsing. She could feel the moisture preparing her channel for him. He lowered his crooked forefinger, and she sucked in air as he inserted it in her opening. "Does that help, baby?"

"Oh, yes, Lucas. But I need more."

"Of course you do. Show me. Show me what you want."

Suddenly, she was timid, but she smoothed over his button fly.

He groaned. "You want that, baby? I want to fuck you so bad right now. Take it out for me, sweetheart. Let me feel your fingers around me."

She undid the top three buttons on his fly. He was commando, no underwear. "You like it quick," she heard herself say.

"No, sweetheart. I like to be ready, is all. Not quick. I like it slow. I like you to ache when I ram my cock inside you."

She had never been more ready in her life. His jeans fell to the floor. She took the enormous girth of him, squeezing him, pressing him between their abdomens. She whimpered when she saw a little of his pre-cum leaking. Her ears were buzzing. He was peeling away all the layers of her ladyhood, all the good girl parts of her, leaving the wild child unfettered and free and aching to perform on a stage for him.

She opened his shirt, popping the buttons.

The rest of the clothes went quickly. As she stood before him completely naked, he dropped to his knees and kissed her leg from her knee all the way up. When he reached her sex, she jumped and her lower lip quivered. She gripped the tops of his shoulders at the intimate act.

"Tell me what you're thinking," he whispered against her mound.

"I'm scared, Lucas."

He leaned back on his haunches, grinned with lips wet with her own moisture, and then dropped his gaze to between her legs again. "You've never done this before?" He reached out and touched her. "Has a man ever played with this?"

She couldn't speak; all she could do was nod. She'd had a man touch her there, once. And she'd asked him to move his hand away.

His gaze narrowed. "But you're not a virgin, right?"

"No, just not—"

"Ah! Now I understand. Just not this. You haven't done this," he whispered as he moved forward, looking up at her while he lapped at the slit between her legs. "Baby, you taste sweet. You like that?"

"Yes."

"You want more?"

"Oh, my God, yes."

"That's my girl. Ride my hand while I take your juices. Just a little." He held her hip and tilted her pelvis back and forth, dipping his head to bury his tongue inside her as he rocked her back and forth.

God, it was getting hot in the room. The backs of his fingers rubbed against her thighs, gently smoothing and parting them. "That little bud is working hard, Marcy. You feel the pressure there?"

"Yes," she whispered.

"I'm gonna take some of the pressure off, so it doesn't ache so much. You okay with that, honey?"

"Um, oh, yes." She couldn't think.

He sucked the lips of her sex and slid his fingers up and down. "You tell me if you want me to stop, and I'll stop." He slipped both thumbs inside her opening, breaching her core, giving him full access.

"Don't—"

His head jerked up.

"God, *don't stop*, Lucas. Please. Don't. Stop."

"I have no intention of stopping. We got all day and no where else to go."

His tongue found her opening again.

She felt an orgasm coming on quickly. She pinched her own breasts, and then looked down on his head buried between her legs, where he feasted.

"Come for me, baby. Let me taste it, sweetheart," he whispered below her.

The friction of his tongue against her clit made her shudder as she felt herself lose control. His deep guttural moan told her he tasted the gold he was seeking. "God, Marcy, more, give me more," he said just before he dove in again.

As the spasms overtook her, she was filled with crazy need to have him inside her channel while she pulsed against him. "I need this so much, Lucas. God, I can't tell you how much I need this."

He withdrew his hands. "I know, baby." He fished for something in his pants, she heard the tearing of a foil packet and then he stood. Her hands went down to his shaft. She rubbed the ridged surface of the condom, and her eyes grew wide.

"Something else new, am I right? Oh, baby, what I'm going to do to you," he said as he picked her up quickly and dropped her back on the bed. "I'd norma like to get you screaming before I come inside, but I think you're there already and I can't wait any longer."

He mounted her, spreading her thighs. He yanked two pillows from the head of the bed, stuffed them under her pelvis and let a finger rub up and down her wet slit so achingly slow; she arched back and spread her legs further apart.

With his gaze locking with hers, he put his forefinger in his mouth. "Ah, baby, choices, choices." The tip of the condom had filled slightly and the plastic looked like it was going to burst.

"Lucas, please. Don't tease me any longer. Please."

"Please what, sweetheart?"

"I need you. Inside me."

He let the tip rub up and down, and then he pushed enough to have just the head inside her and held.

"Please, Lucas," she said, raking her nails over his chest.

"Ask me. Beg me, baby."

"Please, I need you to…"

"To what? What do you need me to do? Tell me, sweetheart."

"I need you inside me."

"Yes, baby, but ask me nice and sweet. Tell me what you want."

His gaze became devilishly dark as he stroked himself, ready for entry. "I need the command, baby."

She inhaled as his large hand squeezed her breast so hard it nearly hurt.

"That, that thing you were thinking. That thought. I want to hear that thought," he said as he smiled, squeezed, and slid his knees under her thighs, readying himself.

"Fuck me, Lucas."

"Yes, my dear. That's exactly what I'm going to do. With pleasure." He grinned again. "Pull me inside, baby."

She leaned forward, gripping his buttocks, and pulled him with her muscles deep inside her, holding him there, milking his length and feeling the hardness of his tip against her cervix. The dull ache had her squeezing her eyes shut. She rolled back and arched her abdomen. His hands held her hips, then pulled her knees up over his shoulders, and he ground down into her, rotating and drilling, holding firm and then deepening his pressure. "Is this what you need, baby?" he asked.

She couldn't speak. He thrust and held her tight, holding his breath as she did the same, then released her and soon thrust deep inside again. Her spine began to tingle as the little precursor to her orgasm began. She desperately needed him to fill every part of her insides. The calm between his powerful hip thrusts left her vacant and needy.

"Deeper," she whispered.

He hitched her knees up again, burying his shaft without holding back. "God, Marcy. I can't get enough."

The soft hairs at the back of her neck began to stiffen. She felt her internal muscles clamp down on him hard. Her breasts felt hot, her nipples engorged. Her body was at the edge of an explosion of passion unlike she'd felt before. Her eyes flew open and through her hair, she saw the smile cross his lips as he felt her pulse against him, as he watched her pleasure, kissing her eyes, her neck, the warm space between her breasts.

Then a sudden frown wrinkled his forehead and his lips formed a perfect O. "God, I can't help it," he said with difficulty as he exhaled, pumped and held, until he collapsed on top of her. As her breathing slowed and perspiration traveled from his chest to hers, she allowed her fingers to sift through his hair, pushing it off his forehead. He kissed her nipples gently, then tucked his head into the space beneath her chin and pressed his cheek to her.

In the last few moments before she fell into a deep sleep, Lucas still buried deep inside her, she played with the damp curls at the back of his neck. Her fingers stroked up and down his spine and she squeezed his butt cheeks. His enormous torso pressed her breasts until their bodies breathed in tandem. Holding him, she'd never felt happier, and she knew, if she ever had to let this man go, she'd miss him the rest of her life.

CHAPTER 11

They needed a cold shower after the third time they made love. Lucas insisted on washing her all over, slipping fingers into every crevice, because it was like seeing her all over again. Her body was like silk. The bubbles over her breasts made them slippery. She was built perfectly for him, and he loved the feeling of her slick body brushing up against his torso.

He tried to envision the faces of other lovers and exciting conquests from his past, but he couldn't see a single one. He couldn't even picture Connie's face anymore. The connection was so strong between him and Marcy he didn't care if they never left the cabin.

Where was it all going? And did it matter, really? He knew Connie would blow a gasket, and he hoped she wouldn't retaliate against this lovely creature he'd found, this woman he barely knew. He wasn't going to fuck it up. Not this time. The bonfire they could build together would be enough to last their lifetimes.

What the fuck am I saying? he asked himself as he watched the water sluice down her perfect back, ending at that perfect ass. She was using his palms as her washcloth, letting him touch every inch of her.

He knew they needed to talk, but he wasn't in any hurry. This was what he knew: The sight of her nude body shuddering in front of him, and her little shouts and wiggles as the cold made her jump, had him smiling and fucking melted his heart.

Oh, he was snagged all right. He was so fuckin' hooked and hog-tied. There was no way out. No way he'd let anyone get between them.

But then he remembered he was a team guy. He was a warrior, and there was a job to do in just a couple of days. They'd have to talk between their fucking. She liked to talk during sex, just like he did. He could pump her little pussy until her lips were so swollen she'd walk funny. And even then, it wouldn't be enough.

"Are you hungry, Marcy?" he dared to whisper. He hated to end their little romp in the shower, but he honestly wasn't sure if they hadn't already drained the well. "We're gonna burn up the pump if we keep this up," he said as he kissed her under her ear.

She turned, and her smile tempted him further. Half-lidded eyes did him in. "I'm starved. What did you have in mind, sailor?"

They ate Thai food on Cloverdale Boulevard. He began to get his bearings, watching people through the dirty glass window. He liked the little town. Things hadn't become all yuppified. There were cowboys, jazz musicians, pot smokers, and little hotties trying to get modeling jobs in San Francisco, so they could escape from their little town. He couldn't blame them. People lived here because they didn't aspire to do many big things. And that meant things were safe—if there ever was a really safe town in the U.S. anymore.

He pushed his leftover food aside and took her hand. "I gotta explain a couple of things to you."

She set down her fork, took a sip of water, and gave him a sober look.

"You know what I do, right?"

"I do."

"So, I don't think I'm breaching protocol when I tell you the world is a much more dangerous place than everyone thinks."

She shrugged. "I know that."

"No, sweetheart," he said as he leaned in, putting his elbows on the table. "You don't know the half of it. Involving you in my life, and I'm assuming we'll be involved—"

"Involved?" She raised her eyebrows.

"Well, pardon me, but I just assumed that—"

She giggled, and it was such a wonderful sound. "You and I are in a boatload of trouble, Lucas. We just jumped out of an airplane without a parachute."

A smile tugged at his lips. "That's a pretty good way to put it, honey." He could see she was hesitant to say something.

"I'd say we're more like blended. Like all those bodily fluids we exchanged all morning."

"I like all those bodily fluids. I want to make more," he whispered.

Marcy blushed.

"What is it? You re-thinking all this?"

"Not sure I can. It's just that I can't believe I'm here, with you. Connie was all wrong about you. I'll bet you never cheated on her either."

"Never. Not after we got married."

"For the life of me, I don't understand why she thought you did, how she could just could walk away."

He stiffened. He didn't want to talk about Connie. "Long sad, story, Marcy. We sure had fun, but we had no staying power. She had one station, Marcy. It was to be all Connie's way. Always Connie's way. She could never understand why I wanted to do this. Looking back on it, I don't think she really supported my decision to become a SEAL. Not really."

"So much for easing into things to find out what's going on, Lucas."

"You and me? I told you it wasn't smart."

"You did. And I didn't listen. I've been a bad girl." Her eyes sparkled as she dipped her chin in an obvious flirtation.

Oh, that was such a dangerous thing to do to him. If she only knew.

"I haven't even gotten started, Marcy, with all the things I want to do with you."

She blushed and looked down at her lap. "Are we going to think about all this before we spend another few hours getting lost in each other's arms?"

"That's exactly what we're doing right now, honey."

She watched their entwined fingers, his thumb caressing the back of her hand. "No, *you* were starting to warn me about something," she said.

He adjusted his hips, rolled his shoulders and tried to get comfortable. "We're deploying in a few months, but in the meantime, we're doing some training out of state."

"What kind of training?"

"See, that's the problem—I can't tell you."

"Are there girls there?"

"Honey, there are girls everywhere. Anywhere there are SEALs, there are girls. But if you don't stop letting those nasty thoughts run naked around that cute little pink brain of yours, I'm gonna spank your sweet ass until it's welted and red."

Her eyes widened. "Another thing I haven't tried before."

It was no use. Only thing left to do was work up a good appetite for that nice steak barbeque he'd planned. The big difference was that this time, he was going to do it all naked.

CHAPTER 12

Marcy called Devon and Nick and told them she was going to stay in Cloverdale and wasn't coming home until tomorrow.

The following day, she and Lucas shopped for provisions in town, and then about noon, went to Nick and Devon's home, where Lucas seemed impressed with the small winery.

Devon was giving them scrutiny after Marcy introduced Lucas to both of them. Marcy could tell she'd figured out who Lucas was, and what they'd been doing.

"I'd heard about this place from some of the old guys," Lucas said. Nick's head jerked up.

"Old?"

"Well, the guys who have been in longer than ten years. You got out at ten, right? About the time I joined Team 3."

"That's right."

"You okay with leaving the teams, Nick? I mean, did it give you trouble?"

"You heard I got injured? It was an easy choice after that. And Devon does really well. I think it would be harder if we lived down in San Diego, seeing all the guys every day. Here, we just blend in, man. It's a good life."

Lucas' phone chirped. "Hallo," he said as he watched Devon and Marcy whispering in the kitchen. He recognized the number as Kyle's.

"We've stepped up the training, Lucas. I gotta ask you to come back home."

"When?"

"Yesterday." Kyle's tone told him not to argue. It was a command.

"What's up?" This wasn't anything good. Something big had happened.

"Not over the phone."

"Okay, well, I'll get going tonight. Be home in about twelve hours."

"No can do. Bought you a ticket; it's waiting for you at Sonoma County Airport."

"Today, as in this afternoon?"

"Yessir. That direct flight leaves at three. You better be on it."

"I got my truck, Kyle."

"So get someone else to drive it home, Lucas. This is something we can't wait about."

It wasn't optimum, but Marcy agreed to drive Lucas' truck back to San Diego. "You can stay a couple of days up here with Nick and Devon, if you want. Makes no difference to me when I get the truck back. I won't be anywhere I'll need it."

He knew Marcy wanted to ask him where he was going. He liked that she didn't even try. He worked to calm his breathing.

He didn't want her to get as nervous as he was. "I can't even go back up to Cloverdale to clear out the place, and there's one thing I don't like leaving there."

"No worries, Lucas. I can bring your things back."

"Cabin's pretty out in the middle of nowhere, Marcy. I don't want you going up without someone to help." Nick was watching nearby.

"Promise."

"You unplug the refrigerator and take home all the food. Make sure the water's shut off. I got a couple of things in the closet, in particular, a heavy black zipper bag full of crap. Don't forget that one, Marcy." Lucas saw the black bag registered with Nick, who added his nod.

"We'll go up there tomorrow. Soonest I can do it."

"Thanks, Nick."

"So, other than making sure everything is locked up tight, nothing else needs to be done." He handed her the truck keys and watched her frown with downcast eyes. "Marcy, honey, no worries. You guys get up to Cloverdale tomorrow. You show them the way, okay?"

Marcy agreed.

"Some of that stuff's heavy. Especially that bag." He glanced over at Nick, and they shared a look. "You don't know the area and there's some crazy shit going on."

Nick gave him another brief nod.

Marcy reached for his arm. "I'll be fine, Lucas. You just come home safe," she whispered.

He held her and felt her shaking as he held her close. "I will, baby. You just keep the truck until I get back into town." He paused. "And I can't tell you when, either, but I'll call when I can."

Marcy took him to the airport in Lucas' truck so she could practice working the stick shift. He showed her all the little gadgets, like the keyless entry and the locked storage compartment she was never to open, which sat underneath the front seat. "You put the heavy black bag here in the back seat and you cover it up with the blanket there. Don't forget it, promise?"

"What's—?"

"Don't ask, Marcy. Just have Nick help you with it."

When they arrived at Schulz International, Sonoma County's only airport, Lucas checked his duty bag separately, having the talk with the security agent. He had to take some of his things with him, since he really didn't want to leave all of his firearms back with Marcy for the road trip home.

As they waited for his plane to San Diego, she brought it up first. "I'm going to have to tell Connie, Lucas. I just wanted you to know."

"Your funeral." The line was getting shorter, and then he was at the x-ray machine. "Tell her we don't get along."

"And what if she sees me driving your truck when I return it. What's she going to say then?"

"The likelihood of that is nil, Marcy. You know that. I doubt she'd ever come over to the place. She never has. You want to avoid Connie at all costs."

"I have to cancel the listing, Lucas, have to give her a reason."

"Don't mess with her, Marcy. If she does find out, don't be surprised if she doesn't try to go after your license or something like that."

"Just such a risk. I'll park the truck at your place, maybe get someone to help me with your stuff. And mysteriously slip away. Geez, Lucas I'm so nervous about all of this. I hate all this sneaking around."

"You go by Gunny's Gym and ask for Sinouk, the owner's son. He can help you with the stuff." Lucas saw she'd been pouting. "Hey, not to worry." He elicited a smile from her as he coaxed another kiss from her lips. God, he hated to leave her now.

"Sir, I'm afraid visiting hours are over," the guard barked. "You're gonna miss your plane."

He gripped the back of Marcy's hair. "We'll talk, Marcy. Not to worry. We'll figure something out."

"But I'm going to give up the listing anyway, Lucas. I just can't in good conscience—"

"*Sir!*"

"Just one fuckin' minute, okay?" Lucas shouted over the small crowd. A mother shushed him and covered her daughter's ears. "She's gonna have a pretty hard time getting my signature now, Marcy." He was rewarded with a smile, and a kiss.

His parting thought as he turned and headed for the plane: *I like the way you do business, Marcy Gelland!* He hoped he had one more time to say goodbye before they deployed in earnest. Finally, he tore himself away and tried to focus on the mission at hand.

She watched him walk out onto the windy tarmac, following a trail of travelers, including one older man in a wheelchair. He quickly turned around and ran past the security guard, who chased him back inside the terminal.

On the other side of the glass security doors, he pounded with his fists and shouted, "Marry me, Marcy Gelland!"

"Yes. Yes, I'll marry you, Lucas Shipley," she shouted back, her heart bursting, crazy, totally crazy for the guy and completely not caring about any of the reality of what she'd just plunged herself into. One thimbleful of rational thought made its way out at last.

"But first, you gotta get divorced."

CHAPTER 13

Marcy decided to go straight up to the house in Cloverdale after dropping Lucas off at the airport. She didn't want to bother Devon and Nick, who would be waiting for her to stay over tonight. Driving all the way back down to Santa Rosa, picking them up, and then going north to the cabin and then back home was just too many trips on the 101 Freeway, and inconsiderate of her friend's time. And she wanted to do the lockup in the daylight hours.

She'd promised Lucas she wouldn't go up there alone, and now she was going to violate that promise. *Always easier to ask for forgiveness than permission.* It had served her well for most of her life. Now was certainly no exception.

Traffic was coming the opposite direction as she headed north. When she pulled into the little town of Cloverdale, she stopped at a coffee shop and picked up a cappuccino and a sandwich, then took the winding road off into the woods north of town.

She took one wrong turn, then doubled back and found the correct trail to the cabin. Using the large brass key, she let herself in. As she stood, feeling the warmth and the wash of memories of what they'd been doing for the past twenty-four hours there, she blushed. It was so peaceful and quiet. On the front stoop all she could hear were the sounds of the tall trees rustling in the wind and an occasional bird. Somewhere off in the blue, cloudless sky a small plane sputtered on its way. A faint smell of campfire and woods was soothing to her nerves. It made her sleepy being so peacefully alone.

Back inside, she washed the dishes and put them away, unplugged the refrigerator and shut off the water main to the house. She made the bed, folded and straightened the towels in the bath, put Lucas' clothes in another nylon shoulder bag she found in the closet, and added her own clothes. She picked up the heavy black bag Lucas had mentioned and gingerly carried it to the truck, depositing it on the rear floor like she had been instructed, covering it with the old blanket. Returning to the house, she took one more look around, loaded the other bags up, and then went back, pulling out all the supplies from the refrigerator and put them in brown paper bags, and locked the door behind her.

Before taking off, she walked around the outside of the cabin to make sure all the windows were secured.

The roadway going out looked different than she'd remembered and again, she took a wrong turn. The drive ended in another cabin nearby, with several metal outbuildings and a stable behind it. A slim man in jeans and a light blue shirt was working with a hoe in the front yard where he was growing a small vegetable garden. A battered red pickup truck and a rusted white passenger van were parked at the side of the structure. The man looked up. He wore wire-rimmed glasses and sported a full beard.

Marcy knew there were communes and pot growers out in the woods between here and Mendocino County. The young man looked like he could have been a settler from a Jewish kibbutz with his full beard and well-tanned skin. He leaned on his hoe and squinted in the late afternoon light at her, frowning, his wire-rimmed glasses glinting in the sunlight.

She rolled down her window, leaning out. "Sorry. I'm a bit lost. Looking for the way out to the highway."

She noticed the front door of the cabin opened and she could see a face, perhaps two in the crack created. The man looked up to the door and shouted something and the door immediately shut.

He walked toward her, pointed with a thin finger, and in accent he said, "Left. Then right. All the way right."

"Okay, so I go out this driveway, turn left, and then take the first right?"

"First right, all the way right," he repeated in his thick accent. "Freeway." He nodded.

"Thank you very much."

The man bowed slightly, smiling as if blushing, averting his eyes down and away from her. Marcy put the truck in reverse, grinding the gears, which had the stranger abruptly raise his head in alarm. She hit the gas and too quickly let out the clutch and the truck stalled. She put the truck in neutral, restarted it, and took off down the road in a cloud of dust. In the rearview mirror she saw two other young men leave the front door, both standing side by side, intent on watching her truck barrel along the dusty drive. Just before she turned left, she noticed a small wooden sign she'd missed on the way in. It was the sign of the cross, with sunlight grooved in and painted in faded yellow. Underneath the insignia were the words, "Sonshine Haven."

Marcy made a mental note to ask Lucas and perhaps Nick and Devon about this obviously Christian camp so close to Lucas' cabin. In a way, it was reassuring to have a neighbor so close nearby, in case anything were to happen with the cabin.

By the time she hit Highway 101, the sun had fallen low. She got a text message that Lucas had arrived safely in San Diego and would call when he could, later tonight or tomorrow morning. She texted back hearts and kisses to him, which he returned.

Next, Marcy telephoned Devon, gave her the news and told her she was on her way back to their house.

Nick was particularly quiet over dinner, causing Devon to ask him what was wrong.

The handsome green-eyed former SEAL gave Marcy a serious look, cocking his head to the side. "Marcy, I don't know you very well but I'm bothered about one thing. And you're gonna have to forgive me on this. I'm a very careful man."

"Okay, shoot," Marcy said.

"Nick?" Devon slipped her arm under Nick's and squeezed herself next to him. "What's up?"

Nick smiled at his wife, but it quickly evaporated.

"Lucas told you not to go up there alone, and the very first thing you did when he was on that plane was go right up there."

Marcy felt her cheeks flush. Nick's direct approach to her disobedience made her feel ashamed, naked in front of them. It was time to beg for forgiveness.

"I didn't want to bother you guys—"

"But Lucas asked you *not* to do that. He made quite a point about it, and probably had good reason for that, Marcy. It has to do with your safety."

"Nick, come on," Devon pestered him.

Nick stiffened, removed Devon's arms from his, separating himself from her, and sat up straight. "It's not funny, you two. If Lucas mentioned it, then it was important. You have to trust him when he tells you things like that, Marcy. You don't know what's at stake."

"I know, but nothing happened. I just got all the things out, did what he asked, and I buttoned up the house so you guys don't have to be bothered with it."

"Except he's going to want me to go up there and make sure it's okay. So you didn't save me a trip after all."

"Nick? What the heck is going on?" Devon asked. Her frown cut deep into the bridge of her nose.

"These are strange times. Lucas even said it. I've been told about all sorts of stuff you guys don't want to know about. It's for your protection you not know. But you have to follow directions. Nothing optional about it."

Marcy knew he was right, but she didn't care for Nick's method of delivery. She felt prickly. Devon had obviously picked it up.

"Nick, get over it, will you? No harm no foul. That's one of your favorite expressions. So just chill. The main thing is that she got it done. Lucas' stuff is safely back down here."

"Not the point, Devon."

"I'm done with this, Nick. You need to go to bed. Now." Devon was getting angry. "Marcy and I will clean up here."

Devon pointed to the stairs.

Nick gave her a hug and quick kiss. Then he addressed Marcy. "Sorry, kid. I'm going to be a stickler about this. Tomorrow we go back up there and double check everything, not that you didn't do everything correctly, but he wanted me to go so I could confirm that it was all done. We're like that. Thorough. Checking, double-checking. Sometimes our life depends on it. No reflection on you."

"I understand." Marcy thought she did a pretty good job of hiding her hurt feelings.

Nick turned and ran upstairs. Marcy followed Devon to the kitchen, and then remembered the food she'd left in the truck. "Holy crap. I've probably got a back seat full of sour milk and melted cheese."

"I'll help you."

The two of them carried the two boxes inside the kitchen. Marcy was going to get the other bags later. They stowed the perishables, cleaned up the dinner and placed dishes in the dishwasher, turning it on. Devon made a couple of glasses of ice water and handed one to Marcy. "Come on, let's sit in the living room for a bit."

"I'm for that," said Marcy settling into the comfortable couch.

"Let's catch up on some juicy gossip," Devon started. "I want to know all about Lucas' wife, or soon-to-be ex-wife. What's she like?"

"She's a piece of work, Dev. Gorgeous, but a basket case. She's bitter, and I don't think he did anything to deserve that. She's jealous of his connection with the Brotherhood."

"From what I've heard, some of the guys play around a lot. Father children all over the place. Many of them lack good judgement. Don't get yourself caught, Marcy. Be careful."

"I might be stupid, but I believe Lucas. I really do," admitted Marcy.

"Some women aren't made for this lifestyle. I might not have been very good at it, actually."

"I don't know much about the community. Maybe you can help me there. All I know is Lucas is on her list. She seems to genuinely hate him. I feel sorry for those kids. Just too bad what she's doing."

"They're pretty intense. But I remember I asked one of the wives about them before Nick and I got married one time when I visited—have you been to any of their get-togethers?"

"No. This happened so fast. I mean, we're only at day three here."

"Right. I forget, Marcy. They rarely let in outsiders, so having you here, involved with him like this, well, it brings you into the inner circle. They have a funny way about them, a code. You're either in, or you're out. You're in, Marcy, and Connie is out. But none of the guys will date her. If she's out, she's out."

"It just seems over the top."

Devon laughed. "In the beginning, I thought so, too. I mean, Nick seemed just like a total asshole at first. So full of himself. But boy, when we got involved, man did sparks fly."

Marcy felt her cheeks pink up again.

"You have to love the way they live, their intensity. Sometimes they're right on, and sometimes they have shit for brains." Devon continued. "They get all this training, all this fantastic equipment. They pretty much feel invincible. Hard for them when they come home. The wives are taking care of everything, running the house, paying the bills, and then he comes home and suddenly he's the king. All she wants to do is get some help. Especially with the kids."

"Makes sense. Connie more or less told me the same thing." Marcy was hesitant to ask Devon so she started softly. "You guys going to try anytime soon, Devon?"

"Have been. It will happen when it happens. At least I don't have to try to space the births around deployments, like some of the other wives do."

"Impossible." Marcy shook her head. How *did* women handle all that, not knowing if their men would come home? But she realized it was what women and families of soldiers have to deal with all the time. Always been that way for those who chose to love warriors, not a stock broker, insurance man, or another realtor.

"So what's her main beef with Lucas?"

"I think the tipping point was a bachelor party, and some of the pictures taken were a little revealing." Marcy giggled. "They had some dancers and such."

"Strippers," interrupted Devon. "Seems to be a custom for these guys. I don't even ask what Nick's party was like."

"Well this one was worse, from what I understand."

Devon frowned.

"Someone posted them on Facebook, and when Connie saw them, she flipped out."

"You can be sure I didn't check Nick's FB page for a month afterward."

"Smart. But, honestly, I think Connie didn't want anything coming between her and Lucas. I think she began to resent the Navy, resent his closeness to the other team guys, perhaps asking him to choose between her and the brotherhood."

"Ouch! Not smart."

"Just my guess, Dev. So when Lucas didn't agree or side with her, I think she decided she was done. I hate to think it's about the money she'll make with the sale of the house, but you know, Devon, I couldn't even rule *that* out. She's one of the meanest people I've ever met."

"And you have to deal with her?"

"I think I'm handing the listing over to someone else."

"Probably wise. I mean, I can only imagine what would happen if she found out—"

"Gives me chills, Dev. Not looking forward to that."

"And you have to drive his truck all the way back to San Diego, too?"

Marcy shrugged.

"How is the market down there?"

"Going gangbusters. That's why I have to get back. Been one of the busiest times I've had. How about you?"

"You know what they say. How do you make a small fortune in the wine business? Start with a large fortune and you'll soon have a small fortune."

They shared a laugh.

"Everything I saved and did has gone into the winery. We start crush soon, fingers crossed for nice temperate weather for harvest. Hoping we get a good yield and the grapes are better than last year. We're at year five now. Another two to go and we'll know."

"Are you still selling real estate as much as before?"

"As much as I can. But Nick needs my help here, too. I represent some big investors who are buying right now, so that part's been good for me. We have investors too, some of the SEAL families are part owners, so that takes the burden off, but adds the pressure to turn a profit."

Marcy looked around the house, hearing the crickets through the screens overlooking the patio. The large harvest moon was just rising over the vineyards in the distance. It was a special evening. Felt like the calm before the storm, for some reason, and she was grateful her college friend could give her the time to just sit and chat.

"You own a little piece of Heaven, Devon."

"That we do. Sophie, Nick's sister, always said so, and she was right. I wouldn't trade my lifestyle for anywhere else in the world. I'd like to raise my family here one day. I'd love this to be a Northern California Wine Retreat for SEALs and their families."

"Wouldn't that be something?"

CHAPTER 14

Lucas was met at the airport by Jake and Alex. The warm night air smelled of the salty inlet, something he'd forgotten he missed.

"So what's up with your truck, man?" Jake asked as Lucas climbed into the second seat of the Hummer.

"It's getting driven back in the next day or two. Kyle wanted me back here ASAP. You tell me, what the fuck's going on?"

"All shit is hitting the fan. We got a lot of chatter about some groups all over the U.S. They're making us do some specialized training with the guys from Little Creek. Team 6 uncovered some stuff in Turkey. And someone tried to take out a military surgeon on vacation in Oregon with his family. They were just camping."

Lucas felt guilty he'd been so head over heels loving Marcy, he hadn't been watching the news. Other than X-rated movies, international news was as popular as sports at the bachelor pad.

"Everyone okay?"

"Cut up, especially his wife, but the kids were okay. Lucky thing he was carrying a gun, though he'll get written up for it." Jake drove them in the opposite direction of the apartment.

"You're shitting me," Lucas said.

"Federal lands. Not allowed to carry," Alex said over the back of the seat. "They might not have survived without it, though."

"That's messed up," said Lucas. No one said a word. Lucas noticed they seemed to be headed toward Coronado. "Hey, we going over to the Team Building?"

"Yup," said Jake.

The injustice of the attack and the fact that the man might get in trouble for defending his family had him fuming. "Just can't believe they'd actually put a letter in his file." Lucas continued to shake his head as he watched the lights of the Coronado base come into view.

"Kyle thinks they'll go light on him, but they have to make note of it." Jake's shoulders rounded as he continued, "A very strange world out there, Lucas."

"That it is. You guys do any training yesterday or day before?" Lucas asked.

"Nope. We start the briefing tonight. Couple of guys coming in tomorrow," answered Jake.

They passed the guard shack, parked the Hummer, and walked toward the entrance to their building. Kyle was locked in serious conversation with a small group of team guys, including T.J., Cooper, Tyler, Rory, and Luke. All of them looked up and behind Lucas as the team erupted in a warm welcome for a dark-skinned man wearing western wear, including cowboy boots.

Kyle put his arm around Jake, as he pulled a group of newbies over to introduce them. "This here is the baddest motherfucker on the whole planet."

The dark-skinned man nodded and looked down at his boots. Though he wasn't one of the newbies, Lucas had never met the man before, even on his DEVGRU deployment.

In a heavily accented voice, the newcomer answered, "Only when I have you guys at my back, or dropping in like flies all around me. Then I can be very, very brave. By myself, not so much."

T.J. and Luke came over and gave the man a bear hug. "Come here you lying sonofabitch," T.J. said to his ear. He made a grand gesture of kissing him on the side of the face. "How the fuck are you?"

"I'm good. My wife's pregnant again. Hoping to create one of those, how you say, 'anchor babies'?"

"Why am I not surprised?" Rory Kennedy said.

When T.J. let go of him, Kyle stepped up and repeated the hug. He turned and presented the man to Lucas, Jake, Alex, and several newbies at the end. "This here is Jackie Daniels, our interpreter. We don't know his real name—"

A couple of the older SEALs started laughing. Lucas hadn't seen so many white teeth since the last time they'd had a bachelor party and half of them were completely shitfaced. Fredo and Armani entered the warehouse building, along with several others Lucas thought looked like transplants from other teams.

Cooper added his hug to the lineup. "Yeah, if he told us, he'd have to kill us, so we call him Jackie. And T.J.'s right, he's the baddest motherfucker in the whole Navy."

"No. Your government will not make me a Navy man. I am working on my citizenship, but soon, they will give it to me, and then I can be a taxi driver like all of my other countrymen."

Jake stepped forward and shook Jackie's hand. "Honor to meet you. Heard a lot about you, Mr. Daniels."

"Jackie," the interpreter corrected. "Mr. Daniels sounds like some guy who is the principal at my daughter's school."

Jackie gripped Lucas's hand, tilting his head and giving him a wide smile, but his eyes didn't blink or waver, and Lucas felt like he'd just had his mind read. Jackie took a respectful step back and seemed to sense the new introductions had some uneasy around him. Lucas also knew it didn't bother the terp, Jackie, one bit.

They'd been told the stories about how he'd risked his life on several missions with their team, as well as several others he'd worked with in the past. Their highest level capture was on a mission that nearly cost six SEALs and a CIA agent their lives. Unlike several of the other interpreters, Jackie was not opposed to be carrying a weapon and protected them on this mission when they freed several SEAL hostages taken captive. This was before Lucas joined the team.

Like a skilled warrior, Jackie didn't force himself on any of them, nor make them show loyalty without it being earned. Lucas knew he was a big-time asset to whatever mission they would be tasked with.

Kyle came to attention, regarding several men in and out of uniform who walked through the Team 3 Building doors. Lucas and everyone else faced them, and several addressed the new audience in hushed tones.

Collins, their SEAL liaison, walked over to a small group of tables and chairs, followed by one Lt. Commander and a non-uniformed, who Lucas judged to be CIA. Kyle took his place next to them, making a fourth. Lucas knew something big was going on as another couple of unidentified, but well-built, gentlemen took to some rear seats in the pit. This was a nighttime briefing, conducted without the whole Charlie Team being present, which meant they were in a hurry. He was glad he'd texted Marcy when he landed, since he doubted he'd be able to be in much communication very soon.

"Gentlemen, take your seats," Kyle said to the group, who had already started doing so before the order was given. Lucas sat next to Jake and Ryan. Looking around, he nodded to Alex, Cory, and several others.

No one standing was smiling. T.J. and Luke sandwiched Jackie, the terp. Danny and Jeffrey sat together in the back row, both wearing sunglasses, though the building was low lit. Rory sat just in front of them.

"This here is Lt. Commander Ian Forsythe, Office of Naval Intelligence. He's going to brief you on a situation we have going on now. Lt. Commander?" Kyle backed up and the highly decorated veteran cleared his throat and took the center stage. Though the SEALs were not required to salute, each man in his own way sat up straighter, uncrossed their arms, and showed they were paying attention, unlike their normal demeanor.

"You've been briefed before about terrorist group formations in this country. I know you had a representative of DEVGRU, SO Thom Grand, speaking with you recently about death teams who we now know have landed here. We have it on good authority some have been spotted in several areas in the southwest, south, and now with this recent incident in Oregon, we believe some are in the Pacific Northwest. We're still scrambling a bit to gather all that intelligence without tipping our hand."

Lucas' stomach lurched as he realized he hadn't eaten anything since boarding the plane, except for some peanuts and a coke. Or, maybe it was the news. He would have anticipated getting geared up and ready to roll if he was with Team 6 again, or even Team 3 in Iraq. But he wasn't sure what the plan of action was for the situation at hand. This was a threat on U.S. soil, after all.

Forsythe continued. "We know members of the military, especially SEALs, are being targeted. Our families are in danger. Our friends too, perhaps. Time to take measures, hopefully preventative measures to ensure our community stays safe."

Forsythe turned to Collins, who stepped up next to him. "Gentlemen, we're going to institute some rules that will not be broken, do I make myself clear?"

Affirmations trickled from the group, a combination of nods and whispers and grunts.

"While we are doing some specialized training, and this will all be explained to you in detail, we're going to organize a com schedule, so no one on this team is out of the loop. And this is going to extend to your wives. And I gotta also mention there will not be the usual recreational use of females, or something that involves you getting shitfaced and making a scene, or getting caught in some place by yourself with people you don't know. We aren't sure how they'll come after us, but we're staying vigilant and, of course, prepared. Being prepared keeps us alive, right, gents?"

Again a wave of affirmations filled the room.

Kyle added his comments. "Newbies especially, listen up. We're doing something that's never been done before. We're going to create an old-fashioned phone list. You are to be in phone contact with five other men on our team every day, morning and evening. And you are to pass along anything you see that is out of the ordinary. Each five-man group will have a senior man who will be responsible for relaying information. But, make no mistake, you can't get hold of someone? You call me, you call Coop here, Fredo, Armani, or Collins."

Forsythe added, "Your training is going to coincidentally take place next to two well-known and documented terrorist training camps. Active camps. Camps we believe have recently imported some talent, and that talent has been kept hidden, which means they know we're surveilling them, and they're still doing it."

A hushed silence fell over the group. Someone let out a loud and long, "Fuuuuck."

"Gentlemen, those of you who've been over in the arena know that not many of these guys fear death. They don't fear getting caught, because that makes the news. Making the news is what they're after. They won't win in the end, but they want to make the US of A feel like a self-imposed prison camp." Forsythe exhaled and paced back and forth.

So that was the gig, Lucas thought. They were supposed to look like they were just living their lives as usual, but they were going to go dangerously close to the bee and not get stung, or be ready for the swarm. They were going to tempt the group to try and snag one of them. But he wasn't sure, so he thought he'd asked.

"Sir, SO Shipley here. May I ask a question?" Lucas stood.

"Go ahead, son," Forsythe answered.

"I'm just not clear, and you probably have much more to tell us, but from what our brothers at DEVGRU, SEAL Team 6, told us, weren't they interested in perhaps doing a reverse snatch and grab?" Lucas could see a couple of newbies had no clue what he was saying.

"That's right. We think they're looking to take a target back with them, possibly a SEAL, and more specifically, one from Team 3 or 5."

More muttering and private discussions continued until Lucas continued. "Okay, then. Why are we going to train near them, if our goal is to avoid being captured or killed?"

Kyle inserted himself before Forsythe could answer. "You mean did we just confirm the CIA and Naval Intelligence is using us as bait? That your question, SO Shipley?"

Lucas nodded his head. "Yes, Chief." He heard a couple of the older SEALs swear, crossing their arms and legs. It was something apparently, several of them were thinking about, but none were excited by the idea.

"Who else would you suggest, SO Shipley?" began Forsythe. "Your wives and children, innocent civilians?" Forsythe drilled his stare into Lucas, his breathing very slow and deep, like he was bracing for a punch and was completely calm and ready for whatever anyone would dish out. All sound was sucked out of the room and nobody moved. "I'm asking you a serious question. I'm as serious as a heart attack, Shipley."

T.J. Talbot snarled out, "Oh yeah. 'Come on over here said the spider to the fly.'" The big SEAL examined the fingernails on his right hand as Jackie and Luke started chuckling. Lucas sat.

Coop was more sober. "I'm going to ask you what I always need to know, sir."

"All ears here," answered Forsythe.

"The women and children. What the fuck are we supposed to do with them?"

After a brief moment of silence, while everyone looked at Kyle, Jones added his comments. "You dumb-fuck." Jones waved his long arms around his head. "You white boys are real slow in the bedroom. You're supposed to keep them barefoot and happy. Nekked I think, too. Yo mamas never teach you nothin?"

Everyone started adding their two cents. But Coop and Kyle were staring at each other like they shared something no one else knew about. Kyle hushed the raucous spouting off. Lucas knew it was nervous repartee, helping to mask how uneasy everyone felt about this whole situation. "Wait a minute guys," Kyle continued. "Coop has a point. So listen up." He turned to Collins and then glanced over at Forsythe.

"I'll take that," said Forsythe. "We're instituting something for them, too. Similar. We're going to embed some extra protection. We're also coordinating with the local sheriff and police, on a very limited basis, not with the rank and file, so while you're gone on training, or, if we don't have a more favorable outcome, we may delay deployment. Just not sure yet what that's going to look like."

"In the meantime, we're traveling out of state," said Kyle.

Fredo shouted out, "Snow gear or swim trunks?"

Some of their jungle training was in Baja, some in Florida, or desert training in Las Vegas. Alaska was always good for cold-weather exercises.

"Neither," barked Forsythe. He took two steps to the side, assuming the wide stance some of the officers were known for, arms crossed behind his back. He inhaled sharply, gave them a half smile and shouted, "Gentlemen, we're headed to Tennessee."

CHAPTER 15

Marcy and Nick drove up to Cloverdale in Lucas' truck mid-morning.

"Sorry about the inconvenience, Nick. I thought I was saving you some time."

"No need to apologize, but you gotta pay attention, Marcy. It comes with the territory."

She knew he was right. "You know we hardly know each other, Nick. There is so much about Lucas I'm just learning."

"Afraid I can't help you there. But even if I could, we don't do that."

Marcy knew it was an uphill battle. It was a long-shot that the two of them would wind up together, and now she began to feel guilty she'd said yes to marrying him. In fact, as she thought about all the decisions she'd made, especially the one about "screwing the husband of the divorcing clients," which was a huge no-no on every scale possible, she was ashamed. She might have even jeopardized her job at Coronado Bay.

Nick tuned on a country satellite station, taking some of the tension out of the air. She crossed and uncrossed her arms and legs and began chewing down a nail. The countryside was green with rows of vineyards, but the brown earth and commercial buildings detracted from the beauty of the several wineries they passed on their way. Traffic bothered her. The bugs on the truck's windshield bothered her. She didn't like one of the songs, and she wished she was back in San Diego, near the ocean, near the blue water and the breeze that was ever present.

Her cell rang. Nick turned down the radio station so she could answer it. "This is Marcy."

"Where the devil are you, Marcy?" Her broker's voice sounded shrill.

"Sorry, Joe. I'm up here in Sonoma County, looking at my client's real estate. She asked me to do it."

"Are you sure about that?"

"Yes." Marcy's stomach flip-flopped, and she squeezed the phone against her ear.

"I've had some complaints from other agents; they can't get hold of you."

"I've gotten no calls, Joe. I'll be back in a day or two."

"Good idea, Marcy. Say, you give that SEAL's wife your cell?"

"I did. Why?"

"Not sure, but she's been talking to Gail here in the office, you know, the new agent married to the football player?"

"Oh yes."

"I guess they're friends. I'd watch my back on that one."

"Joe, there's a little situation there I need to go over with you." Marcy looked sideways at Nick who was pretending he couldn't hear. "I'm going to give up their listing. Coming up here, well, it's changed my perspective a bit." Then she felt Nick's eyes on her as she tried to speak to the passenger window softly, seeking some privacy. "I just can't represent them. I don't feel like I can get along with Connie."

"Then talk with Gail, or someone else about referring it, Marcy. But do it quick."

"Will do. As soon as I get back."

"I'd do it by phone. I'd talk to your client today." Joe hung up.

Was she ready to confront Connie, and do it by phone, not in person like she'd planned? She'd thought she would have the long drive home to San Diego to rehearse and think about how to tell Connie, so it wouldn't blow up in her face. Not being present in person was more dangerous.

"So the wifey doesn't know you and Lucas are an item? That what I'm hearing?" Nick asked.

"Afraid so."

Nick was mercifully quiet. Marcy knew what he was thinking. This also wasn't a very good way to gain points with her college friend and her husband either. Marcy sighed. She was messing up on all fronts.

"I really screwed things up, Nick," she said at last.

"Roger that, Marcy. You got yourself one hell of a problem. And it's going to be a problem for Lucas, too, even if he didn't think about all this beforehand."

No, they certainly hadn't thought about anything. All that mattered at the time, and for the two days afterward, was the chemistry between them, how she felt being around Lucas.

The sounds of the truck filled the deadly silence between them.

Nick continued. "We do so many things well overseas, because we're trained to do it over and over again. All this stuff? Divorce, selling houses, dating? I can't say our community does it very well. We're used to jumping in without thinking. Can't do that at home. And that's a hard lesson to learn. Took me awhile to settle down to being a civilian."

She appreciated his candor and realized she was getting more of a glimpse of the community, way more than she probably deserved.

"But you eventually did, Nick? You eventually made the switch over?"

He nodded, staring right as they pulled off into the woods north of town. "I got injured and that helped the choice. But I couldn't do it back down there in San Diego. It would've driven me nuts. But yes, eventually." He smiled back at her, his honest green eyes giving her a steady hand-up. "Not saying I don't miss it sometimes, though." He splayed his right hand as it rested on top of the steering wheel. "Just being perfectly honest."

Marcy gave him instructions, and in a few minutes they pulled down the now-familiar dirt driveway.

"I can see why he wanted you to come here in the daytime. And you *do* know there are pot growers all over here, right?"

"He told me."

"Used to be a big problem when people would stumble onto someone's field and get shot. Now I think these people grow inside temperature-controlled buildings, the big operations, that is. And they don't do the pot forests like the old days."

"Speaking from first-hand knowledge?" Marcy said as she opened her door and hopped out.

"Not me. My folks, believe it or not."

"You know I got lost coming here yesterday. There are little roads and trails all over the place up here. When I came the first time, I used my GPS. But not everything up here is on that map."

Nick walked to the front stoop. "Nice up here. Very remote, though. You don't ever want to be at this place alone."

Marcy nodded and inserted the key into the front door. Fear coursed through her when she discovered it was unlocked. She was sure she had locked it when she left.

She instantly knew someone had been inside the home even before she saw the mess left behind. The cupboards had been ransacked. Cushions in the living room had been torn open, white pieces of cotton stuffing fell like snow over the floor. A long wooden cabinet door was broken off the hinges, splinters covering the braided rug in front of it. A metal lock was discarded. Nick ran to the bare cabinet first.

"Was this empty?"

"I have no idea."

He peered through checkerboard kitchen window curtains, while Marcy noticed someone had thrown darts, hitting the wall instead of the game board. Nick searched the rest of the cabin, including the closets and the bathroom.

"I'm going to go look around outside. You check for anything that might be missing, if you can tell."

Contents had been removed from the bathroom cabinet and strewn over the floor. Several vitamin and aspirin bottles had been opened and their tablets were absorbing water, turning to paste. Someone had used the toilet, not been very careful about their aim and not flushed it.

Marcy checked the bedroom closet. Every box or bag was opened, and open-ended. Books were removed from the desk in the corner. The cushions on the overstuffed reading chair were sliced open and stuffing was removed just like in the living room.

She wondered what the motive of the break-in had been. The urine left in the toilet made her think druggie kids might be the culprits.

Nick entered the bedroom just as she'd discovered the bedroom window latch had been pried off the wooden sash, which still remained open. "I think this is how they got in," she told him.

Nick fingered the cut marks in the window frame. "I'm not liking this. I've got to get hold of Lucas. You sure you never saw this gun cabinet loaded with weapons?"

"No. I think the weapons are still in the second seat of the truck."

"What the fuck?" Nick's eyes squinted. He cocked his head. "What are you saying, Marcy?"

"The large black bag he was most concerned about is in the back seat of his truck. He wanted me to make sure you helped me. I forgot all about it when I got home last night. It's still there."

Nick ran outside, ripping open the second seat door, removing the blanket and placed the bag over the other items on the bench. As he unzipped it, Marcy could see over his shoulder a huge weapon nearly four feet long. There were several smaller bags, which Nick quickly checked through, and she noticed several contained large sharply-tipped brass rounds in neat rows. Another weapon, much shorter and stubby, looking like a small machine gun, was wrapped in a dirty blue towel. He undid pockets on the front of the bag, pulling out a couple thick knives with serrated edges. Marcy was looking at the bag belonging to a killing machine. Something deep in her stomach churned and her mouth became parched.

The sun was making her dizzy and she stepped back.

Nick made sure the black nylon was well hidden under the old blanket, and turned to address her.

"You're not used to all this, so I have to forgive you for some of your stupid mistakes, but Marcy, no more. You've made a whole boatload of bad decisions, starting with leaving unattended a very dangerous weapon and enough rounds of ammo to kill a hundred people. In the wrong hands, these things are deadly. Could cost you and everyone you love their lives. So, I'm going to give it to you straight. Don't make this fuckin' mistake again. I'm not letting you drive to San Diego alone to return them to Lucas. And I know sure as shit he's going to need them very soon."

"Sorry."

"No. Just doing what he'd do if he was here. Marcy," He stepped forward so quickly she jumped, flinching when he grabbed her shoulders. "You don't do shit like this again. You watch everything. You never leave a weapon lying around where it can be stolen, or found by police, understood?"

"Yes." She couldn't help it, but her lower lip was quivering. If she wasn't so afraid, she'd be breaking down into a sob, seeking the comfort of Nick's arms.

"Okay, gotta call Lucas. You feel okay about starting to clean up in there?"

"Yes. Again, Nick, I'm—"

Nick had dialed Lucas and interrupted her. "Hey, asshole. You wanna tell me what you were doing with an M27 and a fuckin' MP5 in the back seat while your girlfriend and my wife go shopping for bagels and coffee and shit?"

Marcy was glad she couldn't hear Lucas' response.

CHAPTER 16

Moustafa was glad he'd seen the woman who was fated to come into his web yesterday. He'd dreamt about her all night long as he pleasured himself lying on the mattress out under the stars. When he'd heard an owl hooting in the distance, he grew cautious, washed his hands in the hose bib by the garden and retired inside for the rest of the evening.

His two recruits read their books by candlelight. Moustafa was trying to use as little energy as he could, and liked the idea that the boys were learning their sacred studies just as the Prophet had centuries ago, by candlelight.

God is great.

He knew where she had come from, and he'd scouted the little cabin earlier in the month. So he had reason to go back now. As the dawn was breaking he and the others hiked a path through the heavy woods. He chuckled that the recruits would be scratching their skin off the next day, as the forest was full of poison oak.

Moustafa knew the best thing was to take a cold shower afterwards, use his Tech-Nu and then blot his skin dry. He wouldn't get the pox of western man that way. But the boys needed to experience the uncomfortable results while they meditated and did their prayers.

God is great.

He'd seen the gun cabinet on the previous scouting and was most anxious to open it and steal what he thought would surely be some weaponry inside. But that was not to be. The flimsy pine cabinet only held cobwebs and spiders. Even the refrigerator was empty.

He relished shredding the couch pillows, tossing all the dishes and glassware like they were made of paper. His recruits took his lead and destroyed the bathroom. Nothing was found that was of use. The books were unreadable, the magazines worse, although his recruits stole the ones with the naked women in them, thinking Moustafa wouldn't catch them hiding the folded lust books in their clothes. They were like schoolboys upset with being harshly punished, angry that there wasn't anything to eat in the refrigerator, which was still partially cold, justified to help themselves to the infidel's debauched way of life.

He was going to turn on the water and let it run, perhaps burn up the pump and drain the well, but he wanted to watch her shower again, like he'd watched the night before when the big man was there fucking her on his knees with his lips, fucking her from behind and letting her fuck him between her breasts. He would enjoy taking her apart bit by bit, if the opportunity presented itself. It could be a teaching moment for his recruits, who would soon have to do the same. He'd show them an infidel was not like a real woman, one of their believers. They were too used to their mothers and sisters, but they'd learn, in time. Showing them how to properly kill an infidel would toughen them up.

He heard the high-pitched whine of the infidel's truck from a mile away only an hour after they'd started searching the cabin. They'd had just enough time to run back toward the mother house. Moustafa jumped in the shower and put on clean pajama pants and a loose fitting Humboldt State t-shirt, watching as one by one, both of his new recruits began to scratch their skin. He didn't feel a thing.

God is great.

By now, she would have found the cabin altered. Moustafa would wait until nightfall and then creep back and perhaps spy on her sleeping there. Perhaps look for items in the vehicle she wouldn't think to lock up.

He got out his yellow-lined tablet, working on his plan for new recruits arriving this fall, all arranged through a refugee humanitarian program administered by the church group they bought the camp from.

God is great.

America was indeed the land of opportunity. They had no idea what they were willingly giving away. It was a sign from the Prophet they could walk right in and claim what was theirs. The Kingdom of Heaven would reign supreme for all the true believers. And those who did not submit, would be eliminated. There was only one path to Heaven and all roads led there, whether or not the hapless Americans knew it or not.

He smiled as he looked out the window at the bright sunshine. In the dialect of his adopted home, Northern California, he said to himself, 'God is Awesome!'

CHAPTER 17

Lucas hadn't been able to reach Marcy, but the call with Nick got him worried. They'd all been asked to stay off their cells, unless it was an emergency, so he'd had to end the call quickly without asking how she was doing.

"Can't talk, Nick. I'll be dark for a few. Bring that shit home." He hated to hang up like that, do that to a former teammate, even though they hadn't served together. But he knew Nick would figure it out.

Their transport was waiting on the tarmac near lunchtime, the big beast gobbling all sixteen of them, with another group coming the following week from two other teams that were redeployed from the Pacific and East Africa. They landed in Park Field as part of the Naval Mid-South command base. The temporary training hangar and cyclone workout area looked like old prison grounds. A small track bordering a roughly patched lawn with goalposts at the end seemed out of place in the dusty heat of the afternoon.

Tyler Gray was the first to say something after they walked their gear toward the yard. "Holy mother fuck. We got ourselves a soccer field."

Fredo nodded his head. T.J. and Cooper looked toward the sky at the heat of the sun and shook their heads. Lucas stood next to them all, feeling suddenly joyful. "We can have ourselves a scrimmage, gents."

"Gets mighty hot this time of year," said Rory.

Lucas turned back to survey the rest of the base. Old planes and bunk buildings, long since unused, littered the area. It did not look like a high-level SEAL facility, but Lucas reminded himself it didn't take lots of shiny new equipment and paint to make a good target. Even a fresh patch of green lawn wouldn't do it. They weren't there to impress anyone. They were flesh and blood bait on a stick.

The team was greeted by a petite woman in blue camo. She wore a whistle around her neck and a stopwatch. She singled out Kyle somehow and shook his hand. "Donna Grant. I'm one of your trainers here."

Several of the team regarded the diminutive woman, but respectfully not a word was spoken. "Chief Petty Officer Kyle Lansdowne. Where you want us, ma'am?"

She dropped her hand and did an about face, motioning him to follow toward one of the run-down barracks. Several vans were parked nearby and a Skilsaw was being operated inside one of the rooms.

"We don't have much, but what we have is yours, Chief. Had to install internet and some extra plugs, replace part of the bathroom fixtures, some broken windows, and got rid of the crusty urinals. These buildings haven't been used for over twenty years."

She turned to the group, smiling tightly. "Downsizing and all that shit," she said, wiggling her eyebrows.

Kyle angled his head and frowned, but his eyes grew to twice their size. "Good to know." He winked at Coop and Fredo.

Lucas regarded the grins and white teeth surrounding him and knew the little lady had just made one hell of an impression on the whole group. Someone mumbled, "I think I might like this training after all."

Donna walked like a basketball player, but without the tall lanky build. The hallway floor was covered with speckled puce gray vinyl tiles the Navy used boatloads of all over the world. The building was cool and dark. When she flipped on the buzzing overhead lights, some of them blinking and barely glowing behind yellowed plastic covers, it wasn't much of an improvement.

"Okay, you campers can choose your rooms. Trust me, take the ones on the ground floor. Upstairs can be for the poor frogs who have to come next week."

The rooms were not large, but bedrooms opened to a central quad area, so four men could share the common area. Single mattresses in each room were brand new, still in plastic, one set of white sheets and a pillowcase folded neatly and perfectly centered. The rec room at the end of the building was completely sparse. No TVs, tables, or couches were anywhere in sight. A stainless steel all-in-one sink, stove, and dishwasher was bordered by light green Formica countertops with stainless steel, real authentic retro trim. Plywood cabinets overhead had no doors on them.

"Looks like a Costco run is in order, gents," whispered Kyle.

"Do they even have a fuckin' Costco in Tennessee?" asked Fredo.

"Oh yes. We have three," added Donna. "We got more bars, more churches, and the biggest Costco in the whole state not more than a few miles away."

Donna announced the evening dinner would be served at o-eight-hundred and pointed to the hall where it would be served. "And tonight, we have something special for you. Providing you behave yourselves, you'll get to train with the Navy Soccer team. They're joining us for dinner tonight, gentlemen."

Lucas and Tyler grinned at each other. Both of them had played with the boys before and were looking to a rematch.

"When do they arrive?" asked Tyler.

Donna checked her watch. "They're on their way now. Just finished up a game against Tennessee State, and they won, so the ladies are going to want to celebrate."

"Ladies?" Lucas asked.

"Yes. Didn't I tell you? They're the Navy *Women's* Soccer Team."

The announcement had room choices happening quickly and the showers were suddenly full, which limited the water pressure to a trickle.

Kyle conducted a briefing before dinner. "We're about ten miles from the camp run by the MOA group here. Occasionally we'll see members on the freeway, or in town at various places, primarily grocery outlets and secondhand stores. You are not to engage them. I'm good with you looking casual, sharp and military, but no insignias of any branch, please. I'm okay if they think you're a paramilitary defense contractor group here for some specialized training, or, better yet, Army Corps of Engineers working on one of the dams or waterways nearby. But don't volunteer one fuckin' thing. Don't talk to them, or to the locals who have befriended them. You can't trust a one, not one."

Kyle continued with some of the ground rules. "Any of you want to grow beards, be my guest. You know how that registers and identifies us overseas. But again, and I can't stress this enough, you stay off social media as far as posting pictures and letting people at home know you're okay or where you are exactly. Only cell phones, and only if it's extremely important. We have internet just to get and send information about our finds, and not for your pleasure, okay?"

The team grumbled.

Kyle handed out a list of names. "This is your phone tree, like your mom had when you were playing soccer. You check in with your men on this list every morning and every night. You know where they are, when they'll be back, when they get up, and when they go to bed."

"Do we have to find out when they take a shit?" T.J. asked. The group started adding other bits of helpful advice.

"I'm thinking no," said Kyle, who grinned neatly and then turned to all business.

Lucas had chosen a room with Jake, Alex, and Ryan. They'd already made a list of furniture for their crib, as well as the electronic equipment, including a big screen TV and a couple of blenders.

"We gonna be allowed to watch streaming video?" Jake asked.

"Working on it, Jake. Security is our main concern, so stuff like that has to be checked out, and the ONI office hasn't finished their work. We'll work something out."

Kyle distributed pictures of the camp bordered with tall metal fencing covered with razor wire in the remote forested region up the road, which also encompassed a rocky crag nearly two hundred feet tall. Kyle told them the group had twenty-four-seven guards posted in pairs atop this vantage point.

He also told them all areal surveillance was current. The group had purchased a small dozer-tractor and they appeared to be enlarging a large swale or earthen dam, harnessing one of the tributaries into a man-made lake that had begun to fill. "We don't know what's going on here, but if you'll notice they have some small watercraft so we're guessing some kind of amphibious training exercise area." He showed them a picture of a target range and one long metal hangar with no doors or windows in it. The structure looked brand new.

"We are trying to find out what that building is. I'm sending a couple of you over to the contractor's office to find out. Whatever it is, you can bet it's no good. We don't have authority to trespass, so keep your distance, but understand these guys are for real, and they've spent a lot of money getting set up."

The jovial nature of the possible meetup with the soccer players was dashed as the team studied the glossy pictures being passed around. Kyle held up a picture of a graying rotund gentleman in a long Afghani robe and gray pakol cap. His wide face and near mid-chest level beard streaked with light brown made him look grandfatherly and harmless. Lucas had seen many of these tribal members before on previous deployments and it was difficult to tell the good guys from the bad guys.

"You see this guy, you let me or Lt. Commander Forsythe know right away. This is Sheik Hammid Rushti. He hasn't been picked up by birds in a month or more, so he's either escaped without detection or he's still inside. And if he is, we'd guess he'd be here." Kyle pointed to the long, ominous building.

Kyle went over the training schedule as Donna Grant entered the building and announced dinner.

Most the SEALs wore white V-necked t-shirts, and jeans or cargo pants, and canvas slip-ons. There was more aftershave and clean-shaven cheeks than Lucas had remembered at a high school dance. He knew, after tonight, everyone who would be growing beards.

He'd gotten two text messages marked urgent from both Nick and Marcy to call, so he tried to reach Marcy first.

"Lucas, someone's broken into the cabin."

"What? You get my black bag?" He tried to hide the edge to his voice.

"Yes, not to worry. That bag and all your things came back with me. Everything you asked me to get, I did."

"So, what do you mean? Broken in and busted the place up?"

"Yes."

"Nick was there with you?"

"Yes, he went with me to, well, to double-check everything I'd done. I came right up after I dropped you at the airport." Marcy was hesitant to finish. "And I cleaned out your place, like you asked, but I did it alone. So he took me up there this morning—"

He swore and hoped she didn't hear it. "Marcy, I told you not to do that."

"I know, Lucas. I've already gotten the lecture."

"So what did they take?"

"Nothing. Just threw things around the house, broke the dishes, and messed up the couches and bathroom. Nothing that couldn't be fixed."

"How'd they get in? You *did* lock it, right?"

"Of course. Looks like they pried open the bedroom window and came through that way. Didn't break a window, just trashed the contents, the furniture, and…and your gun case. *Was* that a gun case?"

Lucas concentrated and didn't remember checking the case, which had been locked. He'd lost the key years ago.

"It was, but I don't think there was anything in there. Haven't opened it since high school, but my dad and grandpa never left weapons up there. We always brought everything."

"Well, that's good. That's the one thing Nick asked me about."

"I'll bet. So they busted it open?"

"Shattered it."

"Is Nick there?"

"He's outside checking the perimeter. We're preparing to leave here in a few. He's gonna be responsible for that heavy black bag getting to your apartment. That *is* where you want it, right?"

"I'm thinking my locker at the team building. No one's at the apartment."

"Where are you?"

"Can't say."

"You can reach Nick on his cell. We'll be driving all night, so call us anytime you can."

"Thanks, Marcy. Glad you weren't hurt." His mind was racing to think who could have damaged the cabin. It had been there so long without an incident, it was so unusual, but then, lots of unusual things were happening.

"I'm fine. Don't worry about me. And Nick will drive with me all the way to San Diego."

Lucas saw the others gathering for dinner. "I have to go. Tell Nick I'll call later, if I can."

"Will do. Miss you, Lucas."

"Me too, Marcy. You have that talk with Connie yet?"

"Was going to wait until I got there, but don't think I can now. She's already making a little stir at the office."

"Do *not* tell her about us, Marcy. Big mistake. Trust me on that."

"No argument here, Lucas. You take care of yourself. Is it customary to say keep your head down? Like 'break a leg' for an actor?"

Lucas found himself smiling and it felt good. "Would be better if you told me you were in the shower rubbing that gel all over your body."

"Well then, sailor. I'd say it's still appropriate to say, 'keep your head down.'"

"Roger that, baby. Soon. Be safe. Be smart."

"Love you, Lucas."

He hadn't heard those words for at least two years. Marcy's confession of love to him was just in time, too. Not that he needed something to live for. "Love you too, kid. Talk soon."

He hung up, the hard-on in his pants very inconvenient, but easily covered up by a food tray. He hoped.

While they waited for their food, the soccer team bus drew up and one by one the ladies exited, each carrying a large blue and gold leather bag. The players unceremoniously slipped the leather straps off their shoulders and dropped them just inside the doorway. Several disappeared into the restroom while others washed their faces and hands in the cool drinking water dispenser and sauntered over to the food line in their matching blue and yellow flip-flops with the large block letter *N* on the outer edge.

Tyler was the first to speak to them. "Congrats on the win."

One player towered over all the others, being nearly Coop's height, which would make her nearly six and a half feet tall. She cut in front of the line without looking at any of the SEALs, without asking permission. Their captain was still wearing her red armband.

"Thanks," the captain said. "And we beat the *guys* in a twenty minute friendly game too." She flashed a perfect white smile back at Tyler, then winked up at Jake.

Their shorts and tanned legs were scoring big-time points with the team, both married and single guys. All of Lucas' bachelor buddies were pulling out chairs, tucking napkins into their shirts, and asking politely for salt and pepper instead of standing to reach in front of each other. They brought glasses and pitchers of iced tea for the ladies, not paying attention to a couple of SEALs who had their hand out for a cup. The swearing was clipped as well.

Kyle, Cooper, Fredo, and Armani sat together at one end of the table with several other of the married guys. Though married, Tyler sat next to their captain and the two started talking soccer immediately.

Lucas overheard Tyler whisper, "Who's the Amazon?" to his neighbor.

"By the way, it's Lacey," she said shaking Tyler's hand.

"Tyler, this is Jack, Lucas, Alex, Connor, Danny, Jeffrey, and the rest of the guys are married."

"And what are you, Tyler?" said Danny Begay. "Lacey, don't trust him. We're both married."

Lacey began her team introductions, and then added, "Husbands and boyfriends are not suitable topics of conversation on the road."

Jake and Alex shared a smile.

"But I'd recommend staying away from our keeper, Chloe. She's the short one in her family and her dad plays for the Suns."

Chloe lifted a fork and nodded acknowledgement, but otherwise sat expressionless and focused on her food.

One of the pretty blonde-haired brown-eyed players asked the table a general question. "So why are you guys way out here? And how come we've been sent to babysit you? Aren't you guys SEALs?"

The question left the table completely quiet.

CHAPTER 18

Marcy and Nick started to drive Lucas' truck back to San Diego in the afternoon. He called in at dusk, and Nick reassured him he was going to keep Marcy in plain sight.

"Honestly, Lucas, the gun cabinet would have been of interest to anyone. Because it had a lock on it, it was attractive to kids. That's who I think they were. Normal thieves don't do destruction. They just look for valuables. This was a concerted effort to damage and destroy."

She watched the dusk send an orange glow to the western horizon. They'd gotten so busy cleaning everything up and disposing of the broken things, she'd completely forgotten to call Connie. They had another six hours to drive, so she decided to put it off until she could do the *in person* conversation.

Nick chuckled. "Nothing like that. But they did pee all over the toilet." Nick gave Marcy a wink. "Your lady made that place shine when we were done. I screwed the window frame shut because I didn't have a new latch. You'll have to fix that when you return."

He finally asked Lucas the question Marcy was wondering. "You in country or out?"

She heard the, "Yes," in response from Lucas.

"Meaning you are or are not out of country?"

She heard the tinny, "Yes" from the other end of the phone.

"You asshole."

Lucas said something else while Marcy waited to get her chance to talk to him.

"Hey, punk, you have any beefs with your neighbors?" Nick rolled his eyes and gave her another wide smile.

She heard the scratchy swearing and objection on the other end.

"I know, I know. You guys were angels growing up. I can only imagine you terrorizing the little church goin' sweethearts when your dad and grandpa weren't paying attention. No, asshole, I'm talking about the fuckin' neighbors who live in that commune next door." Nick held the squawking phone out to Marcy. "You tell him."

"Nice to hear your voice twice in one day, Lucas," said Marcy. "Everything okay?"

Lucas laughed. "The beach is awesome, babe. Those umbrella drinks are strong. Good music. Missing you real bad."

"That's the only part of this conversation I believe, Lucas."

"Nick said we have new neighbors? What's this about a commune?"

"Well, looks to me like they've been there for awhile. Doing a bunch of things. Buildings out back. Nick said it was an old Christian camp. Sonshine Haven. You hear of it?"

"Nobody has used that place for years, Marcy. I didn't think they even had a road cleared anymore."

"Trust me, it's been worked on. Bunkhouse-like cabin in front and a covered riding arena in the back. Some new metal stables, and hay barns. The guy tending the vegetable garden looked like he could be a pot grower."

Lucas didn't say a word. "You stay away from there, Marcy. I'll check it out when I get home, but for now, no one goes up there."

"Don't you think someone should check on your place for you? How long will you be gone?"

"Not your concern, and to be honest, none of us knows that. But you stay away. Understood?"

"Yessir."

"Seriously, Marcy. Especially with the break-in, you don't go up there anymore."

Marcy agreed with him completely.

They said their goodbyes and Marcy handed the phone back to Nick with a "Thanks."

Checking her cell phone, she noticed she'd missed a call from Connie Shipley. "Oh shoot. I had the ringer turned off. I have to call my client."

"I'm going to pull over for a quick bite. You want a burger or something? There's a great Mexican restaurant a couple of miles west."

"I'm game. Let's go Mexican. I'll finish my call with Connie and then meet you inside."

Connie's phone went to voicemail right away. "Hey, Connie. This is Marcy Gelland with Coronado Bay Realty. I'm—"

Just as she watched Nick walk inside the restaurant, she saw Connie had returned her call. She hung up the message and answered her.

"Sorry to call you so late, Connie. I'm on my way back to San Diego. Thought maybe we—"

"Well, holy shit, Marcy. How good of you to wake the baby up."

"Sorry. I can call in the morning—"

"No. You don't get off that easy."

"Pardon?"

"I've got a screaming baby, but I got a boob that will do just fine."

"Okay." Marcy tried a nervous laugh on for size. Connie was more than prickly.

"All good now. Little shit won't sleep the night, but then that's nothing new." Connie took a deep breath and let it out before she continued. "So, I've been doing a little research. Very interesting what you can find out if you ask the right questions."

"Not sure what you mean, Connie. What questions?"

"When were you going to tell me you were fucking my husband?"

CHAPTER 19

PT started at o-six-hundred with a timed five-mile run around the track. The girls joined them. On the other side of the cafeteria was a small gym with rusty equipment Lucas could smell just as soon as he walked through the old double doors. One window had been duct taped down the middle, cheaply repairing a crack that threatened to destroy the whole frame. Fredo was making a list of things to get at Costco. He'd put down a water dispenser, some white towels to wipe the equipment down with, cleaning supplies and some free weights.

The smell of fresh coffee reminded Lucas of home, causing a twinge of homesickness. He planned on calling his mom by the weekend.

The training went by fast as they focused on pull-ups and sit-ups before they began doing stretching exercises. Several of the team guys remarked they missed the ocean. Coop and Fredo had created a ritual of diving in after an especially long and arduous workout.

Kyle asked T.J., Armando, Lucas, and Jake to join him for a hike up toward the ridge overlooking the camp's compound. It was classified a training exercise.

The five of them made less noise than one of the local deer as they jogged through sparse woods and a meadow with a small stream coursing through the middle. Close to the compound, the terrain was dotted with large granite boulders and became steep. Midway up the bluff, Kyle motioned with hand signals pointing to a sentry. The team fanned out around the back side of the outcropping so his line of sight would miss them. The thin, dark-skinned man was wearing shabby ill-fitting clothes and shoes that laced up, but appeared several sizes too large for him.

T.J. nearly ran into another sentry sitting on a large boulder, an AK-47 resting across his thighs. T.J. signaled and everyone froze in place.

The team waited nearly an hour, settling against rocky crags and high meadow brush, easily camouflaged, to make sure no one else appeared in the area. Since these men were not breaking the law, the SEALs were only tasked with observing, making note of what they found and not to engage. Unless fired upon, they would not be allowed to use their weaponry, either.

They heard a vehicle approach from several hundred yards behind them. Country music was rising into the blue overcast sky. The heat was stifling hot, and Lucas studied the gray clouds with more than a passing interest. A quick shower, even a downpour would be welcome in the nearly one-hundred-degree noonday heat.

The vehicle came into view. Both sentries watched the red Jeep advance into the woods, following the off-road trail. They were speaking to each other from about ten yards apart, their dialect sounding Pashtu, but Lucas couldn't be sure. Kyle held up a small recording device with a plastic cone boost, trying to capture what was being said.

Two young girls in tank tops and cutoffs were in the front seat of the open-air Jeep, wearing baseball caps and sunglasses. One was singing to the words of the song on the radio.

Lucas was concerned at first they were wandering into a den of bad guys, but when one of the sentries waved to the driver of the Jeep, and the other one didn't ready his weapon, he knew it was a planned or announced visit. The girls did not look Middle Eastern, but extremely westernized and young.

Lucas quietly cleaned the lenses on his binoculars, wiped down the scope he'd mounted to his H&K, inserted his fifteen round magazine, and then clicked off the safety, which was all they could do, since they weren't on a snatch and grab or kill on sight mission. Armani was laying flat and had already sighted the camp below, while Kyle was focused on the sentries. That left Jake to be their eyes behind them his Glock at the ready.

Below them, the Jeep stopped, motor running, as the two girls inside began a conversation with the perimeter guards. The ladies turned down their radio and spoke with one of two guards, who leaned over the door of the Jeep as the other scanned the roadway and the hill above. Without knowing it, the guard looked directly at the Team's position, and Lucas heard Armani hold his breath as his finger rested against the trigger mechanism after selecting his firing safety setting. As the guard looked away and the girls were waved through, Lucas noted Armando quietly release his breath, closed his eyes, and then retreated back.

Kyle took pictures of the compound, the approach, and close-ups of the guard gate and the sentries and where they were placed. There were several large trucks with closed beds parked at the side of the long building. A satellite dish and radio tower was installed atop one of the pine trees nearby. Kyle took pictures of that too.

Their LPO motioned for them to make their way back down the hill, and once at the bottom and out of sight, sprinted the way back to the creek, where they splashed water on their faces and down their shirts. Then they continued with the jog until they got back to their camp mid-afternoon. Lucas headed for the shower, for a cold one, soon followed by Kyle and the others.

Alex and Ryan hung around the doorway, waiting for him to finish in privacy.

"So what'd you find out?" Alex asked.

Kyle put his head under the water, rinsing off before he answered. "They're used to having female visitors."

"How'd you get that?" Alex asked, scrunching his eyebrows and forehead.

"They didn't make the local girls cover up. Especially their heads."

"Then there were the cut-offs," Lucas added.

Alex was still not convinced. So Kyle hammered it in. "That would *never* happen to an un-westernized Iraqi." He dried off and threw the skimpy towel around his waist. "Still can't decide what's in that building, but they're moving something in and out of there with those trucks. They're smart not to have people out in the daytime for the birds to spy overhead. We need to get our IR gear and visit them after dark. Begay has natural night vision so he's coming. You in, Alex?"

"Sure, anything, Chief. After all, I don't got a date."

"He's working to fix that as soon as is humanly possible. But the job comes first," added Ryan.

"Tyler's got his eye on Captain Blondie, that married sonofabitch," said Armando.

"I think she's sweet on Jake, from what I can see," said Alex.

Lucas knew Tyler would not go outside his marriage, that the chance to converse with someone about soccer was the real draw. "I agree. Never thought the bachelors would hook up on this training. God is looking out for you guys."

"*You* guys?" asked Kyle. The skimpy white towel barely tucked around Kyle's trim waist and narrow hips. "Aren't you in that league, Lucas? Connie's got you by the balls, I hear."

Lucas nodded in agreement. "Actually, I'm a little attached to my realtor. Got serious quick."

"Holy fuck. You're dumber than I thought, Lucas," said Kyle. "That the realtor Connie hired?"

Lucas didn't see any point to keeping it a secret. "Well, yes."

"You ain't even fuckin' divorced yet."

"That's been pointed out to me, Chief," Lucas answered.

"Unbelievable," Kyle said as he pushed his way past the crowd.

Back at their room, Jake sat down on Lucas' bed. "I need to talk to you a minute."

Lucas was putting on his jeans and a black Team 3 t-shirt.

"He said no logos."

"Shit, you're right. Just second nature." Lucas removed the shirt, tossing it in the built-in cabinet, and unwrapped a new white t-shirt. He slipped it over his head. "Thanks, man." He could see Jake was conflicted about something. "You okay?"

Jake looked at his hands, forearms resting on his thighs. "I've been dating that friend of Connie's, remember?"

Lucas had forgotten all about it, mostly because, since his divorce, Jake never stayed serious with one woman for more than about a month. He figured that ship had sunk long ago.

"So this is serious then, that what you're about to tell me?"

Jake grinned. "You know me. Fucked it up good this time. How did I know she had a sister that didn't look anything like her? Still a babe and all, but man, I had no idea sisters could look so opposite and yet act so competitive. Real catfight. And then they turned it all on me."

"Some people like that action, Jake."

"Shut the fuck up motherfucker. I'm not talking about *that*."

"Come on, Jake, you know sisters are bad news."

"Like I said, I didn't know!"

"Sounds like you dodged a bullet, my man." Lucas slipped on his shoes. He combed his hair and put on aftershave. "Weren't you the one all spouting off to me about staying single? Distrusting women? Didn't we have that conversation? So she, or they, whichever it is, broke up with you. Big deal."

"Well, yeah, that part's okay. I mean, I'm used to it. But boy, these ladies these days talk. They even talked to my ex. Connie gave me an earful."

"Well, you didn't exactly behave, Jake. I mean, mine was just a picture. You went and did the dirty."

"Not with a transvestite hooker."

"*Dancer.* I don't go with hookers."

"That you know of."

"Jake, just where the hell is this conversation going? You know full well I don't date or sleep around at all. And I never did that while married."

"You're married now, asshole."

"Yup, but she served papers on me."

"You're still legally married, you dumb-fuck."

"That's a minor detail. Thing is, Connie got some bad information, and believed I was—"

"That's what I have to talk to you about."

"Okay, I'm listening." Lucas could see Jake didn't want to tell him something and it was eating a hole in his gut.

"So the four of them are having lunch together, and—"

"Jake, you are one unlucky motherfucker. The four of them? Your ex, the sisters you've been banging and who else? Someone *else* you were banging?"

"No. Not exactly."

"Jake what part of '*banging*' don't you understand? That's like being just a little pregnant. We've had that talk, too."

Jake's expression became more painful.

"Holy fuck, you got the sisters pregnant, both of them?"

"Nah, man. Like I said, the four of them were having lunch, and apparently they told Connie—"

"Wait a minute, *my* Connie?"

"She isn't *your* Connie anymore, Lucas."

Alex and Ryan appeared at the doorway, as if on cue. Lucas glanced over at them and then put his hands on his hips. "Fuckit," he said as he grabbed Jake by the shirt. "You fucked Connie, too?"

Alex and Ryan sprang to action and separated them.

"No way, Lucas. I wouldn't do that. Honest." Jake's eyebrows tented upward, eyes squinting like he'd just smelled something terrible. He rubbed his forearm where Alex had grabbed him roughly. "I must have mentioned it to the one gal on our way out here. They wanted to arrange a double-double when we got back. Remember those, Lucas? Like we did before you married Connie?

Lucas could never forget those nights. "Before you were married, too, asshole."

"That's right. So, I told them you were seeing this realtor Connie had hired.

They told Connie you were banging the realtor."

Even though he'd confirmed one of his best friends hadn't slept with his wife, Lucas still wanted to punch Jake as the deliverer of the bad news. Very bad news.

"Why did you have to tell me this?"

"Because it's the truth, man. Thought you ought to know, since you said you were sweet on her. Knowing Connie and her temper, I'd put protection on your lady, Lucas."

"Except I'm stuck in fuckin' Tennessee. How the hell am I supposed to do that?"

"Well, call her, when you get the chance. At least give her a warning."

Kyle stood behind Ryan and Alex. "We good here?" he asked.

Lucas nodded his head while the others just watched.

"We're meeting in five. Rec Room." Kyle said as he left.

Lucas knew it was the end of their private conversation. He was good at burying all his feelings over any deployment. One by one, the team collected in the rec area, as instructed.

Kyle was pouring over his computer. "Okay, I've uploaded the photos and sent the audio clip back to Coronado. Hoping we can get some confirmation on what to do next."

Rory asked the next question. "You make them out to be Afghani? You think they were speaking Pashtu?"

"Yes," T.J. said. His language training was the best in the team. "See if you can amplify it, Kyle and I'll take a listen."

"Roger that, T.J."

The door burst open at the end of the bunkhouse and in walked Fredo, carrying boxes. "Hola, amigos! We got our Costco shit here,"

Accompanying him were Coop, Jeffrey, and Danny. Coop and Fredo unloaded boxes to the kitchen counters while Danny and Jeffrey sat down to assemble two tables and chairs and a TV stand which had all come in boxes. Soon several other members of the team took up positions in a circle.

"Okay, we got nice, fluffy towels," said Fredo. We got two cases of beer, some waters, and sodas and shit. Kyle, got your fuckin' turkey jerky."

"Thanks man," said Kyle.

"I bought condoms, toothpaste, deodorant, and aftershave for those dating, Red Bull, Gatorade, Monkey Butt powder, moist towelettes and some medicated ones for the old guys, hand sanitizer, detergent and dish soap," Fredo continued. "Coop got his dryer sheets and mineral waters too, so he's happy."

"Razors?" Lucas asked. "Forgot to mention it."

Fredo came over and put an arm on his shoulder. "Got you covered, my man, since you're beard is ugly as shit."

Lucas punched him in the arm.

"And for the record, no tofu or fresh vegetables. I figure frozen shit will work, lots of tortilla chips and salsa. Those of you into the healthier lifestyle can go to the fuckin' market tomorrow."

"Awesome!" Jake said as he opened up a box of chocolate bars.

Within ten minutes, all the furniture was assembled without anyone being in charge. The directions were passed around as needed. It was obvious the TV stand needed something on top, which would be one of the missions for tomorrow.

Two blenders and a coffee maker were set on the countertop. Coop filled new ice cube trays and placed them in the freezer. Fredo doled out a towel for each man.

"Okay, I'm going to say this one time, because about six of you have asked me," started Kyle. "Yes, we're having the ladies over tonight for a meet and greet. And here are some of the ground rules."

Lucas and Jake looked at each other and rolled their eyes. The disagreement of earlier seemed to have dissipated.

"First, the bedroom doors are to remain open while they're here. If you're going to be unsociable and go to bed early, you go to bed with your door open and the light on in your quad room. Got it?"

The grumbling continued until Donna Grant showed up to announce dinner.

"Hold on, Boy Scouts," Kyle shouted. "Got two more things to say. I need a volunteer to organize a scrimmage tomorrow afternoon."

Lucas and Tyler's hands shot up.

"Okay, we got two. Perfect." Kyle looked over at Fredo. "You need a donation of how much, Fredo?"

"Hundred bucks, gents," Fredo said.

"That has to happen before the weekend. We have a signup list over on the refrigerator for anything you want that you can share. No promises, of course. Fredo here keeps all the money and there are no refunds."

Lucas noticed a lined piece of yellow paper had been pasted to the refrigerator door with duct tape.

"I'm going to choose several to go up later tonight for a look-see at the camp with some IRs. We aren't telling the girls anything about this, get my drift?" Kyle surveyed his men in front of him. "We might get a visit from DC and Forsythe in a few days, depending on what we find up there at the camp. He's to bring some equipment I've requested. Again, no word of this to the ladies."

Alex asked if the phone tree was in effect tonight.

"What do you think?"

That seemed to settle it.

"I'm sending Coop and Lucas to town tomorrow to talk to the barn contractor. On the way back, they're to pick up a big screen and Blu-ray. We'll wait for them before we start the scrimmage, okay?"

Lucas nodded to Coop, who returned his acknowledgement. They both understood neither would have the night shift tonight. It also meant Lucas might be able to call Nick and Marcy, and perhaps use the internet at a coffee shop.

"Anything else you need to know about?" Kyle searched the room. "Everyone good on the home front?"

Jake and Ryan punched Lucas in the arm.

"Not you, Lucas, you're fucked," said Armando.

Several of the men started to chuckle. He had to defend himself. "At least I'm not the only one. How many times has she taken you to court, Jake?"

"Every time I knocked her up."

Amid the laughter, Kyle signed them off. "Okay, then. We'll have a briefing after PT in the morning. Be safe tonight and get to bed at a decent hour. The midnight hike will be with Armani, Fredo, Danny and Alex."

Kyle let them head for dinner. On their way to the door, he announced behind them, "Last one up cleans up the kitchen."

Lucas knew that meant there'd be a race for early bedtimes, which was probably what his LPO intended.

CHAPTER 20

Nick and Marcy arrived in the early dawn, stopped for breakfast, and then drove to Lucas' apartment, the place he told them was temporary and shared with the other bachelors.

"This is going to be new for me too, Marcy. Never met Lucas before you came into the picture."

"Do you know Connie?"

"Only by reputation. You've got your hands full."

"Tricky part is getting someone *else* to keep the listing. I can't in good conscience represent them. I mean, I *could*, but the appearance would be otherwise."

"I totally get it. Devon has had similar issues."

Marcy checked out Nick's expression. "Not really," she said with a teasing smile, followed by a wink.

"Oh, yes. She gets divorcing couples all the time. About half her business."

Marcy had to laugh at how naïve Nick was, something she also saw in Lucas. Here he was this big tough guy and was completely blind to some personal things. "I think I went a little beyond where Devon has gone. I know her and she'd never do what I did."

Nick blushed and would not look back at her. "Gotcha. Sorry. It didn't even cross my mind."

He set the black clothes bag on the floor near the front door. "Don't know which is his room," he added as he began searching the bedrooms for something that would indicate it belonged to Lucas. "You recognize anything?" he asked as he walked out of one bedroom into the next.

"Afraid not," she sighed. "And I don't know the other guys either."

Marcy unzipped the duffel and pulled out clothes she'd added back at the cabin. Some of her underwear accidentally dangled from one hand in front of Nick.

"You need a bag," he said, and pretended he'd not seen the unmentionables. Returning with a recycled plastic shopping bag from the kitchen, he continued not making eye contact.

Marcy loaded up and dropped the bag by the door. Then she walked slowly through the apartment. The living room couch and matching loveseat looked more than well-used and wasn't anything she'd sit down on. There were nude posters in every room. Several hard-oiled women in handcuffs, blindfolds, and various states of mostly undress lined the walls of the guest bath.

A set of folding chairs sat around a small stained table in the kitchen. The rugs were brightly stained. The slider to the balcony overlooking the valley below was covered with handprints and a torn screen hanging on a bent frame.

Two of the bedrooms had cultures growing from half-eaten food or glasses. The kitchen sink was filled with four bowls with old cold cereal stuck to the sides.

"If I had a couple of hours, I could fix this place up," she said.

Nick smirked.

Marcy continued. "And I'm thinking they'd hate it. Am I right?"

"With those guys? From what I understand, anything approaching domestic bliss would be totally off limits."

"Okay, so what's next?"

"I was thinking I'd get the equipment bag over to the Team building, but I'm detached, so I'll have to get someone else to do it. Can you drop me off? I'll stay there tonight and try to take a plane up to Santa Rosa in the morning."

"Sure thing. Thought the whole team was with Lucas."

"They have someone who injured his leg in a jump and didn't go."

Marcy slipped behind the wheel of Lucas' truck and watched as the sandy-haired ex-SEAL hoisted the heavy weapons bag over his shoulder and resumed a path to his friend's front door. He met another well-built young man with an ankle to hip cast on his leg. Marcy shook her head.

Am I ready for all this? She'd barely knew Lucas, and already she was running guns, cleaning up ransacked cabins, and riding in his truck with another SEAL she barely knew. And somehow, she was *okay* with it?

How my life has changed. With a heavy dose of apprehension, Marcy noted how fast her world had tilted on its axis. She waved goodbye to Nick and his friend like they were people she'd known her whole life. The day was already getting long and she needed a shower and an early to bed.

But first, she had to face the wife of the man she was screwing.

The Coronado Bay Realty office was on a corner in the neighborhood of expensive designer boutiques, high-end burger bars, vegetarian restaurants, art galleries and espresso coffeehouses. Marcy had always enjoyed working at the attractive, highly-visible, upscale office, unlike some of her other realtor friends. Many of the agents there didn't need the income and worked there just to hobnob with local celebrities and wealthy business-men. It was also known far and wide as a great place to pick up a wealthy second or third husband for singles or soon-to-be singles, either male or female. She was one of the few who did not have all the cosmetic surgery to make themselves into sufficient eye candy.

Their lobby was decorated by a designer regularly featured in Architectural Digest. Imitating an abandoned villa in Tuscany, broken pots spilled water fountains and colorful beds of flowers decorated outside the entrance doors. The lobby featured a large, textured steel waterfall, giving a serene and peaceful effect, like a high-end spa. Bird calls and a Tuscan orange room scent piped into the air ducts drifted around the reception and waiting area.

Today, none of those things did anything to cheer her mood.

Gail Burnett, married to the famous wide receiver, Barry Burnett, was the first to greet her. She had been chatting with the young receptionist, her long, tanned form outfitted in a white designer suit. Her blonde hair cascaded over her shoulders and back like spun gold. As she turned to face Marcy, her eyelids closed slightly. She licked her lips and tilted her chin up. Her green eyes sparkled with mischief. On another day and under different circumstances, she would have been someone Marcy could enjoy spending time with. But as a competitor, she was a feral cat used to successfully taking down lions.

Gail was all the wrong kinds of dangerous.

"There you are, sweetie."

It always annoyed Marcy when someone only a few years older could take on the aura of a critical parent.

"Hi, Gail." It was always wise to give the realtor what she wanted. "You look terrific today."

"And you look like you've just come from a demolition derby." Gail winked at her, making it overly obvious she didn't really mean the comment.

Except she did.

"Just got back from up north."

"Yes, heard about your interesting road trip." Gail checked her nails and then fluffed her hair.

Marcy wondered why her broker would have disclosed this little factoid. She put it out of her mind. "How's everything around here? Keeping busy?"

Gail smiled. Marcy held her breath.

"Can't complain. Barry's in Detroit, so I'm actually getting some work done."

Marcy figured Detroit wasn't the shopping destination Chicago or New York or even Atlanta would be. "Well, good. I've got some catching up to do myself," Marcy answered. "Let me get settled, and then could you and I have a little chat in the conference room?"

The receptionist, seated behind the curved bamboo counter, tore her eyes off her computer screen and shot a worried glance at Gail's profile.

"Sure thing, Marcy. Kind of wanted to talk to you as well." The fetching smile she used on her best clients looked dangerous.

"Give me about five. I'll meet you there."

"You bet." Gail turned and continued her conversation with the receptionist. Her skirt could not have been any tighter, revealing she wasn't embarrassed to show she wore thong underwear.

Several minutes later, Marcy and Gail stepped into the warm bisque-themed meeting space. A mural of vineyards and tiled roof spires perched atop rolling hills was painted along the long wall. Marcy sat at the head of the table, laying down her listing information and several other forms she'd dug out.

Gail had a thin file folder she held in long tapered fingers accented with pearlescent polish. Her open-toed sandals made small scratching sounds as she took up her place on Marcy's right, and sat.

Marcy looked at the painting before her and took in a deep breath as if she was vacationing in the little Tuscan village, not staring at a plastered wall. Her nervousness was uncharacteristic, but then, there were so many things she hadn't fully thought out. Normally, she liked to calculate every move in this chess game of real estate sales. Now she was trying to execute a retreat with her job and her pride still in tact.

It was not what she was used to doing.

"Gail, I've taken this listing for a house on Apricot Way, and—"

"Connie and Lucas' house. I know it well," Gail interrupted.

"Good. Well, I've decided I'm going to refer their listing, and wanted to know if you'd be interested in taking over for me." She didn't spell out that normally there would be a referral fee shared between the agents, and just decided to let the implication stand, without bringing attention to it.

Gail hesitated a couple of seconds, tapping her fingernails on top of her file folder, as if she was considering a move she wasn't sure of. Her surgically plumped lips pulled back, without a wrinkle, into a thin line. Her eyes were able to give more expression. "Your timing is pretty good, Marcy." She opened the folder. "Because I got this letter from Connie earlier this morning."

She handed the sheet of paper across the table. Marcy read:

'To: Marcy Gelland

I hereby request that you withdraw my listing at 442 Apricot Way, San Diego, California, immediately. I no longer wish to be represented by you.

The letter was signed by Connie Shipley and dated this morning.

Marcy sat back and waited for the other shoe to drop.

"You know we're always trained to give the client whatever they want, Marcy. I didn't solicit this, not in any way." Gail watched her words sink in. "Marcy, she wants *me* to represent them. Connie feels there's a conflict of interest." Gail's eyes got hard and cold. No smile lines appeared on her flawless face.

Marcy was going to sidestep the elephant in the room, hoping she wouldn't have to bring it out into the open. Instead, she decided, again, to give Gail what she wanted.

"Well, Gail, I agree and have no objection to this. Like I said, I wanted to—"

"And I'm *not* paying a referral fee, Marcy. Don't you think it's a little beyond that anyway?"

"Fine."

"Really?" Gail made a point to raise her eyebrows and bat her big green eyes with the eyelash extensions.

Marcy didn't want to press a fight. If all this could just go away, she'd be fine with the lack of income. She didn't have Barry Burnett's income as backup, but she was the top office producer and could absorb the cut in pay. What was more valuable than the commission earned was her standing in the office, especially with her broker, Joe.

She pulled out a Change Order form and began to fill it out for Gail, when they heard noise coming from the lobby. Marcy had just signed her name to the form when Connie Shipley appeared at the conference room door, her left hand splayed as she slapped the glass, her wedding ring making the metallic tapping sound. She was holding the baby in her right.

Marcy didn't realize Gail had locked the door, so when Connie began yanking on the burnished copper handles, the rattling sound shook most the nearby walls. Connie's face was shriveled in anger. "You let me in there, right now. Where the fuck is Lucas?"

Gail stood to unlock the door, but before she could get there, Connie continued with her tirade.

"Release me from your fuckin' listing contract or I'll tell the whole world you're fuckin' my husband!"

Even through the thick glass, Connie's voice was loud and menacing, but not nearly as loud as Marcy knew it was to the whole office. It would be impossible for anyone present to miss Connie's accusations.

So much for a clean exit.

CHAPTER 21

After dinner, the music began. Jake was the center of attention, often dancing with three or four soccer players. He kept encouraging Lucas to join in, but Lucas was preoccupied with the reveal Jake had given him about Connie, and he worried about Marcy and how she was doing.

He slipped into the bathroom and tried to text her, but couldn't get a signal. In the old days, he'd have been mixing the margaritas and making sure everyone had a generous helping of alcohol, but this time they'd only bought a limited amount and that was mostly beer. He started a list he'd be going over tomorrow when he and Coop paid the visit to the contractor and the shopping trip planned for afterward.

A coed poker game was in full swing. Lucas was normally right in the middle of the action, but his somber attitude prevailed.

Donna Grant wasn't participating in the alcohol, the dancing or the cards. She took a seat next to him and toasted his beer with her mineral water.

"You got a girl at home, Lucas?" she asked. The lady was probably five years his senior, but he'd seen lots of relationships with older military women and the young SEALs. It gave them a problem sometimes with the other branches of service they had to work with closely.

"Complicated, but yes," he answered her. If she wore a little makeup, she'd be pretty. He noticed she had a barbed wire tat around her left wrist. Her hair was cut short, but was shiny brown. With her large brown eyes, she had a classic look and would be stunning if she wanted to be. That had him curious.

"What exactly does that mean?" she asked, without looking at him.

"Means my wife's divorcing me, and I recently found a girlfriend."

"Can't live with them and can't live without them, that right?" she answered.

Lucas rolled his shoulder and cracked his neck. The loud noise had her wincing and even caught the attention of a couple of the card players. "That sounded painful. You better get that checked out."

"I'm fine. You?"

"I like the travel, and I prefer working with men on the job."

Lucas pegged her for being perhaps sweet on women. He nodded, not bothered one way or the other.

She smiled to her shoes. "I like men all right, Lucas. I'm just more of the best friend kind of person. Don't much care for chasing after the steamy romance, if you know what I mean."

No, he didn't know what she meant.

"Sometimes, Donna, it just comes to you. Sometimes you don't have to chase after it at all."

"That happen to you?"

"Sometimes," he answered.

"So that's what happened to your marriage, then?"

"No. That's not what I meant. I'm not like that, although my wife—" He stopped himself until the alarms in his head stopped screaming. "All that was before I got married. My wife is the one who found and chose me."

Donna peeled her gaze from the poker table and looked at him honestly. "And here I would have thought you knew."

"Knew what?"

"The woman always chooses, my friend. That's why you guys have to wait. When you're single, that means no woman has chosen you yet."

He wasn't sure he liked the tone of her implication. She was complicated. Secretive. That was a dangerous combination.

"I still say you be patient. It will happen for you. You just wait and you'll see."

"Great advice, but I'm afraid it doesn't really apply to me."

"But you *are* looking?"

She rocked her head from side to side. "Everybody looks, Lucas. I apologize, but it's a long story. It's not that I'm into ladies, I just have issues with men."

"Except you like to work with them?"

"I know, sounds nuts, doesn't it?" She smiled and he did think she was pretty. "You trying to pick a fight?"

"No, ma'am. I don't fight with women."

She giggled and said something under her breath that sounded like a swear word. "Long story, my frog prince, and I don't know you well enough."

He decided to add a little levity into the conversation, since he was getting a bit uneasy with her secrets, not that he had any right to them of course, but he was used to being direct and forthright, answering and asking questions. He thought he'd just push a little to see if he could crack that tough exterior. "I don't have to worry about you taking a knife to my throat late some night, right? You're not one of those?"

She showed him her white teeth again in a grin. "Only if we're forced to sleep in the same bed and you snore, which I can already tell you do, so give it up, sailor, and leave me alone." She stood and walked away, still looking like an athlete slowly departing a basketball court or a track somewhere. He realized she was probably way stronger than he'd given her credit for.

And lethal.

Everyone turned in before nine o'clock, with the exception of the group going with Kyle to the top of the hill.

"I'm good if you need me, Chief," said Lucas.

"Sure you're just trying to get out of cleaning up? But if you want to tag along, be my guest. You got your FLIRs?" he asked, meaning the SEAL-issued forward-looking infrared goggles.

"Roger that."

"Okay, you still up to the shopping trip tomorrow with Coop?"

"Fuckin' A, Chief."

Kyle and Danny led the team back through the woods. With their thermal gear, they saw eyes of forest animals such as fox, raccoon and deer light up and move quietly out of their path. The sky was cloudy, which was good for visibility. The moon was over half full and very bright.

Lucas was amazed how much easier it was to see the outline of the lone sentry with the equipment they brought. They would be back up as time permitted on other nights, just to verify the single guard was not an anomaly.

Kyle directed Danny and Armando to position themselves higher than the sentry to give the rest of the team cover in case they were discovered. The rest of the team took the best clear vantage point nearly twenty yards below the sentry so they could get a closer wide-angled look.

Scanning the campground, Lucas watched the end on the long metal building slowly move to the side, its large, metal, gear-type wheels squealing as the metal door rolled out of the way. Inside, he saw what looked like a warehouse with tables and storage shelves. But down the center of the building was a lush garden of plants, reminding Lucas of pictures he'd seen of the Panhandle in Golden Gate Park. He counted approximately twenty men, all carrying small automatic weapons similar to their short barrel H&Ks slung over their shoulders.

Lucas heard the whir and click of the scope camera as Kyle documented everything, including the sentry. Lucas adjusted his magnification, got out his vest pocket spiral and jotted down the license plates of every van or truck he could identify. Kyle gave him a thumb's up, adjusted his scope, and took more photos.

Boxes were being loaded onto dollies and placed inside rear doors of two trucks they'd seen earlier that day. Just before the door shut, Lucas caught a glimpse of a sandaled pair of feet peering out of a long kaftan, or robe.

He tapped Alex on the shoulder, pointing straight ahead and saw the faint nod of acknowledgement in return. Alex laid a hand gently on Kyle's shoulder, passing the information along. Lucas could see he'd already started taking pictures of the figure in the doorway.

He wasn't surprised when the gentleman didn't go fully outside, but remained in the doorway. Lucas could see he had a long beard, which the goggles showed in near-perfect detail. With the man's wire-rimmed glasses, the girth of his upper torso, his height, and the tribal cap he wore, Lucas knew he was looking at pure evil.

Fucking Sheik Hammid Rushti!

There was no doubt in his mind this was the gentleman whose picture they'd been shown yesterday. He was amazed at the quality of equipment they'd been issued and the detail it provided.

God bless the U.S. taxpayer and the United States Navy Spec Ops Command.

Surveying the rest of the area, he found someone sitting in a small sedan, under cover of a large willow tree. Once again he gave the signal to Alex, while Fredo watched from Lucas' left side. Kyle took photos of the car.

The howl of a dog of some kind startled Lucas and nearly had him lose his footing. Pitching forward, he braced himself, which knocked a small round rock loose. It slid down the hillside, picking up steam along the way, making too much noise on its journey. The sentry turned in their direction, angling his gun to waist height. Lucas, Alex, Fredo, and Kyle stayed perfectly still, holding their breath.

Lucas wondered where the animal noise had come from since the sound reverberated all over the small canyon. Without turning his head, he glanced to the left and saw two scrawny dogs playing in the dusty campground yard below. The man in the sedan got out, whistled to the dogs who jumped to him and whined as he chained them to a metal clothesline dog run. The movement distracted the sentry, who sat with his rifle across his thighs, studying the compound below.

Kyle and the rest of them stayed calm and within seconds their infrared picked up the shape of Danny backing away from the guard not more than a few feet behind the man. Their only Native American SEAL, Danny made a habit of sneaking up on everyone on the team and playing pranks. Lucas was pretty darned glad he was part of the mission today. If need be, that guard wouldn't have heard a thing before Danny's blade did its job. It was reassuring to know someone so skilled was there to protect them all.

They waited until they could no longer see Danny's outline before Kyle ordered them to get ready to return to camp. His Chief whispered something to Danny, who got out his slingshot, picked up a pea-shaped pebble, aimed without use of the IR goggles at one of the dogs. The animal yelped and started to howl, backing up in circles and trying to get loose of the chain. In the safety of the noise the commotion caused, the team retreated and was halfway down the back side of the hill before it got quiet again.

Lucas realized he'd been holding his breath nearly the whole way down.

CHAPTER 22

The day ended mercifully and at last Marcy got her long bubble bath She retired early, which was also something she needed. She propped up pillows and took out her favorite romance book. She loved the lavender hand and body crème she'd used; it would calmly put her to sleep. Just before cracking open the book, she checked her phone. Still no text or call from Lucas.

She fell into the love story, feeling sad she was missing Lucas. That new scratchy feeling in the pit of her stomach, indicating a new love and desire to grow and explore that love brought delicious anticipation. It was something she'd only felt a few times in her life. This was not just the lusty parts of their steamy and rather sudden crash into each other. It felt like something long sleeping had been awakened. The passion and intensity of this SEAL took her breath away. She knew a relationship with him would be a wild ride, and not all of it would be fun.

But, boy, would it be exciting.

She snuggled in bed, relaxed but unable to sleep. She could still feel his callused hands move up and down her thighs, the way his stiff fingers moved the hair around the back of her ears, or unclipped her hair to let it fall. He didn't make love to her, he *consumed* her like a man who'd been starving. His neediness was something that filled a void. She also realized very few people would ever see that neediness, or how strong his desire was to love and be loved fully. Every other man she'd ever been with was a pale copy of the color and life and energy Lucas brought her. It was something the SEAL training would never drum into him. It was who he was and what he brought to the SEAL team. It wasn't anything a man could learn.

As her eyes closed, the screaming and yelling of this afternoon faded into a sensual dream. Connie's ugly face, the screaming baby and scared to death toddler weren't so scary as she felt Lucas's body behind her, warming her back, his hands around her waist, holding and protecting her, while his lips and tongue tasted the sensitive skin at the back of her neck.

It was what life was all about: the ugly and the beautiful. One woman's horror was another woman's lifeblood. She was sure she was the woman for him, just as she'd felt the first time she'd kissed him and her eyes opened for the very first time to what could be her new future.

The morning light brought fresh appreciation for the warm glow she felt inside. She lay back in the soft pillows, hearing the diffused spray of a sprinkler outside her bedroom window. The day would be a tough one. But for right now, she was savoring one of the first mornings of her new life. Someday, she'd look back on it and remember how she felt, and perhaps she'd tell someone, perhaps a son or daughter, what it felt like to fall in love.

She held that thought, letting her heart beat faster, feeling the blood pumping all the way to her fingertips. She never wanted this feeling to end.

And then her phone rang. It was her broker, Joe Reed.

"Marcy, we need to talk. Can I buy you lunch or a cup of coffee when you can spare some time?"

"Sure, Joe. I was planning on coming in to the office in an hour or so. Have some paperwork to handle."

"Well, you know what? I'd like to talk to you some place private. There's a lot of stuff going on right now, and I just needed a private place to clear the air a bit. That okay with you?"

"Absolutely. The Coffee Bean near the office?"

"Maybe some place else. We'll run into agents on their way in. I just need to talk, Marcy."

Her stomach fell to the floor. His normal friendly tone was distinctly missing, though she could tell he was working hard to mask it. "Okay. Where and when?"

"That new place off the strand? They have ice cream, candy, and coffee? How about that one? Haven't been in there yet and my kids are dying to go there."

"Sounds good. In an hour?"

"Perfect."

Marcy decided to finish shattering the rest of her bucolic morning by asking a question she didn't want to ask. But it would prepare her for the meeting, and that was the best she could do right now. "Is there a problem?"

"Marcy, I like you, but yes, there's a big problem, I'm afraid."

Marcy found a parking place for the truck in a lot behind one of the storefronts that was under remodel. She'd planned on dropping it off at Lucas' place and then taking a taxi back to pick up her own car. Rounding the corner, she walked down the half block to the little specialty shop. She didn't see Joe anywhere until she heard the tinkle of the front door bell and saw him standing right beside her.

Joe had been a good mentor, although they hadn't been close. He'd helped her get started in the business and ran a very tight office for a local celebrity chef, who owned Coronado Bay Realty. One of the things Joe did exceedingly well, and the reason he was such a good manager to work for, is that he had a no-drama policy at work, and so his stable of agents weren't going and coming like so many of the offices in San Diego. Everyone was happy, and Joe didn't hire people without something to bring to the company. Several retired Navy veterans with heavy combat experience, pilots, and sports figures worked at the office.

"Always be the calming voice in the negotiation," he'd taught her. Marcy knew some of the drama now occurring between her and Connie was not anything he'd be happy with. She hoped Gail had backed her up, somehow shifting some of the blame off her shoulders.

"You go get us a table. What can I get you?" he asked with a smile that looked difficult to produce.

"Latte. Medium."

Marcy found a corner and sat against the wall, leaving the comfortable plastic padded bench to Joe. He'd put on a little weight in his middle, but he was still an attractive man with a dusting of gray hair. The office had been very busy with the uptick in sales all summer long, and she thought perhaps he'd not made the time to go to the gym.

He came back bearing two identical coffee drinks, set one down in front of her and slid into the padded seat. After his first sip, he opened his eyes and peered right into hers, slight worry lines developing between his eyebrows that all of a sudden disappeared as he began to talk.

"Thanks for coming, Marcy. I've been talking with Gail Burnett."

"Yes, I met with her yesterday afternoon, and my client on Apricot came by the office. I transferred the paperwork to Gail."

"Okay. She told me as much." He let his fingers scratch at the brown cardboard heat sleeve on the side of the cup. "Your former client, Connie Shipley, has been very vocal, even after yesterday. She barged into the office this morning and broke up a meeting with the staff. I couldn't get her out fast enough."

"Where was Gail?"

"Not in yet. But Connie came in to see me. Insisted on it."

Marcy waited for him to gather his thoughts. She knew this was difficult for Joe. Whatever he was going to say next, she wasn't going to like.

"She's made some rather severe accusations." His sad eyes were apologetic. He slowly inhaled, his chest getting full and his shoulders rising. He leaned over the table and bent down, coaching his words, lowering the timbre to a whisper. "She said that you had sex with her husband, *while* you had the listing." His eyes did not smile. He tilted his head in the other direction, but didn't take his gaze from her. "We don't do that here at Coronado Bay, Marcy. And I know you know that."

She had wanted to return his gaze, but inside she felt ashamed. "I'm sorry, Joe. It was a mistake," she said to the tabletop.

He sighed with the confirmation she'd given him, shook his head, and looked up to the ceiling as if he'd find an answer there. "God, I was hoping you'd say she got it wrong." He looked out the window onto the traffic passing by on the Strand.

"I'm not going to lie, Joe. It was just plain and simple a mistake. I'm sorry." "Damned *right* it was a mistake," he said, his temper beginning to flare. She'd never seen that in him before. "She's talking about suing the company."

Her steely resolve, the fantasyland that everything would turn out somehow crashed all around her like a porcelain doll. Her eyes got hot, and soon tears welled up and started running down her cheeks. Joe handed her a napkin which she used to dab her eyes with.

"What in the devil were you thinking?"

"I wasn't. That's the problem."

Joe sat back and watched her work to repair her composure. With his back erect, he examined the coffee shop, making note of the clerks behind the bar and the new customers who'd entered. His eyes also lighted on the empty seat on his left. "Well, here's the thing, your problem has now become my problem. My problem will be Guy's problem and I don't want to lose my job."

He didn't have to tell her anything more. She was going to try one more time to save the situation. "Is there something I can do to fix this?"

"Not really. I'm in damage control here. I have to tell Guy, and your little lady has a big mouth on her."

"She's mean and vindictive."

"She has some choice words for you too, Marcy. Words she's screamed all over the office. We had clients in the conference room, sitting at agent's desks who heard all this. It was the last thing I wanted to hear at the top of her lungs. We handle a lot of divorcing couples, as you know. That's all we need is to have some divorcing wife hear our agents sleep with their husbands. Get my drift?"

"Yes. I fully understand. I take full responsibility, Joe."

"And you of all people. From a nice family. I mean I have gold-diggers in this office. I try to weed them out before they get hired, but you know this can be a problem. I never expected this from you. You are usually so levelheaded. What the devil got into you?"

If she was crass, she would tell him exactly what had gotten into her, or whom. Now she understood why Lucas wanted her to lie, but that wasn't going to be the way. She knew that was wrong. Why didn't she stop herself from making the other mistake that would, in all likelihood, cost her her job?

"Joe, tell me what I can do, and I'll do it. Anything. You want me to talk to Guy?"

"God no!"

"What can I do to fix this situation for you? Forget about me. What can I do to make it up to you, to the company and its reputation?"

He bit his lower lip, then he smiled. "I'm going to have to ask you to leave."

Marcy expected it, but it still didn't take away the shock of hearing the words delivered to her. Her parents would be so disappointed in her. Every meeting she would go to from now on would be painful. She could feel the whispers behind her back, the gossip. All the embellishments to her character as salacious details were spread throughout the professional community. And it would be more vicious because of the company's long-standing reputation for being more professional and a cut above the rest of the offices in town.

"I understand. I wish there was some way I could get a second chance. Believe me when I say it will never happen again."

"Well, you're right about one thing. It *will* never happen again at my company." He stood, extending his hand to her. "I'm sorry, Marcy. Very, very sorry. You get your things taken care of, I want you releasing all your listings and we'll close the escrows you have, send you a check. But after today, I'm going to ask for your key and ask you to vacate your desk."

She shook his hand and tried to be firm about it. "Okay, I'll get right on it today. Do—does anyone know yet?"

"The secretaries, that's all."

That meant Gail and the rest of the gossip crew knew every detail, and what they didn't know, they were making up. She wanted to go home and just throw herself in her bed, but it wouldn't get any easier than this morning, before the office got busy, to remove all her things. Someone walking out with a Banker's Box full of stuff always indicated one thing: they were permanently leaving. And in her case, everyone would know she was fired.

Marcy watched Joe walk out into the sunlight, the glass door shutting behind him, ringing the tinkle bell. Her stomach was in knots. She picked up her half-sipped Latte and tossed it in the garbage.

Walking toward the burgundy Hummer, her cell phone rang. It was Lucas.

CHAPTER 23

"What's wrong?" Lucas asked.

"I was asked to leave."

"Leave? From where?"

"Basically, the company fired me, Lucas."

Lucas knew this had something to do with Connie. Hell, it had something to do with him, too. Guilt was not an easy emotion to feel, and he found it stuck like black tar in the pit of his stomach. "What are you going to do?" He held off saying he was sorry, as that cow had already gotten out of the barn.

"You mean right now?"

He felt Marcy's defenses rising. Perhaps his making the phone call was a bad idea. But being in town, he had to try.

"What are you going to do about your job?"

"I don't have a job, Lucas. I'm not sure what I can do. First, I'm going to deliver your truck back to your apartment. Then go by and pick up my stuff at the office. Then look for a job, I guess.

"So this have to do with us?"

"Of course it does. Connie found out, you know."

"Yes, that was partly why I was calling. I just discovered that out too. Jake had dated one of her friends. I think that's how it got to Connie."

"God, Lucas, you guys sound like a bunch of gossipy women."

It frustrated him, too. So many uncertainties about relationships, and women were so darned complicated. He didn't have that with any of the guys he served with. But then, it was life and death and a little screwing around in between. They got serious about really serious things. Everything else was like quicksand, something to avoid at all costs, and usually meant someone other than himself would be crying. He'd be left with that uneasy feeling in the pit of his stomach that he'd been a disappointment, but was powerless to sort it out and make things right. He didn't like not being in control.

So now he'd gotten her fired. That was on him, not her. And that just wasn't fair. She'd been a casualty of his desires. Oh yes, the desires were real, but she paid a heavy price for it. And could he be trusted, really?

Now, so far away from her, maybe that was the safest for her. Not for him. God, he wanted to see her, but it was better for *her*.

Her frustration speared him through the long, tired sigh he heard over the phone. He'd wanted just to touch base, yet he couldn't tell her anything about what he was doing. Nothing like, "Oh, we're just having a normal day, checking out terrorists, searching for bad guys at midnight, fraternizing with the Navy Women's Soccer team. We're buying big screen TVs and checking out contractors and little hottie Nashville chicks who want to hang out with these assholes we're watching. We're locked and loaded and nearly cut a guy's head off last night, but other than that, we're fine."

He really didn't know what to say. And he knew he should say something, and quick, too.

"That's too bad, Marcy." He winced, doubling over, socking his thighs with his fists. Coop looked up from his computer and grimaced at him. The tall SEAL held his palms out to the sides as if telling him, '*What the fuck are you doing?*'

"Too bad? Did I hear you right, Lucas?" He deserved every bit of her frostiness.

"I mean, what do you want me to do?" He tried to be soft. He was listening for every little detail over the phone, any sigh, anything at all telling him she was okay with it. But he had a really bad feeling about their chemistry right now.

The silence sliced down on the back of his neck. *Shit. Here it comes.*

"You know, I might be some minor inconvenience to you, Lucas, and I do appreciate the call, but right now, I've got to sort out the rest of my life, since I don't have a job and I won't be able to afford to live in my place for more than a couple of months and no one in San Diego will hire me anyway."

"You're being a little dramatic, aren't you?" He bit his tongue at what an asshole he was being, but if there was nothing he could do, why pretend? She needed to calm down and solutions would come to her. In any high-stress situation, making a decision while upset could get you killed in the battlefield. And this was beginning to feel like a war. The love wars, like the boys had been telling him. But he also knew he was sounding like a royal jerk to suggest it. He didn't know what to say to her. He cared about her so much and wanted to spend the rest of his life with her, but he freakin' didn't know what to say right now.

He could feel what her face probably looked like. He knew she'd be bright red now. Her chest would be blotchy and she'd be shaking like a leaf.

The last line she delivered, he knew he fully deserved.

"You know, Lucas? I didn't understand how Connie felt until today. Now I do. You are every bit the asshole she said you were—"

"Marcy, wait—"

"Wait? Wait for you to come back here to California so you can charm the pants off me again? You know, Connie warned me about you. I didn't believe her. Now I'm thinking—no, I'm *knowing* she's right."

"Marcy, calm down. You don't have to get upset—"

Coop was looking at him like he had black warts all over his face.

"No, of course not. Who needs a fuckin' job, Lucas?" She sucked in air. "I could go stand on a street corner here and pick up SEALs who want to screw, maybe make a few bucks to tide me over—"

"No, Marcy. That's just nuts."

"You know what's nuts? Believing your horseshit. You remind me of the guy my sister dated. He'd put a big fuckin' engagement ring on someone's finger so he could get all the sex he wanted. When it broke off, she gave the ring back. It was the best deal in the world for him."

"I didn't get you a ring. I have no ring."

"Which means it was an even worse idea to agree to marry you."

"Marcy—"

"Please, Lucas. I don't want to hear another word. Let me cling to that tiny ounce of self-respect I have left. I thought you really cared."

"I did."

He realized he put closure to their entire relationship with that one. Coop covered his face with his hand and was shaking his head.

"Oh yeah? Well listen here, sailor. I never did."

The line went dead.

"Fuck," he said and almost tossed the phone.

"You are a seriously stupid asshole, Lucas. I don't think I've ever heard anyone at your level. Ever. So all the stories are true. You and that stripper?"

"Dancer."

"The trani dancer?"

He was going to argue the point, but looking at Coop, he knew he should just shut up and get drunk.

Lucas was still festering, consumed in his head as they drove over to the building contractor's office.

"Would you stop with the fuckin' sighing, Lucas? You're acting like a teenager." Cooper downshifted the van and pulled around the corner, sending Lucas into the passenger door. "Get your fuckin' seatbelt on, man."

Lucas complied.

"And get your mind off that phone call. We have to concentrate here."

"I know," he said softly. He told himself he wouldn't have taken it so personally if he'd been overseas. Over there, you knew you had to concentrate. Here, on home soil, it was something he was having a hard time getting used to. Terrorists here. Possibility of danger. Here. In Tennessee, of all fuckin' places. It just didn't fit.

Coop drove them to the office of the contractor who built the barn at the complex.

Inside the front door, a large fuzzy-haired dog slept by the metal reception desk. He rose up, blinking his dark eyes underneath soft bangs, regarded them casually and then laid his head back down over his outstretched paws.

They were greeted by a young, ponytailed blonde girl who appeared to be high school age.

"Can I help you?" She wore tight blue jeans, ones she looked poured into, and a pink flannel shirt in a plaid design, and pink cowboy boots. Her drawl was soft and sexy and Lucas again cursed his lack of judgment.

Coop cleared his throat and took out a piece of yellow-lined paper with a building design drawn on it. "We're looking to get some quotes on a building for my friend's ranch. He drew this from a magazine."

She took the paper, regarding Lucas briefly, and then studied the drawing.

"Let me get my dad. Just a minute." With the drawing in hand, she exited through the glass door to the shop area in the rear. Lucas couldn't help but follow her perfectly formed ass through the doorway. He told himself it reminded him of Marcy, but he cursed himself for the lie.

A country station was playing in the background. Pictures of stalls, hay barns, and paddocks adorned the walls. The owner apparently supported several kids' baseball and soccer teams. Framed letters from satisfied customers also cluttered the walls in small black frames. Although clean, the office was sparse. Two imitation leather chairs in an olive green color sat in the corner, bordering a corner table with a large amber lamp that looked like it had come from someone's living room thirty years ago. A space heater in the opposite corner next to the dog kicked in, but the dog didn't move.

"Where did you get the picture?" Lucas asked.

"Traced it from one of those farming magazines."

"Looks like the one—"

"Shhh. Sort of. That was the idea."

Lucas took three steps to the side and bent down to pet the dog, who promptly rolled over and exposed his full underside, including an empty ball sac.

"Sorry there, boy," Lucas said to him. "You're a friendly thing aren't you?"

A red-faced gentleman with a belly bump walked through from the back with the paper in his hand. He extended his hand. "Hunter Boles. I'm the owner."

His thick accent was difficult for Lucas to understand. Coop returned the shake. "Calvin Cooper here, and this here is Lucas."

Boles pursed his lips, a frown developing on his forehead. "Hey, Jake, get over here," he ordered the dog. The animal scrambled to obey. His legs were long and thin, with a slim waist and large chest. Lucas thought he might be part Greyhound. "Some guard dog, right?"

Cooper gave him a half smile. "I got a dog, Bay. About the same size, and he's real friendly when I'm around. Not so much when I'm not. I'm sure your dog is the same way."

Lucas saw Jake hang his head as the door was opened and he walked slowly to the back. "Yeah, well, he's supposed to earn his keep. My wife doesn't like him at home because he sheds on everything, so this here's his home and he's workin.'"

Boles put the paper on the desk, smoothing it over.

"This is just a rough drawing of what he saw."

"This your friend here?" Boles said, pointing to Lucas.

"No. My friend lives west of here."

"Um hum." Boles studied the drawing again, tilting his head to the side and scratching the back of his neck, then stood to address Coop. "So what's he doing with the building, then?" Boles squinted up to Coop's considerable six-foot-four frame.

"Hell if I know. Gentleman farmer. Grows pot? He hasn't told me. And I don't ask."

"Gotcha. Yeah, we got a few of those around here."

"He's got money."

"I would expect he'd pay cash." Boles said as he narrowed his eyes.

"Sure. He's just looking for a good deal."

"So how did you get my name?"

Coop shrugged. "No clue."

The owner pulled his pants up onto his waist, which was wider than his hips. "So don't 'spose you know what size he wants, either."

"Big."

Boles grinned and Lucas could see a wad of tobacco stuck to his upper teeth, staining them a dark brown and making him look like he was missing them.

"No windows, I guess."

"That's what he drew. I thought he just forgot to put them in here. I mean, why would anyone want a building like that without windows?"

"Well, it kinda depends on what you're doin' inside, Mr. Cooper. If you don't want anyone to know, whole lot safer not to have windows."

"You build anything like this he can take a look at?"

"Sure. Baptist Free Will Church over near Paris, but that one has windows. This here is really a warehouse. No animals?"

"Again, Mr. Boles, I have no idea."

"Well, I need to know that. Ventilation? Air conditioning? He want it on a slab?

"I'm guessing so, yes."

"Well, keeps the varmints out, too. Until it rusts." He held the paper up. "Can I make a copy of this?"

"Help yourself," Coop said.

Boles handed him back the drawing. "I'm a little uncomfortable talking price without the owner, you know, the guy who's paying for it, being present. Don't like to talk to representatives, no offense."

"No offense taken, sir."

"You shopping this around?" he asked Coop.

"You're the first person we came to."

"Why don't you let me have a first crack at it? I'll see if I can find you an overrun or slightly damaged building, if that's not important to him?"

"Sounds good to me. If I don't have to drive halfway across the state, I'm happy with that."

"You fellas aren't from around here, are you? You sound like a Midwestern boy."

"That's right. Nebraska."

"I knew it."

"And I'm from California," added Lucas. Boles completely ignored him.

"Well, Mr. Cooper, I'm going to need the size, though, so you'll have to get him to give me a call with that. I'll have to see the site, study the road access for the trucks carrying the steel."

"Of course."

"How soon does he want this?"

"He said as soon as possible."

Boles studied both of them slowly, focusing on their shoulders, forearms, taking special note of their tats. Cooper had turned his forearm toward his side, as did Lucas, to hide the identical frog print tats that nearly everyone on Kyle's team had from inside their elbow to their wrists. Lucas made a note to himself to wear something long sleeved the next time.

"You boys military?" Boles had taken on a somber tone, trying to sound more casual than he was thinking.

"Ex," said Coop.

That seemed to satisfy Boles. He handed Coop a couple of business cards. "That's got my cell phone on it. Use that number. I pick it up all the time, day or night, but never when I'm on top of a building doing an erection, okay?"

"Thanks, sir. I'll have my friend call you."

They both turned to go, Lucas opening the outside door first. From behind them, he heard Boles shout out, "What's your friend's name?"

Coop slowly turned. "Kyle. Kyle Lansdowne."

Boles shook his head. "Never heard of him."

CHAPTER 24

Marcy drove Lucas' Hummer to the complex the bachelors lived in. Of course, she felt completely different now than when she and Nick had returned Lucas' items. She had been in some fog then, clinging to some oversexed belief this was true love and Lucas was The One.

Thank God for reality, she thought. Though painful, she made a mental note that a fresh start was what she needed. And maybe San Diego would remind her too much of the failed experiment that was her SEAL, Lucas. It would be a good thing if she never had to talk to another SEAL for the rest of her life. Except Nick, of course. But then, he wouldn't really count, since he was out and Devon was her friend.

Thinking about Devon's career in Sonoma County gave Marcy an idea as she turned off the truck. She fiddled with the keys and saw what looked like a front door key on the fob. Perhaps that was to the apartment. She decided to try it, and perhaps call the Taxi from inside Lucas' place.

She examined the area, including the parking lot that was near drained of cars. *That's right. Everyone's at work.*

She told herself it would get easier. Shrinking from the reality of her firing wouldn't help. She'd face it head-on. Get used to the idea that, unlike the rest of the world, she was on a precarious footing, but she would definitely find a way out. And whatever was out there, was going to be a good thing. *Not* a bad thing. When had she not landed on her feet?

Marcy knocked on the front door, and when no one answered, used her key. "Hello? Anyone home?" she said out of practice. The place smelled just like before. It was still a man cave. If she still harbored any warm loving feelings for Lucas, she'd stay and clean the place up, but she figured they wouldn't notice any tidying up, and it would send the wrong message. The men had nothing living in the place that needed tending, like plants or fish tanks. Everything could be left to rot or dry up as she was sure they were used to doing.

She examined the sagging ugly brown couch, and got the impression perhaps this was Lucas' bed. *Serves him right.* The SEAL was freeloading on his buds too.

She walked toward the dirty sliding glass door entrance to the balcony overlooking the parking lot. The barbeque was still covered in plastic, but the wheels and undercarriage were getting rusty from the salty air. The view was nice, seeing the bay and a large cruise ship pulling out, getting ready for a grand voyage.

Maybe I should sail away. Take a vacation.

She thought of Nick and Devon's place, the winery, the beautiful scenery she'd seen on her way up to the house in Cloverdale.

She did have a California Real Estate license, so relocating up there might work. Might. Maybe Devon could grease the way a bit. Hanging around Nick would be safe too, since he wasn't really close to Lucas and probably wouldn't have much to do with him. And somehow, she trusted him.

Marcy discovered there was no apartment phone, but she did find a phone book and called a Taxi with her cell, instructing him to meet her next to the Hummer. She peeked one more time at the four bedrooms, and again at the disgusting hallway bathroom with the raunchy posters and, as if she was saying goodbye one final time to Lucas, did a complete 360, not finding anything she wanted to memorialize. She was done. Time to go. Next fish to fry was moving all her stuff out of the office. She dropped the keys under the sand-filled ashtray pot standing guard by the front door.

Halfway down the hallway, she ran straight into Connie Shipley, who was carrying a Banker's Box. She had the baby in a front backpack and the little girl was tugging at her impossibly tight jeans.

"You just keep turning up like a bad penny, Marcy," the SEAL's wife said.

"Just dropping something off." It was a partial truth, though she really had no reason to be inside the apartment.

"Well then, you can open the door so I can give Lucas this shit."

"He's not here."

"Do I care? Did I ask that?" Connie balanced the box on the metal railing. The toddler was yanking on her leg, begging for something.

"Well, I'm just leaving." Marcy tried to walk past Connie, but her former client stepped into her path.

"Hey. You got a key? Then I don't have to leave these outside the door."

Marcy cursed inside at the thought Connie would leave a man's stuff outside for anyone to steal. She knew Lucas wouldn't be back right away, and she guessed Connie did as well. "Yes. I have a key. You don't?"

"Of course not. So you can let me in, and then leave it with me."

Marcy wasn't sure what to do with that one. She whirled around, walked past Connie, stooped down and found the key and unlocked the door. She stood next to the frame while Connie and her box and two children entered. The way the woman wandered around, Marcy ascertained she'd never been inside the place before.

"Where's his bedroom, Marcy?" Connie asked, pursing her lips and raising her eyebrows. She was still holding the box, while the little girl began running from room to room. "Lindsay, stop it," Connie yelled.

"I have no idea. I was never here when Lucas was."

"So how come you have a key?"

"Because I drove Lucas' truck home from Sonoma County with Nick, his friend."

"Oh, so now we're working on another SEAL? Is that right? He *is* another SEAL?"

Marcy wanted to get herself as far away from this woman as she could. She was having unclean thoughts about saying or doing something unladylike. "Connie, Lucas was called away so fast, he had to fly back. That left the truck behind, and I was conveniently available to drive it back."

"With your new boyfriend."

"I don't *have* a boyfriend. And what difference does it make to you, anyway? Let's just get this over with, and then we don't have to speak to each other again, okay?"

"Fine." She dropped the box beside the entrance to one of the bedrooms. Marcy could hear something clatter inside, perhaps break. "Lindsay, we're going."

The little one grabbed onto her mother's hand and continued looking back at Marcy with wide eyes, her little feet running to keep up with her mother.

Marcy locked the door, tucking the keys back into her pocket this time, and followed behind them. At the parking lot, she stood by Lucas' Hummer to wait for the taxi she'd called. She would ask Nick for the name of someone in the area she could safely leave Lucas' keys with.

Connie hadn't forgotten her earlier request. Holding out her hand, she gave a triumphant smile. "The keys."

"I'm sorry, those weren't Lucas' instructions."

"You have no right to my husband's truck keys or the keys to his apartment!"

Marcy's fury didn't interfere with her judgment and she bit her tongue, swallowed, and reeled in everything she had to stay calm. "I'm afraid you'll have to take it up with him. I'm merely following orders. But in case it matters, I'm not coming over here or taking his truck anywhere."

The unkind scowl Connie gave her did nothing to her already churning insides. Marcy was confused, hurt, angry, and tired of everything, ready to put it all behind her as quickly as possible.

"You know, Marcy, my divorce attorney has suggested I sue your broker."

"Really? That surprises me," Marcy lied. She thought perhaps the woman wanted to gloat about something. "I'd love to stand here and chitchat," she said as the yellow taxi pulled up and she waved to the driver, "but I have to go over to the office to pick up my things. As you may or may not know, they fired me because of the stink you caused. So I get to move on with my life. I guess I should thank you. But I do have work to do."

She didn't look back at Connie as the taxi did a U-turn and came back the way it had entered the parking lot.

In fifteen minutes, Marcy was at her own apartment, located within walking distance to the Coronado Bay Realty office. Once inside the door, her defenses dropped and she ran to her favorite overstuffed reading chair. Her tears had begun before she hit the cushions. The familiar hollow angst in her chest, the hole through her heart, was something that began to spread all over her body, causing her to shake. The tears desperately tried to wash away the hurt and memory of something lost, perhaps something that never was. Her neck ached.

She leaned her head on the padded back of the chair, staring up at the watery ceiling. Big gulps of air helped, and she began to calm with each deep breath she drew in. At last, the warm familiar aura of the place she'd enjoyed living in finished the soothing job of bringing her back to herself—the self that she'd relied on, the person who had been successful, enjoyed life, and made good decisions. Not the reckless self so easily influenced by that wrecking ball of a man. He was like an Alaskan ice breaker ship, crashing through all her defenses, making a waterway for himself where there wasn't one before.

She'd been so dumb. She'd been no match for his intensity. And yet, being perfectly honest, that intensity was what she had been attracted to in the first place. She was like a moth to the flame, and, unlike her usual self, powerless to stop it.

Marcy decided to call Devon in the privacy of her own space. She made herself a glass of ice water, brought it back to the chair, and dialed.

"Hola, Marcy. How are things?"

"Nick get back okay?"

"Fine. He had a good time driving down with you."

Marcy's stomach lurched. She'd not had breakfast, just the coffee. "He's a really nice guy. You're a lucky woman."

"Hey, hands off."

It was a light-hearted comment, but it cut to the bone. She covered the phone in case Devon would be able to hear the heavy breathing that came along with more tears. She tried to speak, but the words were more like a whisper.

"Marcy? Are you okay? What's wrong?"

"They fired me." There. She'd said it.

"Oh my God. When did this happen?"

"Just today, just now really. It's a mess, Devon."

"Yeah. I can imagine. Your broker is taking a hard line. You gave up the listing, of course?"

"Absolutely. But Connie—that's the wife—she's a real pistol. Lots of drama with that lady, and, well, she caused a scene in our office, with all the high-end clientele, celebrities, and such. My manager worries about—"

Oh hell, who am I kidding? I made a mistake!

"It's all my fault. Never should have happened." She tried to laugh, but it didn't come out right. "Devon, I was such an idiot."

"Love is blind."

"And stupid. There isn't anything there. I gave up my career—a good career too—for a couple of days of self-indulgence. That's the long and short of it. I'm ashamed."

"Oh stop it. I think you guys are great together."

"Except that's not happening either."

"What?"

"Lucas called right after I met with my manager. I know I was upset, but he sounded like such an asshole. I ended it, Devon."

"Oh no! I'm sorry to hear that."

"Well, Dev, this has been a couple of just terrible days. I'm working to get my head on straight. And I was wondering—"

"*Of course.* You get your butt up here. You can stay as long as you like."

"Under the circumstances, I've had to turn over all my listings to the office, so there isn't any reason for me to stay down here. I really appreciate it if I could bunk up there until I sort out what I'm going to do. But I'm not one to impose."

"Nonsense. You can help me with the crush and all the holiday party planning, Marcy. Get your mind off everything. Just get the soonest flight out you can."

"I think I'm going to drive, bring a few of my things, if that's okay. *Not* moving in, of course, but I will need a car. I plan to look for work up there. Maybe, you know, a winery hiring?"

"You can use ours—the old beater or the Kubota, of course!"

They both laughed.

"I'll get your room ready and you just let me know when you leave. We'd love to have you."

"Thanks, Devon. Really appreciate this."

"You'd do the same for me."

"I would."

Marcy was about to sign off, when Devon added, "Hey, and sorry about the comment about hands off on Nick. I didn't realize—"

"I'm so over that, Devon. How would you have known? Eventually, I'd like to find someone just like Nick. When I'm ready. Right now, I just gotta land on my feet, figure out what I want to do."

"I got it. And where, right? You need to figure out where you're going to live? You're not giving up real estate, are you?"

"Well, perhaps we could talk about that too, but let's just wait and see where this takes me. I do appreciate all your help."

"I'm going to talk to my broker, or do you not want me to do that?"

"Hold off for now. I'll see you in a couple of days."

"No problem. But get up here so I can keep an eye on you, okay? I'm going to worry myself sick until I see your smiling face."

Marcy was so filled with gratitude, she nearly started crying again. It wouldn't totally fill the hole in her heart, but it lessened the size and gave her the doorway to another future, so she could turn her back on the poor decisions of her recent past. In time, she knew she'd scratch her head and wonder what had come over her. It would look like just a little blip on her timeline. She'd be able to notice it without feeling like she'd lost something.

After all, she *was* gaining a future, somehow. It just wouldn't be with Lucas.

CHAPTER 25

Lucas didn't like the contractor. "You trust this guy?"

"Well, we're not going to fuckin' build a building on the Navy site. Not sure how much trust we need."

Coop's steps were longer than Lucas' He began to speed up to stay slightly ahead of the tall medic.

"But with the proper encouragement, I think we can get his cooperation."

Lucas stopped in his tracks. Looking up to Coop, he asked the question: "How we going to do that?"

"Up to Kyle. He has ways, believe me, and he knows more about this whole thing than he lets on."

Lucas nodded. He knew Coop was out of sorts about something. He could ask the giant about it, but decided he'd wait for Coop to seek him out. He didn't have to wait long.

"Look, Lucas. I'm going to say this once to you, and then I'm going to shut up about it because I really shouldn't be having this talk with you."

Oh fuck, here it comes.

"Ladies. This is about ladies."

"I don't need it, man." Lucas wondered why everyone felt they had the right to tell him where he'd fucked up. "I'm not a perfect man, Coop. I make mistakes just like the other guy. I don't need to hear all about it, is all." His shoulder ached and he rotated it while cracking his neck.

"Holy shit, Lucas. You gotta get that looked at."

"Shut up and go ahead, tell me what I can't stop you from saying. Just for the record, and for the second time, I. Don't. Need. It."

"Oh, you're gonna need it, or you won't make it on the team. I've seen guys…" He was quiet as a couple of young girls passed by them, giving them a long hungry stare. Coop turned around to make sure they were out of earshot, and Lucas heard their giggles. "Girls are funny," the tall SEAL whispered.

"I don't get that same reaction, Coop."

"You know what it is? They know I'm nice to them. I've never mistreated a lady. Worst thing I ever did was turn them down, and that's hard. But sometimes, it's the most compassionate thing to do."

Lucas tried to let Coop think he was considering his words, but he didn't believe a word of it.

"A man wants to do things, you know, sweet talk himself into a little nice situation. A little pleasure party, you know. It makes us feel good. Makes us feel like a man when the ladies fall for us. Flirting is one thing, being a gentleman is another thing. *Not* being a gentleman or not realizing the consequences of your actions is very dangerous."

Lucas was hoping Coop would shut up soon or he was going to lose it.

"Then you'll be like your friends at the bachelor pad. Hating women. Leaving them crying all over the place. Kids in every port, you know what I'm sayin'?"

"Coop, that's not me. I used a condom."

"Fuck's sake, Lucas. I think you're the dumbest frog I've ever met. You seriously think that ends your responsibility? How the hell'd they let you on the teams with that attitude?"

"No one asked me about condoms, man."

"I can't believe what I'm hearing," Coop said. "Unbelievable."

Lucas was starting to get pissed off. "Coop, could we just stop talking about all this shit and go buy the fuckin' TV and maybe some groceries, including some beer—a lot of beer—and then you can leave me to have my own pity party?"

"Sure. I expect you'll be rooming with those guys for the next ten years. Better start looking for a five bedroom place, or you'll start sleeping with each other."

"Asshole."

"I've been called that before. I expect you'll be called that a whole lot now. Good luck with that, by the way." Coop stopped in his tracks. "One more thing—"

"You said that already. This makes the second thing."

Coop ignored his words and punched him in the chest with his forefinger. "You stay the hell away from my wife, Libby, or any of her friends. And if she's real nice to you and tries to fix you up with one of her lady friends, you just say no. You stay away from all of them, you hear?"

"Sure, Coop." He had to look up to the tall Nebraska former farm boy, but he wasn't intimidated. "I can do that. Your lady and her friends are probably way out of my league, anyway."

"You just have to learn the facts of life, Lucas. Don't listen to Jake and Ryan and those losers."

"They're not losers. And Connie and I had a great time in the beginning."

Coop started laughing. "I'll bet you did. Not doubting that."

Lucas still didn't like the advice giving, but Coop was senior to him on the team and he knew it was smart to show him the respect he was owed, even if he didn't agree or like the advice.

"You'll figure it out, kid."

He didn't take offense at Coop's comments, even though they weren't even ten years apart. But Coop had paid his dues, and Lucas had one third the deployments the tall medic had.

That counted for a lot. He figured he could put up with some of Coop's shit and then go his own way. No need to start another confrontation, or a fire.

They brought the large screen TV into the temporary team building to much celebration. With quiet concentration, the Blu-ray and cable was connected, and soon the 55" screen was streaming action-adventure films. Another poker game was started, but Lucas grabbed a couple of beers and retreated to his bedroom. He thought about his conversation with Marcy, especially her words that Connie had been right. Were they both right? Perhaps he had no business being with a woman.

When he'd moved in with Jake and Alex and the rest of the boys, he thought it would be a temporary gig, that Connie would tire of her single life, she'd start to miss him, and voila, they'd be back together again.

He'd been wrong on that one.

Then he found himself attracted to Marcy. That was not only wrong from her standpoint, it made things worse with Connie. And it ruined Marcy's employment situation. He never intended for this to happen. He didn't wish any ill to come to either of them. Was he really that dangerous?

He finished his first beer, set the bottle down on the concrete floor, where it tipped over. Jake was at his doorway in an instant.

"You're being rather unsociable, my friend."

"Bad news. That stuff with Connie is a real mess. Wish Connie hadn't been told."

"Hey, I wish a lot of things. I wish my ex hadn't gotten the hots for the pharmacist. I wish I hadn't been on such a long deployment. I wish I hadn't dated the sisters—"

"That one," Lucas said as he pointed to Jake while still holding the bottle, "that's the one that fucked us both up, and got Marcy fired."

"Fired?"

"Yes. Fired."

"Wow, that sucks."

"Jake, the company she worked for is real high-brow and everything. Not everyone understands these things. I mean, we do, but it didn't go over very well with her boss."

"Geez. I'd never make it there," said Jake.

"No kidding."

"Half the population screws around, and here it was just one night of sin and all."

"It was a couple. But that's not the point, Jake. She was working for both Connie and I, and how do you suppose Connie took it?"

"Yeah. I knew that." Jake sat down with his beer. "So what's your plan?"

"What do you mean?"

"Well, what did you tell her?"

"Oh that." Lucas sat up, rubbed the back of his neck and took another long sip of the second beer, finishing it as well. "We're done."

"Done?"

"Yup. I screwed this one up royally. Really great lady. I wasn't thinkin'. She's better off without me." Lucas looked at the bottle and set this one down carefully beside the first one.

"If it makes you feel any better, I've been told that a time or two."

Lucas nodded his head and he imagined Jake had been told that many times over. "We aren't the type who are good for women, Jake. I didn't believe it at first, but you know, in the brief time since I've been bunking with you guys, you've got me convinced."

"Well, glad we could help on that score at least," Jake said as he stood up. "Come on, it's going to be time for dinner soon, and then maybe we can wreck some hearts on the Navy soccer team. You game for that?"

"Not sure about the girls, but the food? Yeah. I could take some right about now. And then I'm going to have a few more beers and see where it leads me."

"That's a good plan, Lucas."

Lucas watched him leave the room while he stayed behind, sitting on the bed, with the light of the day waning, waiting for dinner, considering having one more beer before.

It was a shame Marcy had to pay the price for his stupid mistake. But hell, at the time, it sure didn't feel like a mistake at all. It felt like one of the best couple of days of his life. Everything was possible. He was finally into a woman who was just as into him. How in the world could that be a bad thing?

CHAPTER 26

Marcy was going to attend to her office things, but after the call with Devon, she started making a plan, writing a list of things she would pack and take up to Sonoma County. To heck with the prying eyes of the office. Besides, if she went in there right now, she would be the talk of the place. Marcy decided to wait until late in the day when she knew the office would be completely deserted.

She picked through her clothes, thinking there could be a few boxes she would give away. She straightened up her apartment, changed her sheets and towels. Something about this little ritual made her feel more like a whole woman. She lit two new candles and played a streaming Spa Radio channel. She made herself a light lunch, brewed some fresh, strong coffee, sat at her tiny dining table overlooking the flowering crepe myrtle tree that went up three stories, its showy deep rose pink flowers blooming happily just for her. It had been a nice place to stay, but she realized she would move on without regret. Some place equally as nice in Sonoma County awaited her. And in the meantime, Devon and Nick's home was a safe place to land for a few days.

She called her hairdresser and found out she'd had a cancellation, so Marcy took the time to have some highlights and a trim. Next were her nails and a pedicure at her favorite Asian spa with the waterfall. She even managed to return Lucas' keys to the friend who had taken the heavy duffel. She no longer trusted leaving them at Lucas' apartment, where Connie had watched her retrieve them.

Strengthened by doing all the things she liked, she decided to go face the office, just as the sun was hanging low and threatening to melt into the ocean. Tomorrow morning she'd get up early and go to the gym in the complex, finish her packing, and then perhaps leave for up North early the next day.

All the good self care she'd done buoyed her mood, so that when she pulled into the parking lot at the Coronado Bay Realty company's lot, squeezing her Nissan between large Mercedes, Teslas and Bentleys, the three cars of choice for the Realtors in her office, she felt strong and ready to take on anyone or anything.

Until she rounded the corner to her semi-private office. Someone had already started moving her things and had brought in several boxes of their own. Marcy's plaques and awards, even the oil painting a client had done for her as a thank you, some of the celebrity photos she'd had signed, were all stuffed roughly into a couple of cardboard boxes without being careful about the quality of the packing job. It was an obvious slight. The painting had a small hole in the bottom right corner of the canvas where a sharp cornered black-framed award had poked it's way into it.

Son of a bitch. She worked on keeping her emotions in check, the painful memory of Lucas' advice to do so washing a prickling wave over her skin surface, making her hot, frustrated and needing to take it out on something. She kicked the brown box belonging to a stranger, heard something inside tinkle like it had broken and frowned.

"Hey, Marcy. That's my stuff," Gail said to her back.

Of course it would be Gail.

Whipping around, Marcy stared back at the woman who was dressed in skinny jeans and an expensive designer t-shirt, showing her ample surgically enhanced cleavage, dressed for a designer work day. "Who gave you authorization to take my stuff down? You put a hole in my painting."

Gail sneered, reared her head backwards like Marcy's comment had an odor. "Geez, Marcy. That thing? I'm sorry. I thought a little kid did it. I was careful with your awards." She crossed her chest, arms revealing long white fingernails. "As for who gave me authorization? Joe did. He said he'd *fired* you." Her eyelids lowered and Gail didn't seem to have any trouble using that "F" word. She examined Marcy's face through the bottom half of her eyes, head thrown back again. "Sorry about how all this has happened."

"I'll bet," Marcy mumbled. Her composure had flown right out of the room. "I need a little privacy to go through my things, if you don't mind." She took two steps toward Gail, pulled the door away from the wall and swung it in front of the agent's body. Gail had to step back to avoid getting it slammed in her face. Marcy made sure she gave it an extra push for the satisfying sound effect as it rattled the other doors and windows in the building.

She pushed Gail's boxes to the corner and out of the way first. Then she loaded up the items on her desktop so she could use it as a staging area for other things she needed to quickly go through. Gail stood outside the glass window overlooking the bullpen of other agent's desks, talking on her cell phone, while giving a disapproving look back to Marcy. The agent's lack of consideration for anyone else's feelings actually helped with the process. Marcy was looking forward not to have to deal with Gail and the other whispering hens who could say whatever they wanted, once Marcy was safely away, living a great life in Sonoma County.

Surprised it only took barely a half hour to complete the sorting, Marcy brought a large box of papers and folders to the shred bin in the reception area, unlocked the box, and dumped her things inside. The rest of her things fit into three remaining boxes. She'd been short one, so removed the contents of Gail's things from one box and placed them on the near-empty desktop.

A picture of Gail and Connie caught her eye. It was taken in Hawaii, in happier times. The two ladies were tanned, drinking umbrella drinks at sunset. Behind them were two tanned men: Lucas Shipley and Barry Burnett. The visceral reaction she had seeing Lucas' face was a surprise to her. His wide smile and white teeth contrasted the twinkle in his eye. She could see all the way through to his bad boy soul. It made her heart beat faster.

Damn.

Carefully, Marcy grabbed the framed picture and turned it over on the desk top. She loaded up her items and took each box out to her car. Before she removed the last box, she righted the foursome picture, turning it to face the side wall, surrounding it with other things from Gail's collection, turned around and left without searching back.

"All yours," she said with a quick smile. Gail stood in the lobby area alone, without expression.

"Good luck to you, Marcy. Where are you going to work?"

"Not sure yet."

"Well, I can call your cell, then?"

"Excuse me?" Marcy set the heavy box down on a reception chair.

"If I have questions about your other listings."

So Joe had given them all to Gail, which felt like a stab in the back. Suddenly her trusted feeling towards her broker was gone.

Better. You are so outta here, Marcy. Who cares what any of them do now. Not. Your. Concern.

"I'm probably not going to be available, Gail. It's up to you."

"Oh."

Marcy was planning on calling all her former clients, to say a proper good bye. Perhaps lay the seed they could still use someone else from the office if they were unhappy with her replacement. Something like that. Do it classy and quick. Let them know it wasn't her choice.

"Where are you going, then?"

"Gail, I have no idea." One of the receptionists was leaning to the side to watch her communication with Gail. Marcy walked up to her and presented her office key. "Give this to Joe, okay?"

"Sure will."

Marcy walked out the lobby doors, past the scored faux columns and broken pottery vases bursting forth with color, down the crushed granite walkway to the parking lot beyond and set the box down in the trunk. Marcy and her Murano drove off. She had no impulse to want to see what the office looked like. There was nothing there any longer she wanted to remember.

The trip up to Sonoma County the next day began after Marcy did one last hard workout in her complex gym. The morning commute was thinning. She texted Devon before leaving and then promised she'd let her know when she was near San Francisco. She double-checked messages and confirmed Lucas had not called, which was as she expected.

Near dusk, she was close to San Francisco, stopping by an Italian place she knew about, had some soup and good San Francisco French Bread, a cappuccino, and then texted Devon she was an hour and a half away. Devon texted her back a smilie face and a heart, *'Can't wait.'*

Near eight o'clock she turned down the winding Bennett Valley Road, into the crushed granite driveway of Sophie's Choice Vineyard. The stress of driving the distance and the awkward meeting at her office lifted as she pulled up to the beautiful modern home, golden lights from the many windows illuminating the silent green vineyards tucked in neat rows.

Devon ran outside, grabbed her Murano's door handle and swung it wide. "Welcome home!" She nearly pulled Marcy from the little SUV and then gave her a big hug. "So glad you made it safe and sound."

Devon was quickly trying to struggle with Marcy's bags when Nick appeared. "Hold it there. You get your butt inside the house, little one. I got this."

Marcy started to take one of the bags and Nick swatted her hand away.

"I *said* I got this." Then he broke a smile. "Welcome." His familiar blue-green eyes were warm and friendly. With his straight jaw, slightly unshaven stubble, his blond hair wildly growing like cropped golden hills of California, he exuded confidence, health and a good dose of sex appeal. She had trusted him since the first time she'd met him, but now, she realized she'd missed their easy conversation and banter on the trip down to San Diego.

As the tingling began forming in her belly it dawned on her that the person she was really missing was Lucas. The loss of that sexy friendship she had with him hurt like a wound that would never heal.

She and Devon laced their elbows together as Marcy slung her red computer case over her shoulder and walked arm in arm with her best friend. Her eyes filled with water with the welcoming she'd received in just under a minute. It was something that helped take away the bitter sting of her firing and painful scrutiny in San Diego.

They were playing soft music that echoed up throughout the house. A melodic soft African singer's voice filled the large rooms with warm sound.

"You have dinner? Want anything?" Devon asked.

"I'm fine. I stopped in San Francisco and had some soup and French bread."

"Vesuvio's?"

"What do you think?"

"How about some hot chocolate?"

"Sounds perfect."

Devon pointed through the sliding glass door off the kitchen, "You go on outside to the guest house and get yourself situated. I'll brew you some hot chocolate with a little chili, okay? Come on in after you get settled."

Marcy set her computer case down and crossed the kitchen in three long strides to hug Devon. "Thanks so much, Dev. You guys are a lifesaver."

Devon's body was warm, returning her hug with a squeeze. "I'm just so excited to have you here. We've got some wonderful news I'll tell you all about it after you come back. Now scoot." She said as she spanked Marcy on the rear.

The cottage brought back the memory of when she first came up to Sonoma County, the day she met Lucas. It was the cottage she'd hoped to spend a few nights with him in, before he was called away. A single lemon-scented candle glowed on the glass coffee table in front of the burgundy loveseat at the foot of the bed. Bright oil paintings adorned the walls as well as collages of work done to the winery. She examined one picture with a bunch of boys working shirtless, spraying each other and dancing. She saw Lucas among them.

"Where do you want these?" Nick asked, standing in the doorway behind her.

"Just put them on the bed. I'll unpack later tonight and tuck them away." She smiled up at him as he lay the suitcases down on the bed, waved and started to leave.

At the doorway, he turned to ask her a question, "So Marcy, you hear from Lucas?"

"No. Not sure I will ever again."

"Ever is a long time." He was right, of course, but his wicked red eyes bored into her like she was target practice.

"I know, Nick. I appreciate all you guys are trying to do for me. This was very generous of you."

He departed.

The property had been Sophie's struggling nursery and Marcy could still feel her presence, her spirit somewhere. Sophie had been Devon's mentor and friend, but she was also the older sister of Nick. Marcy knew the story of how she'd died at the old home, had been poisoned with arsenic in the water tank. Shortly before her death she had to endure the fire that nearly burned everything to the ground. She looked at a picture of Nick and a very frail and thin Sophie, which must have been taken just before her death.

Marcy washed her face, put on a stretchy top and bottoms she could sleep in, hung up a few things and placed underwear and other items in the dresser drawers she'd been provided. She removed her shoes and slid into some felt slippers, making her way back outside along the pathway nearly overgrown with honeysuckle, to the rear kitchen door. Devon had just poured them each a steaming mug of hot chocolate.

"Here you go. Let's sit here for a bit," Devon pointed to one of the overstuffed chairs in the living room. A fountain outside bubbled and spattered loudly, working it's magic on Marcy's soul and she relaxed further. Nick sat on the wide arm of Devon's chair, making her look like a child easily lost in the big cushions. Devon's feet couldn't touch the ground when she was seated all the way to the back.

"So, can I ask you what happened with you and Lucas?"

"Nick, stop it. None of our business," Marci interrupted him. It elicited a shrug from Nick.

"Sorry."

"If it makes you feel any better, when Lucas gets home, I'm sure we'll talk. But only if he initiates it. Not holding my breath," said Marcy. "In all fairness, it was just one conversation, a long-distance conversation." She examined her fingernails. "Nothing I can do about any of it until he's back. I could tell his focus had changed. He was a bit stressed."

"I'll bet," Nick whispered looking far away.

"What's happening, Nick?" asked Marcy.

"Crazy sh—stuff." He shook his head. "We are living in strange times."

"Well these are certainly strange times. I meet Lucas, and less than a week later, I'm without a job, relocating to Northern California. I'll be lucky if I still have my real estate license left when all the dust settles."

"Lucas is a one-man wrecking crew."

"We all are," Nick corrected her. "Remember, Devon? We get this tunnel vision, especially when we're on deployments. I've seen guys lose it when they get into arguments with their girlfriends or wives. Here they are, hiding in some boxcar of a home, hot, tired and maybe a little scared. Waiting for all the action to start and wham, a call to or from home, puts them on their ladies' shit list. Not a damned thing we can do about it, either."

"So, maybe it's best that everything is over before too much is made of it." Marcy's words trailed off and she slowly felt herself getting sleepy. "I gotta turn in."

"Me too. We'll talk in the morning. I have a Noon appointment in the office, so why don't you plan on going in with me and I'll introduce you to my manager. That sound good?"

"Thanks, Devon."

On the way back to the cottage, Marcy saw a shooting star, and made a wish, just as she'd always done as a child.

"If there's a way, and a reason for it, bring him back. If you can. And only if he wants."

CHAPTER 27

The soccer game after lunch between the Navy players and the SEALs was a complete wipeout—for the SEALs. The girl's goalkeeper wasn't afraid of a muscled hero coming at her. What she couldn't stop with her body, she would push back with her spikes. She drew blood on three forwards, tackled another and did a from behind slide tackle as her only defense of the box when she'd been caught off guard by a quick pass. With no refs to call a maybe questionable foul, she got away with it. What was apparent was that, for all their strength and stamina, because the SEALs had not worked together as a team on the field, the girls would be able to kick their butt each time they played. And the games wouldn't be close either. They called it quits after an hour, and although there was a dispute about the actual score, what wasn't in question was that the girls scored at least ten times, and the SEALs had only made one.

It was something that would eventually even out, but it would take several more games than they had.

A party was arranged to go up to spy on the training camp in the daylight. This time, Lucas stayed back at base. Jeffrey had brought a prototype of his new Battlefield Zombies video game Lucas and Jake lost themselves in.

"Holy shit, Jeffrey, do you suppose you could have any more blood in it? Alex asked the handsome former Bachelorette contestant.

The game had blood spurting in every direction when one of the good guys died, and greenish black ooze that worked like acid on the good guy's skin for the zombies. Lucas laughed when a new zombie appeared dressed as a cheerleader, complete with a couple of heads she used as pompons she held by long stringy hair. He wasn't so sure he'd have much of an appetite for dinner. It didn't affect his ability to drink red bull and beer in alternate doses.

"Red sells really well in China," Jeffrey answered.

"That's death to Chinese."

"Prosperity and long life, good luck too," he answered. "That's what they asked for. Lots of red."

"Who the fuck is supposed to win?" Jake asked. "Looks to me the zombies have an edge."

"Can't make it too easy. I think they expect for a novice there'll be lots of red. They asked for that. Then we get the kids to watch the online tutorial I'm working on now. You tell me what parts you like, would like to see more of."

Lucas switched with Rory and T.J. while Lucas, Jake and Ryan went outside, sitting on foldup lawn chairs he and Cooper brought back.

"So you guys think we can find a five bedroom in the complex?" Lucas asked.

Ryan sniffed the air, "You smell that, Jake? I can smell it a mile away. This here is a kiss-up."

"Nice and sweet," He smiled back at Lucas. "You stay the hell away from me in the shower. Recent breakups can do a lot to a guy, and you got two inside of one week, my friend."

"Shut up. You should talk."

"Seriously, Lucas," Began Ryan, "You're lucky man. I'd say you dodged a big ol' bullet. These married guys, they can talk all they want, but we all know what some of those ladies can turn into. And as you've noticed, you don't get any warning or chance to plan."

"Ryan's right. You're much better off playing the field."

They all turned their heads when Rory screamed, "Fuckin' A" so loud it nearly rattled the windows. The video game was getting lots of attention. The noise made it difficult to talk, so the three bachelors retired to Lucas and Jake's bedroom.

"In time, it goes away, and then you wonder what the big deal was," said Jake, pulling from a bag of chips.

"What goes away?" Lucas wondered.

"You know, dreaming about your ex, and trying to get back together. That goes away in time."

"What about your kids, Jake?" Lucas had identified what the real pain was.

"I get to see them. They're actually happier to see me when they don't see me every day. Our times are special now. And they can't say no."

Lucas had to laugh again. "You should see mine. Connie's scared the shit out of them. They cry whenever –well I've only seen them once since the—the—"

"You just got served man. You haven't had enough time for them to adjust. Now for another piece of advice?" Jake started. "Get back in good with that Realtor, and make Connie jealous. She'll start trying to get you back, Lucas. Women like a little competition."

"You don't know Connie."

"No. Sadly, no," Ryan said.

Lucas threw his beer at him and the arc of amber liquid sprayed across Jake's chest. It started a pileon—Jake was on Lucas immediately and then Ryan jumped the pile, causing them all to hit the floor.

Rory and Jeffrey appeared and quickly separated the brawl by pulling Jake and Ryan up to standing position, then shoving them out into the common area between the two bedrooms.

Lucas tore himself off the bed, straightened the mattress that had been dislodged from its base. He wanted to watch some news, feeling a little isolated from the rest of the world, but the game players were monopolizing the big screen. Depending on how long they were there, another TV might be in order to satisfy all camps.

Kyle and the rest of the men who had gone with him up to the hills made their entrance. Kyle headed for the bedroom he shared with Coop, who was burdened with some equipment in a pack that looked heavy. In his other hand, he held a camera with long lens attached. Lucas walked over to his LPO, leaning into the doorway. Kyle sat at a makeshift desk, and was writing some notes, copying some measurements from a crumpled piece of paper they'd prepared in the field.

"What's up, Chief?" Lucas asked, but he looked at Cooper.

"No sign of Rushti. Kind of a quiet day," Coop said. Kyle's back was to the two of them, until he turned around to face them.

"I gotta call CentCom, gentlemen. I'm gonna need a little privacy."

"Sure thing." Coop set the equipment on a table against the wall, which also housed three black duty bags Lucas knew to be filled with ammo and IEDs. Lucas entered the hallway with Cooper right behind him, closing the door.

"We saw him though, right? I mean they know that back in San Diego?"

"And D.C."

"You know what the plan is?"

Cooper grinned.

"There is a plan, right?"

"Oh yeah, there's a plan."

"Spill."

They heard the hallway door open. Lacey and several members of the soccer team sauntered in, freshly washed, looking lovely, and smelling even lovelier. Lucas momentarily forgot his question to Cooper, until the giant stepped on his big toe.

"The plan is that we focus on what the plan is, young froglet. Keep your eyes and ears open."

Several of the girls shuffled slowly past them, their running shoes barely making a sound. Cooper nodded. Lucas mumbled, "Ladies."

"We weren't sure we'd be welcome after today's game," started Lacey. She gave Lucas a wink.

Jake and Ryan had joined the group. "Apology accepted. But you owe us," Jake said. The two accompanied the girls to the living room/kitchen. Rory demonstrated the new video toy.

Coop cleared his throat. "So the plan is that we don't do anything to provoke them. Can't do a damned thing until we get the okay. Now, if they pick a fight, well then, all bets are off."

"You don't think they'd be stupid enough to—"

"Stupid's got nothing to do with it, Lucas. They're worked up with the heavenly fever, I call it. That knife cuts both ways."

"That it does," Kyle said behind Coop. "We stop talking about this right now. We have company."

"Roger that," Coop said. "Lucas, you hang with Kyle and I and stay away from those friends of yours or you'll go crazy. There's a reason they're single and we're married."

Lucas thought about the comment from Jake about being better off, and he agreed with his buddy one hundred percent. That's when he decided Cooper wasn't nearly as smart as he thought he was when it came to women. Eventually, he'd find out.

CHAPTER 28

Devon and Marcy rode together to Devon's office for a scheduled appointment with her Broker/Manager.

"I know about Coronado Bay. Good company. We've shared referrals over the years, although we don't get many coming up here from San Diego," Ted told the two women.

"Just want to be totally honest and above-board," Marcy began. "I made a terrible mistake, and this lapse in judgment isn't something I'm very known for. I've never been close to this. Ever. I think this couple just rattled me. I've worked with very high-end and powerful people, Admirals, CEOs and heads of hospitals who are used to hiring and firing doctors, and never had a problem."

Ted smiled. "Well, Devon's husband is the exception, of course, but most these guys are pretty wound up tight. I can see where that would bring some extra tension into an already stressful situation."

"Thank you, sir."

"So is there any fall-out about all this? Are you being sued? The company being sued? Anything like that and I need to know? Anything that comes up, I have t be kept in the loop."

"Of course. No. Nothing like that. I've turned over all my listings to another agent in the office, as instructed. I have nothing that should pull me back there. I need—" Marcy's left eye twitched as she stared down at the carpeting. "I want," she corrected, "to make a fresh start of it. I know Devon. I hope to make friends and get involved in the community and perhaps forget I was ever in San Diego. Besides, it's lovely up here."

"It is. Don't let the people fool you. Lots of money here. We are what they call the blue jeans tofu crowd."

All three of them chuckled.

"Down south, they try to show their opulence. Opposite up here. We don't like that sort of thing. We hate scandal, drama, too much rushing around, being cutthroat or unfair. Most agents here don't care how much they do, as long as they do it right. And I couldn't agree more. Lucky, really, to live here."

"I can see that. Well, if you'll give me a chance, I'd like to join your team."

"I think you'd fit in well, Marcy. Welcome aboard." He leaned over the desk and gave her a firm handshake. "I'll have the Independent Contractor agreement drafted for you in the morning, and of course we'll have to request your license."

Marcy held out her business card for him to get the broker address and her license number. "That's my cell."

"You want a desk here? Or, are you working out of Devon's house, like she does?"

Marcy smiled at her friend. "I'm going to impose as little as possible on Devon and Nick, although I'll be staying there until I can find my own place. So yes, assign me a desk and I'll try to start as soon as it's arranged. That way I'll be around your staff and people who can show me what to do until I learn.

They got up to leave, shaking the Broker's hand, and he tilted his head to the side. "You still seeing the SEAL?"

"Well, he's on deployment, but no, I don't think so. Part of the reason I need a fresh start."

"I understand completely. It's a shame, Marcy. Sorry for all this mess. But I figure you'll want to get busy to bring in some income. That works for me."

The two women had lunch downtown at an open-air pizza restaurant, watching people, sitting in the late autumn sun.

"I'm going to go looking for a place to stay, Devon. I intend not to be a burden to you guys."

"Don't be ridiculous. You've been through a lot—"

"Everything of my own making."

"Yes, that's true, but what kind of a friend would I be to dump you out on your own? You take as long as you want. Why don't you start making some calls for me? We could share the listings, if you get the appointments for me. We can work as a team."

"I don't want to impose."

"Now you're just being silly. I've got phone lists at home. You could even get started today, if you wanted."

Devon stopped for a newspaper, handing the classified section over to Marcy to search for properties.

At home, Marcy called on several rental cabins. Not being familiar with the area, she ran the addresses by Devon, who immediately eliminated those that she wouldn't find to her liking. Marcy was left alone when Nick returned and took Devon shopping.

Her rental car had GPS, so when she found a cabin up in the woods near Lucas' cabin, she decided to head up to Cloverdale area and check it out. Along the freeway she passed rows of vine-yards, splaying out in order, leaves beginning to turn yellow and red at their tips. Assorted white tents were set up in the rows as a sun shield for field workers picking the grapes for harvest. Underneath the green and golden leaves, the grown was a rich charcoal color. Bins of grapes stacked up between rows. Several large estate wineries were perched like crystals atop rolling golden hillsides.

Cloverdale came up soon after. The two lane road through the center of town was nearly devoid of traffic. A dog made his way across the highway, barely glancing in Marcy's direction, sensing she'd slow down and let him cross without him having to make a run for it.

Before she made it off the highway, she stopped for a cof-fee. Espresso machines squealed their protest. The heavily tatted barista was playing light jazz in the background. Marcy exam-ined artwork hung along the bright orange walls of the little coffee house. A lending library stood in the corner with a full two rows of books, several of the romance. It was a place she could sit and think about things, on another day when she wasn't on a mission. Some day, when she could ponder the complexities of life. She got in her car and headed left when she passed the outskirts of the town, as her GPS had instructed.

The drive through the redwoods was lush and green. Unlike the scrubby oak and madrone wilderness where Lucas' family home was located, this area was cooler, closer to the ocean by a few miles, the damp green carpet of foliage making a perfect place for a nap in the forest. The tall trees were thicker and let in little light. The road soon turned to a red-brown color. Her GPS instructed to go further, when all of a sudden, something hit her rear bumper from behind. She dared not look into the rear view mirror since she was having so much difficulty maneuvering her car, but one quick glance and she saw a dirty white van with tinted windshield. In the limited light from the forest, she couldn't tell who was driving. The van continued to push her car as she fishtailed in front of it. Unable to keep up with the switching back and forth. Eventually she was forced off the road, down a small embankment and into the path of a redwood tree.

In a flash of color, she saw the impact. Her windshield cracked and burst forth into a rain of crystals while her head was forced into the steering wheel, and then ripped backward from the impact of the crash. The airbags deployed before her head could hit the steering wheel a second time.

The last thing she heard was a door opening with a squeak. It wasn't from her vehicle. She smelled gasoline and wondered if she'd be able to move if the auto should catch fire. Black spots appeared in front of her eyes. She felt something warm trickle from the side of her mouth as her forehead pressed into the sticky wet plastic of the white airbag. Blackness shrouded her in a deafening silence.

CHAPTER 29

Lucas tried his hand at Jeffrey's game after dinner. He noted Donna was sitting just a little too close to him, and her thigh stretched the length of his. While he didn't think she meant anything by it, he also felt it was more than a sexual advance. Her close proximity, her scent, the way she laughed and so expertly worked the controls of the game when it was her turn, and competitively tried to beat him at every round, intrigued him. But he also felt something dark was looming just under her surface. She wasn't a woman to talk much, and she'd been blabbing all evening, and drinking more beer than he'd seen her do the previous two days.

Something had shifted. She trusted him. He wondered if that was very wise.

Kyle went outside to greet someone who drove up in what sounded like a large diesel truck. Lucas tried to angle a way to see through the building windows, but couldn't make out who it was.

"The barn builder," Coop said.

Lucas excused himself and followed Cooper outside. When Boles laid eyes on them, he didn't smile or extend his hand like he had in the shop.

"You guys got a lot of fuckin' nerve getting me to come out here after dinner. Urgent, you said. What the fuck's so urgent about this place? This is government land. I don't want any of that goddamned paperwork filled out in quadruplicate cluttering up my system. I deal with small time rural farmers." His face was bright red. One eye had a popped blood vessel, which was new. Lucas saw he could have a temper. "I don't have to wait months and months for my cash. I get it before or the day of installation."

"We had to do it this way, sir," Coop started in. He peered over at Kyle, asking for help. They'd not discussed him coming over today. Kyle must have gotten the urgent call from Forsythe and made the invite himself.

His LPO sat down on a picnic table, leaned into his thighs and spoke slowly to the man, who was scanning the scene in front of him. Boles scratched the back of his neck and breathed hard like he had a medical issue.

"We're looking for information about our neighbor over the hill there." Kyle pointed to the ridge of dark green trees casually. By the way he studied the builder, Lucas could see he didn't trust him either.

"Not sure what you mean by that, son."

"You know, the people who have the little group thing over the hill. You've been there I'm sure. You helped them build it, am I right?"

"Of course. But if you think I'm going to go gossip about them—you guys have no right coming in here under false pretenses. I keep to myself. I don't ask questions and I certainly fuckin' don't answer any asshole's questions unless I got a good reason to do so."

Kyle stood up and was toe-to-toe with the man. The contractor's belly pushed into Kyle's abdomen but neither man backed up. "I got a good reason. Trust me I got a good reason," Kyle said between his teeth.

Boles managed to take a step back. "You guys military? You look military. What, we gonna have a fuckin' war on our hands here in the great state of Tennessee?

"Not if we can help it sir, and that's where you come in." Kyle's voice was practiced and gentle. Calming. It did little good.

"Like I said, I don't want any trouble."

"And we're not looking for trouble either," answered Kyle.

Boles scanned the three of their faces. He nearly jumped out of his pants when the back door to the building opened and out poured several SEALs. Lacey came behind them, kicking a soccer ball. Two of her teammates had removed their jerseys, exposing their sports bras underneath, and stuck the t-shirts inside the backs of their pants. The SEALs were bare chested, having tucked their shirts in similar fashion. Within seconds a lively pickup game of grab ass ensued, both sides trying to capture jerseys while others members attempting to bury the soccer ball into the post nets on either side. One goal was well defended, the other had no keeper.

Fredo had been on the sidelines and at last jumped in. With his speed and superior ball handling skills, he was dodging other players and easily scored a goal. He was on his way to scoring a second, when Chloe tackled him and left him limping for a bench.

"Who the hell are all these?" Boles finally asked.

"U.S. Navy Women's Soccer Team," Kyle answered.

"Navy, huh? So you guys are Navy?" Boles squinted into the remaining sunlight. The lights on the field came on as the dusk sensors kicked in.

"Um hum," Kyle answered him and didn't break his line of sight.

"Fuckin special forces. That's what you are." The builder spit on the ground.

Lucas cracked his neck again and all three turned quickly, alarm written all over their faces.

Kyle refocused on Boles. "So all we want is information." He brought a picture from his vest. "This man. Did you see this man?"

"Never saw him before."

Lucas didn't believe him. The telltale widening of the eyes before his uber-quick response told him the contractor had seen him, maybe even talked with him.

"Try again," Coop said as he picked up the contractor by his western style denim shirt. Lucas heard a loud rip in the fabric. His feet nearly dragged in the dirt although he probably outweighed Coop by forty pounds. Coop let loose of him, brushing the fabric flat against the man's chest. "I apologize for ruining your pretty shirt. I'll see to it Uncle Sam brings you another one."

"Get your fuckin' hands off me. You think I'm stupid?" Boles adjusted his clothes, stepping back for a safe distance.

Kyle looked at Cooper and then to Lucas and shrugged. All of them shook their heads. "No sir," Lucas said. "None of us thinks you're stupid. That's why you're gonna cooperate with us."

"This isn't fuckin' Afghanistan or Iraq. You can't just come in here and manhandle me!" His voice was attracting attention from the field. Fredo limped over to add assistance. Two of the girls stopped and put their hands on their hips. Even Chloe stopped, holding the ball at her hip with one palm.

"So, I'm gonna ask you one more time. Have you seen this man?" Kyle held the picture of the Shiek up to the builder's nose.

"He was there. Didn't talk to him, though."

"How many are they?"

"How the fuck do I know? They have some young ones that stay in the other buildings. Saw them through the windows. Never saw them outside. I only went inside their bunkhouse one time when I got paid. We made a point not to stare, if you know what I mean."

"Sure." Kyle sighed. "So guess. Humor me."

"Thirty? No telling how many inside those other buildings."

"So what's the scene like? You were there, what, three days?"

"Four."

"Okay, so what did you see that you remember? Anything unusual?"

"What, besides the fact that they pray several times a day? They wear long white robes in the fuckin' ninety degree afternoon? They got sandals instead of cowboy boots? You wear sandals here when you're a full grown man and you're, well, we don't do that here."

"I got you. So they're different. What else. What about this guy?" Kyle tapped on the picture.

"His look. The way he looked at me."

"How was that?"

"He looked like he fuckin' hated me." He pulled his jeans up, bringing his belt buckle up into the middle of his "pregnant" belly. "After the first day, I had the creeps. I asked for all my money. I gave it to my wife in case I didn't make it out of that place alive.

The Mexicans in my crew didn't seem to have a problem with them. They're used to not understanding the conversations I have with clients."

"So what gave *you* the creeps?"

He looked up at the trees as if the camp's spies were looking down on all of them, and bit his lip, following along the horizon. He watched the soccer players for a few silent seconds without showing any expression, his lips pursing in fleshy puckers, and then smoothing back into a grimace. At last he took a deep breath and made a line in the dusty dirt with the side of his cowboy boot. When he looked up at Kyle, the man's eyes didn't stray a quarter of an inch from side to side. Lucas could see there was a little courage, a little fight left in the man. But not much. And though he was trying to mask it, Lucas could tell he was more than a little intimidated.

"One night we were working late. I saw this guy walk between the buildings. The sun had gone down. They'd finished their prayers. We were picking up our tools but the moon was bright so we could see. I wanted to get out of there so fast it made me sick to my stomach. We knew we'd be done in one more day, and that was one day too long."

"Okay. So what happened?"

"He walked into one of the houses. Before that, I never once saw or heard a woman. But that night, I heard a woman crying, like things were being done to her, you know? Those animals were doing things to her."

Lucas could see Kyle wanted to punch the guy, but his mission was more important than his own satisfaction. Instead of chastising him, Kyle showed mercy. Not many men, especially men who weren't trained to see the kinds of things they saw over in the arena, would know how to deal with this. It wasn't something people in the U.S. were used to seeing. Unfortunately, it was something all three of the SEALs standing before this man knew without a doubt occurred in the world of evil men. Lucas knew it hit all three of them the same. Someone innocent was being violated. Someone needed rescuing.

Kyle spoke softly, making the man lean towards him to hear. "Now you know why we must be here."

CHAPTER 30

Marcy's head hurt with a dull ache, which is what woke her up. She was confused, but gradually the fog lifted and she remembered what had happened before she'd passed out. She also remembered hearing voices in a strange dialect, and hands holding her body, carrying her somewhere. But the splitting pain forced her to keep her eyes closed, keeping the room from spinning, knowing even limited light would hurt worse. And then things would go black again. This happened several times before she woke in earnest.

Now, nausea plagued her. She needed to roll over and vomit, but when she tried, discovered she couldn't move. As she struggled with her own mind, trying to will her legs to slide off the bed, and found she wasn't on a bed at all, but a hospital gurney. She smelled the sweat from her body and knew she'd been there more than a day. She had to go to the bathroom.

The tiny room was cold, like a closet off a main living area, without heat. Someone had covered her with a blanket that smelled like it hadn't been washed in months. And then she discovered she was nude underneath the blanket. So where were her clothes? Did she require surgery? Was she in a hospital or clinic of some kind?

Light crept under the doorway, where she heard muffled talking, again in a foreign tongue.

She checked herself over, closing her eyes and concentrating on what hurt and what didn't, discovering her head was still the most painful. She willed her bladder to hold and to her surprise, it worked. Wiggling her eyebrows up and down, she felt the welt on the right side of her forehead. The rusty taste in her mouth and clots of blood on her lip made her heart beat faster. It was one thing to be involved in an accident. But to be drugged and kept in a storage closet, without any medical care, meant only one thing: the accident had been anything but an accident, and the same people who caused it now held her.

They hadn't gagged her, so Marcy deduced they weren't concerned about her screaming for help. She guessed they were somewhere out in the boonies, since she could hear neither traffic, airplanes or other sounds of civilization, except for the faint middle eastern music and the sing song of the unfamiliar dialogue in the background.

The room smelled of bleach, or some sort of pungent cleaning fluid she didn't recognize.

Because one ankle strap immobilized her left foot, toes pointing down, Marcy developed a calf cramp in her left leg that began to drive her wild. She focused on the cramp, pushing into it, while her other leg developed another cramp. She willed herself into accepting it and stopped fighting, which gradually sent the dual cramps into remission.

She steadied her breathing, promising herself that, as more and more memory began to dawn on her, that she would not panic. What had Lucas said?

'Aren't you being overly dramatic?'

"Fuck," she muttered softly. She hated to admit it, but being overly excited *would* interfere with her problem solving, and she most definitely had a problem. A life or death problem. She harbored no illusions as to their intentions.

Marcy struggled against her foot binding and a small metal tray fell from the gurney, crashing onto a concrete floor. The door to the lighted room opened, flooding her with bright white light. She squeezed her eyes shut.

Someone closed the door partially, giving her eyes time to adjust. Standing before her was a young man in white robes. His full beard framed the smooth, young face of the man she recognized near Lucas' cabin from three days ago. He saw in her eyes the recognition she bore.

His teeth were white and perfectly straight. His smile tilted upward to the left as he scratched his chin. But the eyes of this man carried a coldness she'd not seen before.

He removed a large ugly knife, brandishing it from palm to palm, showing off the highly polished glint of the blade. His eyes studied her as he peeled back the top of the blanket and lowered the tip of the knife to her abdomen. He jerked it upward, tickling her skin without penetrating. Still dangerously clutching the handle in one hand, the man pulled back the blanket to below her belly button. His sharp inhale told her he was turned on by the violence he anticipated. She braced for a stabbing, a deep cut, or perhaps a beheading.

One more time the blade was lowered and this time she felt the cold metal on the flesh of her upper abdomen, causing her to shiver. With a flick of the wrist her captor scraped her left nipple. He stared down at her chest, licking his lips.

He was muttering a prayer. Marcy accepted the fact that there was nothing she could do, except perhaps throw her weight to the side and topple them both. But being strapped to the gurney would put her at a disadvantage.

And then it hit her. They wouldn't kill her until they abused her. The way this man looked at her flesh, she became convinced his pleasure would be extracted from her pain. If she showed fear, or struggled, it would enhance the experience for him.

She vowed to hold out for as long as she could.

The robed man shouted several Arabic names and instantly the room was filled with several young boys barely old enough to shave.

He waved the tip of the blade at her while he spoke to them. None of them would look her in the eyes, but remained focused on her breasts. The robed one squeezed her left breast first, muttering something in a sneer, citing a verse the rest of the room repeated. He fondled her right breast, but this time, tweaked her nipple, twisting it until it caused pain.

She arched up as much as she could, but did not scream. That action drew a reaction from the young boys. One by one, they each took a nipple, twisted it until Marcy finally cried out. She watched in horror as the boys were encouraged by her terror.

Her stomach finally could hold out no longer as the nausea swept up from her abdomen, quickly sending bile and contents of her lunch up and out her mouth, spraying the group with her vomit. Pandemonium spread over the little gathering, as the room emptied, no doubt sending the boys to the showers to wash up.

She got what she'd been hoping for and didn't have time to brace herself against. The robed man's hand came crashing down against her left cheekbone and again the room went black.

CHAPTER 31

Early next morning, Donna Grant went for her usual five mile run. The faint scent of burning leaves was in the air. Heat from yesterday's sun had soaked into the soil and the asphalt she ran on at the side of the country lane, but the air was crisp and cool, perfect for her run.

As the road veered off to the left, she heard a vehicle approach from behind so she moved further onto the shoulder to make sure to give the driver clearance. But the motor slowed and began following close behind her. She tapped her watch, sending her personal signal through the Apple device. The watch would clock her location and send that information as well.

The motor continued to run but when she turned to look behind, three dark-skinned men in green camo caught up to her, despite the fact she'd put on the speedburner sprint most men had difficulty keeping up with. They grabbed her arms, one of them put his hand over her mouth where she was able to bite down and take a sizeable chunk from the man's palm. She could feel freedom within reach when suddenly a moist rag was placed over her nose and mouth and she succumbed to spotted dizziness fading to black.

"Forsythe is coming today. We're gonna show him the camp. He's bringing sat photos, and another special honored guest," Kyle reported to the group before breakfast. "We do our PT here. No one leaves the compound until Forsythe okays it, understood?"

"Who's Forsythe bringin'?" asked T.J.

"T.J. because I'm not totally positive he's coming, I'm going to wait. But you'll find out when all the rest of us do."

Tyler raised his arm and was called on. "How about a rematch with the ladies? We're looking at O for three."

"Not a fuckin' chance. Besides, I think they're leaving soon, maybe even today. I don't want Forsythe to get the impression this is a Club Tennessee all inclusive fucking resort, catch my drift?"

Lucas noted how disappointed Tyler was. "I'll kick the ball around with you after breakfast, if you want. We can do that without the girls, right? You still remember how to play with men, don't you?"

The team laughed at Tyler's expense. Tyler took off his sweaty shirt and threw it at Lucas.

Breakfast was somber. The girls obviously noted none of the SEALs sat with them, as was the custom. Everyone on Team 3 had one eye on the entrance to the mess hall's doors, looking for Forsythe.

Lacey cornered Tyler when he went back for seconds. "You guys sore losers?" she asked loud enough for the entire room to hear.

"Nah. We got—" he looked at Kyle for reassurance he could mention Forsythe and got the nod, "We got brass coming in today. We're supposed to show our bad-ass side, not the fraternizing side. Nothing against you ladies."

"What a load," Chloe said under her breath as she walked past the men on her way to hand in her tray. Lucas thought it was funny as hell.

"See, that's what's wrong with women," Jake started. "They win a little bit, and then they take over. Mess with your head. Talk about sore losers. They hate to waste an opportunity to pound us into the ground."

"Fuck sake," said Alex. "It's their job to win. That's what they train for. We train for something else. They get in your head, Jake, because you let them get inside your head. Your fault, man."

Cooper leaned forward to be able to deliver his message to both Jake and Alex. "Boys, I'm having a hard time imagining you ever being married. I mean ever. This isn't about winning. You don't treat a woman like that. You continue with that shit and you'll be jerking off to the TV when you're seventy. Broke and lonely."

"Fuck, already broke," Jake said after standing. Tyler nodded to Lucas and the two of them cleared their spots, then headed over to the bunkhouse to retrieve the soccer ball.

A black SUV with darkened windows pulled up and three men stepped out. The security team consisted of the driver and two details. Ian Forsythe extricated himself from the rear passenger side, while Jackie Daniels got out on the other side behind the driver. Kyle was quick to appear and give the man a shake, and give Jackie a bear hug.

Jackie was roundly welcomed. Lucas knew then, that if the mission was successful, they'd be interrogating the Sheik or his underlings, and that would require someone with native language skills. Jackie was the only man any of them trusted for this job. And he had saved their lives on several other missions. Not only was he deadly with his interpreting, he was deadly with any weapon they gave him, and never hesitated to use it. He was as close to an Afghani SEAL there was.

Several minutes later, the team was briefed. Forsythe showed photos of satellite surveillance on the camp.

"You'll see these trucks are in constant use. We've tracked them as far as we can. Gonna have to paint them somehow, or install tracking devices. We're bringing in some drones, but understand only Coop operates them. I don't want any incidents, or alerting the camp to our presence."

Coop nodded. "Can I take pictures?"

"Being fitted now as we speak, Coop. Daytime only, I'm afraid, though."

"We'll do the best we can."

"Chatter is up, indicating we got something coming very soon. The Oregon incident was apparently orchestrated by a group in Northern California, but you know as well as I do, there are over thirty training camps operating in the U.S. today. Our leadership hasn't been comfortable spying on them, although God knows they should be. I mean what the fuck do they want with training camps, learning how to shoot while crawling on their bellies, breech boats and blow shit up."

"Wonder if that guy who got away—remember that guy, Rory?"

"Sure do. The sidekick of the dude Megan went all Bobbitt on," said Fredo.

Jackie piped up. "I do not understand why your government does nothing. They know. It's like they want to allow these people to do evil things to the good citizens of the United States. This should never have been allowed."

"And it's getting worse," Forsythe said.

"Not like it's a church or Boy Scout camp," added Jackie. He continued to shake his head.

There was a general mumble of approval from the group.

"You know what they say. Evil exists when good men do nothing." He paused. "When Kyle reported your builder guy heard a woman crying out, that escalated this mission into a primary target. We can't engage unless they engage first. Be very clear about that. We in no way want to bring in local news crews or garner criticism about SEALs doing work inside the U.S. borders, so we're still considered a training mission. Doesn't hurt to take pictures, and if need be, stage a rescue if we can get the approval."

Armando stood. "Sir, wouldn't it be a good idea to inform the locals? Isn't this something the Sheriff's Department or Marshall's Service should know about?"

"We're studying the situation. Not sure it will work that smoothly. We got three jurisdictions and they don't always cooperate. But yes, we will if we can. If we have time. That would be ideal. But gentlemen, we're here to learn about this verified threat of militias kidnapping and taking hostages—SEALs, *not* civilians. So we're taking the broad interpretation it's our mission. But again, I have to underscore we keep it tight. We say nothing to anyone. No one. Understood?"

The Team was in agreement.

"We will have to verify there's a hostage situation. We can't just send guys in there, even locals, unless we can verify this. So far, we have nothing on what we've taken by air. Hope the drones work better, Coop."

"If she's able to be seen, we'll find her."

"I'm working on VIR equipment for your two drones, too," said Forsythe.

"Two? Hot damn!"

Lucas knew Cooper was their gadget guy and could rig up anything to look harmful or not harmful, depending on the requirement. In his single days he lived in a motorhome by the beach, outfitted with more devices than some small police departments had. His home on wheels, before his marriage to Libby, was affectionately called the Babemobile and had been used on some surveillance and rescues in the past, before Lucas' time on the Team.

Jackie Daniels spoke up. "You get something to record their conversations, and that will be more incriminating. They have to speak to someone by cell. They probably have computers, which would be good to try to capture."

"I got some little devices with a pretty good range. Problem is, we need to be line of sight to work them. That means someone has to stay buried up on top of the mountain."

"Then we'll plan that. You look today for what you'd need and plan where we put them. We'll do the rest," answered Kyle.

"Okay, then. Kyle, give me the grand tour," said Forsythe.

Lucas accompanied Forsythe and Kyle, Cooper, Armando, Jackie and Fredo to the top of the ridge. They were surprised to find two guards posted on the hill today, and, unlike before, one was upper ridge, one was lower ridge. With his high-powered scope, Armando was able to determine there were two other sentries across the small valley overlooking the camp. This meant they had beefed up security, for some reason. Nothing could be discussed until they were away from earshot.

Lucas heard the buzz of a high-flying drone before anyone else did, and he pointed it out to Coop.

"Shit," he said softly. He pointed to his chest, shook his head, "Not ours," he whispered.

Armando finished taking pictures. Lucas noted the vans were lined up as they always were, with the exception of one backed up to the end of a building. The doors were not visible.

Forsythe was comparing their photos with what he was seeing live and made a couple notations to Kyle. Lucas kept scanning the skies for evidence of the drone's return. Movement down in the valley piqued his attention and he found a drone operator using a small laptop computer was guiding it home. He handed his scope, taken from his H&K, to Coop. After several seconds of study, and watching the drone land near the lake's shore, Coop nodded and handed him back the scope.

"All good," he whispered.

Lucas gave him the thumb's up.

They began to leave the site when they heard a car approach the guard gate to the camp. The occupants were two ponytailed blonde ladies, both wearing short shorts and tank tops. Lucas examined the ladies as they were ushered through the gate. What he saw made the hair stand up all over his body.

"Holy fuck!" he whispered.

Kyle faced him and angled his head.

He whispered, "Builder's daughter" to Kyle's ear. Armando had them in his site as well.

"Wonder if papa knows," said Armani.

"I'm guessing not." Kyle added, "If he felt the creeps when he was there, I'd have a hard time thinking he'd let his daughter go there."

"He must have told her, right?" Lucas asked.

Armando shook his head. "I say no. She's doing her little wild child thing, but that's a dangerous game. Very dangerous."

The ladies parked outside one of the buildings and were shown the way to the building doorway. The girls looked at each other, shrugged and walked inside.

The SEALs waited a half hour without further incident. It appeared no foul play was at hand, or whatever the girls were doing was consensual, so Kyle and Forsythe checked with Jackie for any clues, and then called their surveillance off and the group headed back to camp.

After they arrived at the meadow at the base of the ridge, Lucas asked Coop what he was dying to know. "What the hell are they doing with that drone?"

"Same thing we are. We gotta hope to God they don't know we're here," Coop answered him. "Hard to tell, but I didn't see any equipment saddled on her, so I think she's not taking pictures, but you never know. They get hold of one of those micro cameras and we may be on their evening news."

Forsythe turned to them. "We're going to have to consider not going up anymore in the daytime. At least at night, we aren't as discernable."

"But our signature will stand out more," said Kyle.

"Only reason you'll be there is if we can't get the air support, if we go in. We need eyes on the ground," said Forsythe. "I'm going to get on the horn and find out if there are any updates. But I think our next mission will be to verify there is a hostage there."

Lucas didn't like the fact that, due to it being on U.S. soil, they'd have to be extra careful before they were granted permission to go forward. Going in and still having to get permission to go forward didn't seem tactically sound. But he wasn't the one calling the shots.

CHAPTER 32

Moustafa intended Marcy would be the training whore for his young men, something to use as reward for jobs well done. He cleaned her body and even put first aid salve on some of her scrapes and the bump on her forehead. He enjoyed washing her, preparing her. The training would be long and delicious.

He found that forbidden fruit was the best kind of motivator. They studied it was wrong to have sex with an infidel, but an infidel being used to train boys into becoming men, was allowed. The fact that she would never give her consent made the whole scenario complete. Consensual sex with an infidel was punishable by death. Rape with a subhuman infidel was not only allowed, it was doing the Prophet's work and moving them all toward the Kingdom of Heaven. Moustafa knew he'd be rewarded.

In the meantime, he'd be quiet about his designs on the woman. He would let them touch her, pinch and lick her, perhaps draw a little blood, but the first entry into her body would be performed by him. He'd like to do it in private, but it was important to show the men how it was done. In the old days, they would have themselves to practice on, but now they had a live woman, a woman they could defile and not be punished.

God is good.

He'd given her another dose of heroine, when she started to come to as he was washing her. She quickly succumbed to a deep sleep and he could do anything he wanted to her. Such a thought was thrilling.

The heroine was part of the supply they were leaching out into the local high schools in Northern California, which accomplished two things: they raised funds for their cause, and they got the local population hooked on the substance. As far as he knew, they were off the radar.

The government was not only letting them operate these training camps, which emboldened his leaders back in Iran, but had expressly put out public communications to law enforcement they were to be protected. How the Prophet managed to arrange this, Moustafa could never figure. But it was a fact, they had nearly full immunity from prosecution, or persecution. Being isolated in the woods made them virtually invisible. Only thing missing was a fence. Every other compound had installed one. His would be coming soon.

God is good.

Marcy was in such a state that the restraints were not necessary. Besides, he liked having her drape over his body, her limp form still lusciously curvy in all the right places. He loved the smell of her perspiration, and the scent of old cologne behind her ears, on her wrists and between her breasts.

Today, while the boys were delivering their drugs to Cloverdale High School, he locked himself in the room with her, removing all their clothes and let her sleep on top of him. He fingered her clit, stuck a thumb into her anus and she moaned like it was pleasurable. But he knew better.

It had been a stroke of luck when they'd found her at the coffee shop. He'd hungrily watched her athletic body order her coffee, watched her out of the corner of his eye as she added cream and stirred the liquid mixture. Her backward tilt of the head exposed the silky white flesh of her neck. The more he watched her, the more he felt he owned her. His fantasies came in wild colors as he imagined things he could do to her, things like that warrior had done. He knew what her skin looked like at midnight, in the shower, even when she was relieving herself. He'd watched her shave her legs, shave other parts of her more intimately. Just for him.

They'd followed her at a distance, but when she drove off the main road leading to the coast, and onto the dusty dirt roads of the redwood forest, he decided on his bold plan. He would take her and the taking would happen nearly five miles from where they were living. It would surely take a week or more to find her car, locate her body, if at all. That was more than enough time for the events he knew were coming.

Capturing her was thrilling. He allowed someone else to drive while he made sure her body was sufficiently intact. Her arms were strong, thighs unharmed. Her forehead was bruised, but her abdomen was flat and unmarked. Her butt cheeks smooth and squeezable. He took just a few liberties, when the students were not looking over at him.

Soon it would be time to use her the way the Prophet intended.

His erection was deliciously hard. She was unconscious. He grasped her hand and squeezed her fingers around his shaft, jerking off into her belly button. He longed for the day he could take her several times and spend an entire day doing it.

When he heard the boys' van drive up, he quickly clothed himself, gave her another dose of heroine, placed her still naked body under the fleece blanket he'd taken off his own bed, and left her alone in the dark.

"Have you found anything?" he asked his young apprentices.

"Nothing."

"Then have you developed our next target?"

They nodded. "She's under age, Moustafa. Does it still count?"

"It counts double."

His young students beamed with delight and anticipation, handing him all the money they'd raised.

"Tomorrow, then. We will continue our training with the infidel whore. Later in the week, you all will become men together. Then you will have the chance to choose your own vessel. After that, we will kill them all. Together."

God is indeed good.

CHAPTER 33

Reverend Travis Banks ministered to his flock at Riverbend Maximum Security Prison, ten miles away from their base camp. Banks had met T.J. Talbot at the request of T.J.'s dying father, who was an inmate at Riverbend before he passed.

Because the SEAL team was asked not to leave camp, T.J. asked for and was granted permission to have him come visit at the camp the next morning. A year ago, Banks had informed T.J. about some of the activity that had been going on in the greater Nashville area, and the trending toward radicalization in the local prison population. T.J. thought perhaps Banks could be of some use.

The giant of a man with the gold front tooth made even T.J. look small, something that never happened.

"You never did stop by and I been waitin', T.J. We gots some catching up to do," Banks said, showing off his tooth in the wide smile pasted to his face.

"No excuses. But with little Courtney, it's been tough. We're expecting again."

"Halleluiah. God blesses those who do the good work."

"If that was the case, you'd have a dozen kids."

Travis stopped a bit, tilted his head and dropped his smile, as if offended.

"Oh shit, Travis, I'm so sor—"

"Jes messin' with ya."

Lucas could see T.J. was relieved. "Honored to meet you, Reverend Banks. T.J. has talked about you non-stop since we found out you were coming out here," Lucas said as he shook the pastor's massive hand.

Forsythe was going over some photos and stopped to greet T.J.'s friend. "We're most grateful for any help you can give us."

"That's partly why I'm here."

Kyle showed Banks the photo of the Sheik. "This is the guy we're looking for, reverend."

Banks studied the photo. "Hmm. Reminds me of a real bad dude came through here last year, just before Christmas, but it wasn't this guy. Big, grown bad-ass men at the prison were bowing on their knees to him. He swept through here, had a couple huge services at the Mosque and there were crowds clear across the street, blocking traffic. Police had to shut down the whole area and it was on the news. I don't remember his name, but he was someone big, very big in their circle."

"Like an advanced guard," Forsythe commented.

"Kyle," Jackie slipped between them. "You guys find some news footage. Let me listen to what he's saying and I'll tell you exactly what he was all about. This guy I don't know, but he must be a powerful Imam from Iraq, maybe Syria," offered Jackie Daniels.

Forsythe indicated he'd get someone working on it.

"So you wanna catch us up as far as what's been happening in the community?" T.J. asked.

"Word has it there's going to be a coordinated effort at a strike, or something of that nature. But the thing that bothers me is that this prison isn't the only place. I got a friend out west works in the central valley of California, and he's run across the same thing. This Imam I was telling you about went to all those places, too." Banks looked around him at all the SEALs. "So what're you doing here in Tennessee? Not exactly a place I'd expect to see this kind of crowd."

"Training mission," Kyle said. His voice was flat, but Lucas knew it belied apprehension. Kyle wore the mantle of leadership well, but anyone who spent any time around him knew he carried more than they saw publically.

Reverend Banks was hesitant to offer more help but finally agreed to check the visitor logs, which was a violation of his volunteer agreement.

"Now can me and T.J. here just sit and shoot the bull a bit? Or is this all serious, being that it's a *training mission*." He winked at T.J.

After getting permission, the two men headed to the corner. "Your sister looks good, T.J." Lucas heard the pastor say as they left earshot.

"How did we not know this, Forsythe. You guys uncover this?"

"I'm sure the Bureau has knowledge of it. Politics, Kyle. Stay as far away as possible from politics. No winners there, except the most ambitious, the ones who will do anything."

"That kinda fits us. We'd do anything to save this country," said Coop.

"Ambitious here, to make sure everyone stays safe. A lot of our guys are dying out there and it's still coming this way," said Lucas.

"Well, that's geography catching up to us. We can be thankful for that big old Atlantic. Pacific too, for that matter," answered Forsythe. "With limited resources and the public retreating from their taste for war, as opposed to 9-11, we have to decide what to put to good use. Can't do it all. People need to understand that."

"Until something big hits us," whispered Kyle staring off into space.

"And maybe that's coming," said Forsythe. "Either that or we'll be ready. That's why you boys are here, mainly to watch and learn. We weren't putting you into the middle of a fight, but right next to the bad guys."

Lucas couldn't help but think about the timing of all this. Someone knew a confrontation was brewing. With over thirty camps in the U.S. it wasn't going to be possible to stop them all. Maybe, just maybe, they could stop one here in Tennessee.

He thought about Marcy and was glad she was some distance from harm's way, living in San Diego, where there were more military and retired military per square mile than just about anywhere. Even if he couldn't, some soldier down there would make sure she was safe. Of that he was sure.

CHAPTER 34

Donna Grant heard the voice of another woman, which was odd because she lived alone. But within mere seconds, she heard not one voice, but several. And they were all women's voices. One was sobbing uncontrollably.

She wondered if one of the soccer players had managed to call a meeting with several of the others while she was sleeping. It felt like she'd slept a whole week, and then remembered she'd been drugged. Then Donna recalled the strange truck, the rag across her mouth and nose, and the odd noises while she fell backward into someone's arms.

She'd been running. That was the part she was sure about. And they'd come up behind her and—and they'd kidnapped her! She remembered sending off the text SOS just before they came up behind her with the rag.

The sobbing continued. Several women's voices tried to soothe the pain, but if anything, the crying continued at an even higher decibel. Donna was now wrestling with two conflicting feelings. She felt perhaps they were all in danger, but before she could do anything, she needed to know whether or not she was intact or gravely injured. It was her training: to assess the damage to her own person first before attending to someone else's.

Her left shoulder was sore. Her head felt groggy, but other than that, she was good to go, provided they stopped giving her the heroine. She assumed that was what it was from her previous experience in Iran.

That had been nearly four years ago when their convoy had been picked off by a warlord and his small band of militia. While most of her unit was killed, they'd taken her captive. The days and nights blurred into one long nightmare that lasted nearly a whole month before she'd been rescued by SEAL Team 5.

But now it was happening all over again. She was a captive this time in the U.S., not some foreign hellhole. And there were other women here as well.

She arched her back and found she had no pain. She brushed the hair from her forehead, opened her eyes and began to feel her life had been spared so she could exact revenge. That required clear-headedness, planning. Taking in a deep breath, she pushed the screaming voices of insanity rattling around in her brain all the way to the back of her skull, where it could sit in a corner until she was ready to call it out. It was time to focus on what lay in front.

The zip ties they'd fastened to her wrists were easily removed by wiggling the ends back and forth until they crumbled in her fingers. She did the same with her ankle restraints.

"Who's here?" she called out.

The sobbing stopped immediately.

"I'm Jenna, and I'm here with Shelley. There's another young girl here, very young, but she doesn't speak English."

"Anyone know how long I've been here?" Donna asked.

"They brought you in this morning."

"Okay, I'm Donna. Coming over. Don't be afraid," she said.

She felt her way on the concrete floor stained with water and what smelled like blood, until her eyes adjusted and she could see the outline of three women in seated position.

"Anyone hurt?" she asked.

"She is," one of the girls said. We just got thrown in here. But from the feel of her face, she's been cut and beaten."

Donna reached out to the girl and immediately the poor thing jolted and pulled away, working against her restraints.

"They even have a collar around her neck," one of the girls said.

Donna used soothing words like she would do to a frightened young child, holding out her hand until she felt the familiar leather collar she knew all too well. The pictures of her abuse flooded her brain until she closed her eyes and willed them to be gone.

"There should be a buckle at the back, or perhaps a lace up device. Do you have use of your hands?" she asked them.

"Yes." She heard the clanging of metal as the collar was removed. The young woman spoke in a Pashtu dialect. Donna remembered the word *whore*, and *animal*, shouted to her multiple times, and she heard those words again uttered by a frail young girl.

She spoke a few words to the girl, and got some single word answers she could barely understand. Donna put her palm on the girl's shoulder and told her that there were people near who could help them all. It was the truth, however, getting word to those people, her SEAL friends, would be a whole other problem.

Her wrist hurt and that's when she discovered they'd not taken her watch, probably not realizing it had internet and wifi capacity. Donna pushed the light button on the right of the small screen and noted she had a decent signal. She tapped in an SOS to her procurement officer's cell phone in Norfolk. She didn't have time to look for a return signal, but started to focus on the other women.

Donna removed the zip ties from the others while one of the American girls held the light for her. Her fingers were stiff and swollen from the drugs, but eventually the plastic ties fell away.

The young girl looked to be no more than a preteen, which sickened her. Her clothes were in rags. Her pretty face was marred with large purple and blue bruises that had been dished out over multiple incidents. The girl's right wrist also appeared to be broken, the swelling forming a lopsided red lump that was hot to the touch. If she had time, Donna would make a sling to immobilize it, but for now she had to address the issue of where they were and what their options were.

"Why are you here?" she asked the American girls.

"Well, we know these guys. We've been coming here for weeks."

"Where is here?"

"Their retreat, you know, this is where they bring in the people from the cities and give them some country experience."

Donna couldn't believe what she was hearing.

"So this is the camp on Pine Flat Road?"

"Yes."

They heard voices outside the door. Donna scooted over to the other wall, lay on her side and pretended to be sleeping.

The door opened and a slice of yellow light fell on the room. Donna heard the young Middle Eastern girl whimpering as two men yelled at her and threatened to hit her about the face. Donna could tell they wanted to know how she'd managed to get out of her restraints. The girl didn't have to act to be scared, and didn't give them an answer. They grabbed her by the elbows, lifted her up, and despite her protests, carried her out of the room.

Donna heard the distinctive beep of her watch, thankfully just after the door was closed behind the enemy. She disabled the sound and then looked at the words on her tiny screen.

Message received. ST3 en route.

She doubted no text message would ever make her so happy again as those few little words.

"Okay, we got help coming I think."

"That the special forces guys?"

Donna's hackles stood up. "Who said anything about special forces guys?"

"My dad. He built this complex, well most of it."

"Okay. So he knows you've been coming over here?"

"No. He'd be pissed. We just like to hang out, you know. They have some awesome weed. They've been really nice to us."

"You call this *nice?*"

"Up until today," the other American girl said.

"Yeah," the other one whispered, her voice fading.

"So that should tell you, what?" Donna answered. "How long have you been here?"

"Since yesterday afternoon," one of the girls said.

They were silent. Finally one of the girls spoke up. "We came over to warn them. We thought they were friends."

"Friends?"

"People don't understand them. Once they get to know them—"

"No. I don't want to hear any more of this folly," said Donna. She looked for a window and found none. The only way out of the room was the door they'd come in through.

The air was punctuated by the sounds of their young co-captive screaming. "Still think they are friends?" Donna willed her nerves to calm, but terror was looming at the edges of her mind. She knew what a full on panic attack felt like, and she was close. She needed to be able to think.

The room was some sort of storage closet. With her wristband light, she was able to see cleaning supplies and an old mop, a broken wooden chair. All of a sudden she remembered what the girl had said. "Warn them about what?"

"We wanted them to know about the Special Forces guys who came in to town asking questions. I think they put us here just to ask us some questions. They're not going to harm us, you don't think?"

"They've been holding you against your will."

"Maybe they were provoked. They almost seemed happy about what we told them."

"I'll bet. Part of that devious plan they have. You've put yourself right in the middle of extreme danger. These are bad men. This is a terrorist training camp, not a Boy Scout camp for R&R. I can't believe how stupid you were." Donna took the broom, laying it against the wall on the floor. Her fingers squeezed the wooden handle, as if there was some support there. She sat back and tried to breathe. There wasn't anything in this closet she could defend herself with, except for this broom. After a few seconds she sent another text.

4 of us here. One young girl badly beaten.

Donna's eyes began to water. Her face began to flush, her fingers swollen and stiff. Her mouth was parched. Her heartbeat nearly threw her against the wall. She wondered how long before she'd completely lose it. She had to get out. Being confined for any length of time would kill her, not to mention what the group's intentions were, and she had a pretty good guess at those, too.

Memories began to sift into her head. Those long thirty days came flooding back again and she knew it was useless to try to push them aside now. Donna began to shake. She closed her eyes and banged her head against the concrete walls of their prison, like she had done before. After awhile, she knew it would no longer hurt. The back of her head would hurt later, if she survived.

But today she couldn't knock those visions out of her head. The trauma she'd suffered, the acts of debasement she'd had to undergo were so horrible, she'd become grateful for the heavy doses of heroine they'd given her that day and the days after.

Donna watched the outline of the two girls who had been unwilling accomplices. More memories poured in, her shakes became more pronounced. All of a sudden, she was transported back there as if it was happening all over again, right here, right now. She inhaled and braced herself for what she knew was going to happen next.

She remembered on that worst day, when she'd been forced to have sex with multiple men in an endless stream of hell, she wished they'd just given her an overdose. She'd tried to fight the effects of the drug, to make them give her more. She'd sought death with everything inside her. The more she fought, the more they beat her. She fought the cattle prods, the foreign objects forced into her mouth, her vagina and her ass, defying them, seeking to draw their anger to perhaps finish her off.

That day, she crossed the threshold between life and death. It wouldn't matter what they did to her. She felt like she was dead already. There wasn't anything further they could take. She was sure they'd already taken away her womb, cut and disfigured her such that her life as a normal woman would forever be lost to her. But while they'd altered her physical appearance and capabilities of her body, they didn't change the woman she was on the inside.

At the end of that day, she'd come up with a slogan that sustained her, "Dead people feel no pain."

She'd lived through that. She could wait the time it might take for the SEALs to stage a rescue. She hoped the tipoff didn't mean the SEALs would be running right into an ambush.

Donna left one more message for her boss.

They know you're coming.

CHAPTER 35

Jackie threw his headset down on the table. "This is definitely the Sheik."

Lucas ran to find Kyle, who was on the phone. He gave his LPO a thumb's up.

"Okay, Jackie says it's him," Kyle said into the phone.

Jackie came up behind speaking over Lucas' shoulder. "The girl they are holding is from Michigan," he said in his heavily accented dialect. "I cannot make out the name, but she's been given in exchange for favors. She herself was a ransom."

Kyle relayed the information into the phone.

Lucas couldn't believe what he was hearing.

"Chief Kyle, she's only thirteen years old," Jackie added.

"Fuck me," Lucas said. "Sorry."

"No I completely agree," said the terp.

Could this mean they were getting permission to actually perform a rescue mission in the states? As far as he understood, this was the first of its kind performed by a SEAL Team on U.S. soil.

"How's Donna holding up, do you know?" Kyle was looking right at him while talking on the phone with someone from SOC.

Lucas felt like the air had been knocked out of him. Could Donna be in danger?

He ran to the poker game. "Anyone seen Donna?"

"Last I saw, she was going for a run," said Rory. "But geez, that was hours ago."

"Kyle's talking to command, and asked how she was doing."

Cooper shot up to his feet and ran to where Kyle was just finishing his call. They shared a private conversation, then Cooper departed to his room. Lucas guessed it was to retrieve his medical kit. That meant something big was happening.

Lucas began letting the other members know something was up. The faces of their team went from relaxed to stoic attention. The games were left right where they'd been played. Cards left overturned at each man's seat. The activity level began to intensify.

"Jake, we're gonna go do something. Get your shit together," he said to his roommate who was outside reading a book.

"Gotcha."

Lucas changed his clothes and put on his full camo gear even though it would be hotter than hell. He heard Kyle shout orders and they all came running to the common area.

"Okay, I've just been given the go-ahead for a mission to rescue confirmed hostages, one of whom may need serious medical attention over at the training camp."

The audience of SEALs were silent, except for some muttered cursing.

Lucas interrupted Kyle. "Excuse me, sir, but is Donna among the hostages, or do we know?"

"That's a confirmed yes. And we don't believe she's injured at this point, but we really don't know. There appear to be four."

The room erupted in every man's personal choice of profanity, so Kyle had to draw them to order.

"Listen up! We have permission to engage only if fired upon first. This is a rescue, not a search and destroy mission, and I want every man to fully understand that." Then he added, "Get your shit together and let's be on the road in thirty."

"We're driving?"

"We're borrowing Donna's two vans. I'm hoping she won't be too pissed."

Everyone grinned.

As the orders sunk in, the group got vocal, as had been their routine on deployments. Conducting a mission was what Lucas lived for. All the cares and concerns for his personal life, including Marcy and his kids, were secondary to the mission. It pained him that there was no one to call, no one to leave a message for. Before he allowed it to rot a hole in his heart, he sucked it up, took on a deep breath and started packing gear.

Kyle pulled the barn builder's card out of his pocket. "Lucas, go call him and find out where his daughter is. See if she's missing, okay?"

"Roger that."

"Hold it there, son. Get your gear together first. Then you call him. We think we already have the answer."

"Got it. So the girls we saw yesterday are still there, then?"

"That's what I want you to find out. There are at least four hostages right now. We just don't know who anyone is, except Donna. You get on the horn when you're done getting you shit."

"I'm on it."

Lucas moved down the hall, walking just outside the barracks doors and dialed the number. He got a recording.

This is Hunter Boles. I'm not available to—the phone message was interrupted by Boles' gruff voice.

"Mr. Boles, this is Special Operator Lucas Shipley. We have a situation here and wondered if you could give us some information."

"I'll do what I can." Boles sounded pissed he'd been interrupted from something and was helping out begrudgingly. "I'm a little short staffed here today, so you'll have to forgive me. Let's keep this short."

Lucas could hear another phone ringing in the background.

"That's partly what I'm calling about, sir. Do you know the whereabouts of your daughter, sir?"

The silence on the other end of the line screamed volumes.

"I have no fuckin' idea where she is. She's not at work, that's for sure. You know anything I should know?"

"When was the last time you saw her?"

"Yesterday afternoon. Just after lunch. But she's not here today. She and her girlfriend took off to run some errands yesterday, and I just figured she stayed with her friend Jenna last night. She does that all the time."

"Have you tried to call her?"

"Well, of course I have. Her phone doesn't pick up. Is she in some kind of trouble, Lucas—was it Lucas?"

"Yes, sir. We think we may have located her."

"Where?"

"Not at liberty to tell yet, but as far as we know, she's not injured and she went of her own will."

"What the hell's that supposed to mean? You mean like she wasn't kidnapped or something? That what you're sayin'?"

"In essence, yes. We'll let you know as soon as we have anything further."

"So if I was going to go look for my daughter, give me a guess where I should start."

"Does she often stay out of communication this long, sir?"

"No."

Lucas knew he couldn't reveal anything to the girl's father. "Her phone's probably dead. When we can, we'll have her contact you. Keep the phone by your side, okay?"

"Will do."

Lucas was going to hang up when he heard Boles ask him another question he didn't want to answer.

"Should I be wearing a gun?"

Lucas decided to give the man something to do. "I'd say stay armed until we find her. Now, if you'll excuse me—"

"Wait, wait, where is my daughter? You gotta tell me!"

"I promise to let you know just as soon as we confirm a few things."

When Lucas returned to Kyle, he shook his head.

"She didn't come home. He hasn't seen her since yesterday after lunch."

"That's what I was afraid of. Hey, thanks, Lucas. You packed?"

"Yup."

"Okay, see you out front in a couple."

"Chief? Can I ask a question?"

"Shoot."

"So are other places, like San Diego—are they experiencing this type of behavior too? I mean, how safe is it near one of these camps?"

"Right now I think your girl, the girl you broke up with, is safe, Shipley. We don't have any intel this is going on in any coordinated effort. We just know they're up to something. But as far as I know, no one else has experienced a hostage situation."

"Except there is that girl Jackie says was from Michigan."

"And that's a different story. Unfortunately, that was cultural blackmail. Any way you slice it, we gotta rescue those ladies quickly. We can't wait for a terrorism task force to get assembled."

"Thanks."

But Lucas decided he would have to swallow his pride, and as soon as they were back from whatever mission this was, he was going to find Marcy, apologize for being a complete dickwad.

CHAPTER 36

It wasn't the nakedness that bothered Marcy, it was the fact that she'd been injected with so much heroine she could hardly think.

The "boys" in the compound were getting bolder, showing their disgust of her, which of course she did in return. She felt like a piece of meat in their eyes. She was a plaything for amusement, similar to what a person would do if they were going to torture an animal. But she knew the longer she held out, the better chance she had of survival. She had no illusions the wait would be in any way pleasant.

Thinking about these men, she understood a little more where Lucas went on deployments, mentally. There was evil in the world. She'd seen her share of wicked people, but pure evil—until now—she'd never been exposed to it. If the world knew what she knew, what Lucas and his brothers knew, they'd spend less time being politically correct trying to run a gentlemen's war and more time seeking results. She knew that she was the least of those being tortured, held captive just for believing what they believed, for being an American, for having a lifestyle worthy of the envy of the whole rest of the world.

Lucas was part of that line of defense of the Homeland. And he was paying the price for it. He did and always would come to the aid of his brothers in arms, even though it would look like he was abandoning his wife and children. He had to have that singleness of focus. She understood that now more than anything.

How ironic, she thought, that now, after they'd broken up at her call, not his, that she should figure that out. She was grateful for what he had to do. She understood now what he needed in life: a woman to help him heal, bring him back, not make him jump through a bunch of hoops of her own selfish choosing. She also understood how Connie felt, but she was sure the woman had her own set of issues that warped her worldview and made it impossible for her to be the support he needed. Being totally honest with herself, Marcy wasn't sure she had it in her either. But she knew she'd feel like a complete heel if she didn't at least try. She owed the man an apology.

She closed her eyes and pretended to be asleep when she heard footsteps at the door.

The familiar voice of her oldest captor spoke in broken English. "You are awake I think. Time to prepare you for your new life as the vessel of our pleasure."

"I'm not the vessel of your pleasure, or anyone's pleasure. I'm a woman whose freedom has been taken from her, but who still has her dignity left. Nothing will ever make me a vessel."

He smiled and patted her arm. "We'll see about that." He pulled back the blanket and peered down at her naked body. "I can help you with a shower, if you like. Would you prefer to wash up before we get started?"

Marcy calculated what she'd have to give up for the chance to have her wounds cleaned and decided the most important part of her current survival plan was her health. She attempted to sit up and found she had been bound about the waist, to the rolling hospital cart. Her arms felt heavy and though unrestrained, were useless to her. She suspected her legs would be the same as she couldn't feel her toes.

"Yes, the effects are wearing off, so I had to restrain you. That means I will have to help you to the shower."

She wished she had more choices, but needed to see what was outside the room, and she needed to get as clean as possible.

"Yes."

"Yes, what?" he asked.

"Yes, I'd like a shower."

"Very well. The boys will be pleased when they get back, that you have prepared yourself for them." He pulled back the brown blanket that stunk of him, unbuckled the large leather strap around her waist, and slipped an arm beneath her, lifting her to sitting position. She tried to lean away from him, but there was nothing to hold her up. He adjusted her balance so she didn't do a backward roll off the gurney, bringing her forward and against his chest and abdomen.

His hand softly thread through her hair while she drooled a bloody mixture down his shirt, unable to stop him. His wild scent as pungent, without cologne, smelling more of rancid oils mixed with days of sweat. Her stomach churned and she heaved, but without anything in her aching stomach, she produced nothing.

"Yes, a little nourishment, too. Would you like that?"

She didn't trust his feigned sweetness. She tried to imagine what he'd look like eviscerated, or hanging from a tree, or torn limb from limb. The violent thoughts came easily, her fear fueling her imagination. Or perhaps it was the effects of the drug he'd given her.

"Water. I need some water," she managed to mumble.

"You can drink in the shower."

He was a small man, and had difficulty getting her out to the living quarters off the storeroom, down the hallway to the bathroom. Her toes dragged on the concrete surface and she knew they were bloody with patches of skin scraped off. Again she tried to raise her elbows, and was more successful than before, but at last her strength gave way and she allowed them to flop down over his arms wrapped around her waist. As he moved her into the shower, her head bobbed back, and although she tried, she was unable to hold it upright.

He sat her on the tiled handicap bench seat, leaning her back against the cool tile wall of the shower. She looked at her bloody feet as he disrobed, slipped off his sandals and then stepped close to her.

"I have watched you shave yourself."

She tried not to react. The water began to flow ice cold, and she shuddered. "Sorry we have no hot water here, but I think you'll enjoy this anyway."

He hoisted her up, into the spray and she stiffened, found the cold sent blood pumping to her legs and for a minute, she had enough traction to fight him off. But it was short-lived. Her knees collapsed and he was once again propping her up, facing into the spray. She opened her mouth and drank the cool water. It smelled of sulfur and rust. The drain and shower floor was light orange.

Marcy felt tingling in her extremities and allowed her heart a moment's triumph. It did feel good to get the sweat and remaining vomit from last night off her. It felt invigorating to have a drink of water. When he positioned her back onto the wooden bench seat in the corner she looked at his face for the first time that morning.

Though the young man smiled, his eyes were hard and did not smile. The covetous stares seemed to inflame something inside him that did not appear human. She could see how mad he truly was. He was living in a bonfire of hell, and it was of his own choosing.

She slumped forward involuntarily, and he pushed her back again as her head lolled forward.

Her eyes were focused on the tiled floor, fixated on something that was blurry at first. As her eyes came into focus, she saw a bottle with a large plastic pump spout in the corner. He bent and squeezed some of the clear gel into his palm, rubbed his hands together making a lather and began to rub his palms over her now-slippery flesh at the shoulders and then on to her breasts. She couldn't react as he squeezed her flesh, as he pinched her nipples. Her eyes continued to focus on the shower gel in the corner.

Slowly he lathered her arms, her belly, her thighs and legs, kneeling like a servant in front of her. Though she didn't show it, her spine became rigid. She could push her feet against the floor of the shower, felt the cool water and for the first time, she was able to squeeze her fingers into a fist.

Staring at the bottle still, she pushed herself forward over his shoulder, draping her body over him, and then allowed herself to topple, sliding down to the floor. He was frantically trying to right her, but with her slippery skin not giving traction, was unable to lift her up to set her back down on the bench. Her right hand reached for the shower gel and she watched as she tried to hold it one-handed, which would have been impossible even without the drugs, and the bottle tipped, scooting out of reach. She released the support from her legs and she collapsed to the floor under the stream, her back curved against the wall, her feet pushing against the wall perpendicular to it.

Her captor began to say things she didn't understand. But he was unhappy and getting more agitated by the minute.

Bending over her, he managed to get his arms around her lower back and tried to pull her up, but Marcy resisted, feigning lack of control. She rotated to her upper torso, to her back, looking up to him. His feet were slipping on the slick shower surface. He was focused on his arms, and when he squeezed his eyes shut to pull her limp body up, Marcy put both palms around the shower gel bottle and with all her might, forced the spout into his neck just below his chin. Even after the spout entered his skin, she pushed, feeling the delicious crunch of cartilage that was his windpipe.

Her captor screamed. The spray from his blood covered the walls and poured over her, coating her with the deep red of his precious fluids, momentarily blinding her. She pushed with her legs and managed to head butt the man out of the shower, where he fell onto the bathroom floor, still struggling to get the spout from his neck. His legs frantically bicycle-kicked as he tried to find something else to push against. He was trying to get air. His gurgling screams got less intense. His almond-shaped eyes stared back at her in panic, and she realized the same time he did that she had just successfully inflicted a mortal wound.

His struggle was over. A light bloody spittle leaked from the right side of his mouth. With brown eyes fixated on her, she saw the moment when life left his body. She continued to lay on her belly, gasping for air, the water sluicing over her backside and upper thighs, sending her ribbons of calm and bursts of hope. She didn't know how she was going to function against the men who would be coming back, but she knew she couldn't wait around to find out. Somehow, she had to get out of the cabin and to some place safe. Some place that had tools and sharp objects she could use to defend herself.

Carefully she sat up. Her legs were coming back to near full strength, the activity in the shower and adrenalin pumping through her veins apparently aiding this process. Marcy grasped the wooden slats on the bench and because it was bolted to the side, supported herself as she stood for the first time. She placed her palms on the tile, pushing until she was balanced and was standing on her own without aid.

Each movement was slow motion for her. She allowed the water to wash off all the blood, rinsed her mouth, taking more drinks of the precious liquid, and emerged, trying to avoid the growing pool of blood forming from the gash in her captor's neck.

Using the doorway as a brace, she stepped out and into the hallway she new led to the living quarters.

Her own clothes were left on the floor in the storage closet where they'd been discarded next to her purse. Though they were dirty, she welcomed something familiar, something that smelled like freedom, grateful for shoes she would need to run through the forest to find help. Pawing through her purse, she found her cell phone and anxiously checked for service.

Her stomach leapt as she realized the battery was dead. She placed the phone back in her purse, slung it over her shoulder, picking up a couple of bananas and a half-full bottle of water and exited the dwelling.

Outside, she heard Middle Eastern music pumped loud, echoing throughout the long building on her right. She was grateful for this. Whomever was inside, then, could not have heard the screams of her captor. She bent her knees, crouching, and slipped into the edge of the forest. Once protected by the cover of greenery, she began to run. She knew right where she was going to go.

CHAPTER 37

Lucas helped Coop bring the drone cases. Kyle had Fredo continue to monitor with SOC, so he could lead the team. They all had their specialties. Armando was their best shooter. Coop was their medic with the most deployments with SEAL Team 3, but if he was working the drone, T.J. would take over in that department, with nearly the same experience.

Lucas was also trained at the Army course at Ft. Bragg, certified by the SEAL instructors there. He was also their second sniper. Fredo was their communications and explosives expert and had lovingly said to Lucas one time when they were relaxing, "If they don't want to talk, I send a little fire their way. And guest what? They talk!"

As a unit, everyone was trained for one specialty, but cross trained to be able to work in more than three others, if need be. Lucas breathed slowly and deep to calm his nerves. He was put up on the ridge out of sight, but nearly fifty yards from Armando.

Fredo was next to Armando working the comm. Coop was over on Lucas' side, getting his drone out, clicking the wings into place. With a flick of the switch they heard the soft whir of the drone's belly. The small tablet screen lit up as the drone was readied for it's mission.

Coop searched his spot, searched the sky and then leaned over to Lucas. "Eyes for their birds, Lucas. I got interference, I need to know."

"Roger that, Coop," said Lucas.

Cooper stood, leaned back, clutching the drone in his right hand, then propelled it forward and let it go. At first the white bird swooped down, then was corrected to stay high until Coop got her tracked. With a thumbs up to Fredo, Kyle was told, "Eyes in the air, Kyle. Good to go."

Jake and Tyler had disabled the sentries when they first took up their positions. The sentries were bound, gagged and tied and wouldn't wake up for several hours. They now joined the plateau where Lucas and Coop were perched.

With his high-powered scope, Lucas followed the two teams below, who separated, coming from different directions. Two SEALs were left near the entrance to disable the guard shack after their breech was discovered. Everyone else was going to go through the holes they were cutting in the fencing material. One breech was behind the long warehouse, the other was in the area of the camp's vehicle storage, well masked behind a fleet of white vans.

Their Invisios clicked to life. "On three, two, one, go!" Kyle's voice commanded.

The front gate exploded, the doors bursting wide open. Small explosive devices and smoke bombs were tossed into the long warehouse, starting a fire as chemicals began igniting, ending plumes of flame nearly fifty feet high. Several earth-shaking explosions took out the side of the metal building, sending burning debris and pieces of twisted metal all over the area. The thick black smoke nearly made it impossible to see.

The team near where the hostages were was taking on fire. Armando picked off three combatants within seconds, sending others, who had ventured out into retreat. Lucas followed as several of them hid behind a storage tank of some kind. Lucas' one well-placed round caused the tank to explode in a hail of fire. Tires on several of the vehicles began to burn.

He studied the area where they knew the girls had gone yesterday and saw the front door to the structure open slowly. One gunman had the girl with a forearm across her throat, a pistol aimed at her temple. The sheik, whose robes were bloodied, walked behind one of the local girls. Lucas recognized her as the daughter of the contractor.

Armando was shifting position, adjusting his range, checking the wind and then, as the young girl stumbled in front of the gunman, took his shot. The blonde girl and the Sheik behind her were covered in the spray from the man's exploded head. The Sheik was armed with a small automatic and as he pointed it in the direction of the screaming young girl, Lucas took the shot Armando wouldn't be able to make and the tall man dropped to his knees first before one of the SEALs did the double tap to his head.

Having lost the two leaders, the rest of the group dropped their weapons.

Fredo was giving out information. The SEALs pushed the captives to the ground on their faces.

Lucas had only seen two hostages, but both appeared to be out of danger, for now. He spoke to Kyle in his headset. "Where are the other two?"

"We got 'em. Donna's okay."

Lucas breathed a sigh of relief. Something about Donna told him it was important she didn't have to stay overnight in the camp.

They unloaded the girls over at the dorms where the soccer team was staying. Coop worked on the girl from Michigan while Donna sat by her side, holding her hand, speaking to her in broken Pashtu. Donna herself had a pretty good-sized bump on her forehead, but was completely focused on the girl.

She nodded up to Lucas and smiled her thanks.

The blonde girls were brought food and drinks by the soccer girls, allowed to shower and were given changes of clean clothes. Jenna called her dad, who was on his way over. Sheriff and fire crews were on their way to relieve the SEALs who had stayed behind with the prisoners.

"I think she's gonna be good to go here," Coop said. "See if you can get me an ambulance, Lucas."

"Sure thing. What about Donna?"

"I'm staying with her. I'm fine. But let's get her to the hospital," Donna answered.

Lucas ran the hundred yards to their buildings and sent an EMT crew over to the ladies dorm.

Decompression was a bitch, Lucas thought. Easier to stay pumped up, but when you went through a firefight, and usually they were short and sweet, like this one, it took awhile for the adrenalin to subside. Everyone retreated to their own brand of recovery while their bodies adjusted. The mission was a success, but wasn't really cause to celebrate. This was, after all, an operation on U.S. soil. They had gotten all the way over here, had set up a camp—hell, had set up multiple camps—and nearly pulled off a tragic loss of American life. It was all handled small, which was their way of saying it caused as little disruption as possible.

When his cell chirped, Lucas jumped, having forgotten he even owned one. It was Nick. That's when he realized there were two other calls from Nick as well.

"Hey, what's up, Nick?"

"Man, you're not going to want to hear this, but we just got a call from Marcy. Devon and I were sick with worry when she didn't come home last night."

"What do you mean? Marcy's in San Diego."

"No, she's not. She's up in Sonoma County. She left yesterday to go look for a place to stay—"

Fuck me. I've messed up again.

"—escaped, she thinks she killed one of them. We've called the cops."

"Where, Nick?"

"Cloverdale, man. She's at your cabin."

"What the fuck?"

"There's one of those groups up there. She escaped, but she's all alone in the cabin waiting for the cops. Just wanted you to know."

Lucas searched his memory

Immediately Lucas' heart began to race. He had to find Kyle. Somehow he was going to have to get to her, even though he was clear across the country. He knew he was probably too late, but nothing in the world would be able to keep him away. He just hoped the Navy would understand.

CHAPTER 38

Marcy watched as the bars went back down to zero on her phone. She knew Nick would send the police. She knew she'd feel more relaxed when her cell had enough power to be in permanent communication.

She looked through the windows, searching for evidence the camp members were coming after her, and wondered if they even knew about this place. She'd broken the bedroom window, the same one that had been used for the thieves—and then it hit her. They *did* know about the house, because they were here!

The remaining captors were all young, and she doubted they would have done the damage to the place without their leader, so perhaps she was safe. Maybe they had outside help. Maybe they'd be blinded by revenge. Every bird, every sound coming from the forest put her at edge.

Lucas told her earlier that there were no guns stored in the cabin. So that meant she was going to have to improvise. Other than knives in the kitchen, she couldn't find anything else that would work as a weapon. She did have a broom handle that looked solid. She picked up pieces of glass stuffing two of them into her pockets where she could safely hide them until needed.

Nick told her he'd be right there, but Cloverdale was nearly an hour from their home in Bennett Valley. She just had to get through the next hour, or however long it took for the police to arrive. She hoped they'd not get lost.

Her eyes wandered over the cabin where she'd spent a beautiful two days. She could smell him. When she closed her eyes, she saw what he looked like when he talked to her, the angle of his head, the way he smiled, what the touch of his kiss on her lips felt like. So many little things came racing through the fog of fear.

She prayed she'd have the chance to tell him all this.

It startled her when her cell phone rang.

Lucas!

"Is that really you?" Her heart was pounding, and surely he would be able to hear her ragged breathing.

"Absolutely, baby. Are you hurt?"

"I'm okay."

"But did they hurt you?"

"No. Big goose egg on my forehead."

"God, Marcy, I've been a total and complete fool."

"Where are you, Lucas? I'm all alone here and—"

"Nick called me. We just finished up an operation and I'm coming to California right now as we speak. Waiting for the transport. Won't get there for a few hours. Nick says the police are on their way."

"Good."

"You have battery on the cell phone?"

"It was dead, charging it now."

"Okay, nothing to do but hang tight. Let's hope they decide to bale instead of coming to the house."

"What do I do if—" Marcy saw three of the young boys come out into the clearing at the kitchen side of the house. "They're here!"

She heard Lucas swear on the other end. "Get a knife. Hide in the bedroom closet. There's a hatch there in the floor of the closet. See if you can get yourself in there before they come. Leave the phone on, but try to hide it."

"Right. Bye." She placed the device on top of the refrigerator where only part of the cord showed at the attachment to the plug in the splashboard.

Marcy wanted to say more, much more, but she knew they'd find the broken window and she didn't have much time to get herself hidden.

The closet floor was covered with empty bags and a suitcase. She brushed them aside and found the ring of the hatch, pulled it toward her and saw the dirt beneath the cabin floorboards. Carefully, she pulled the closet door closed, and tried to distribute the bags so they would fall over the hatch opening, perhaps giving her more time. She was small enough to slip down through the square hole and then touched the ground, stopping to listen.

Chatter from the young men trickled down to her from on top as she heard them climb through the window and begin searching the house.

She wondered why Lucas had asked her to leave her phone on, but she guessed he wanted to listen to whatever was going on, since he couldn't be there.

Fingering the glass chard in her left hand and the serrated knife in her right, she sat on the cool dirt and waited without making a sound. Her stomach growled so much for a second she wondered if they'd be able to hear it. She wished she had the water she'd left on the counter, or the bananas she'd brought from her escape. No doubt the boys would find them and realize she was near.

Orders were being given between the men. They removed themselves from the place the way they'd entered, and soon all was quiet.

Except for the crackling she could hear. Then she could smell it.

They'd set fire to the house.

CHAPTER 39

Lucas heard the unmistakable sounds of fire raging through the cabin. Already at thirty thousand feet, there wasn't a thing he could do, except text to Nick and Devon and let them know. He'd lost connection to Marcy' cell. He hoped she'd be able to get out before the smoke got to her, as this was more of a threat than the fire itself.

> *Lost contact with Marcy. House on fire.*
> *Holy shit. I'll call the PD. They should be there by now. You in the air?*
> *Yes. Taking direct to SF. Renting a car.*
> *Hold it, let us pick you up.*
> *If you can, sure would appreciate it.*
> *Okay BRB.*

Lucas was crammed into the oversold airplane, but because he was active military went to the head of the standby list. He texted

Kyle to let him know he was on board. Kyle let him know the soccer team was leaving and Donna still wouldn't leave Alfari's side.

Good. I think she needs it, Lucas texted him back.

Thinking the same.

He decided not to add any further worry onto his LPO's shoulders, so didn't tell him about the fire.

He relaxed the seat back and pulled his baseball cap down over his eyes, and attempted some sleep. No telling what he would be doing later. He'd be no good to anyone if he was exhausted.

An hour into his rest the phone pinged with a message from Nick.

Fire out. No sign of Marcy or the others. Will update if any news.

Lucas managed to sleep the whole rest of the flight. The stewardess tapped him on the shoulder and asked him to reset the seat to its upright position. He barely had enough time before the wheels hit the pavement, in a landing far from smooth, the big plane swerving and rocking as if driven by a fighter pilot landing on a carrier. He checked his phone as they taxied to the gate and there were no further texts. His stomach turned over. When he mentally counted the hours since he'd last eaten, he discovered it had been nearly twelve.

He followed the line off the plane, his legs and neck stiff from sitting in one position for so long, but all the same, he was grateful for the shut-eye. Now he needed to find Marcy. He was hoping Nick had something he could go on.

Nick was waiting by baggage claim, but since all Lucas had was his carry-on, they made it out to the curb just in time for Devon to slip by and pick them up. The two men sat in the back seat of Nick and Devon's Land Cruiser.

"Not going to lie to you, Lucas. The cops in Cloverdale and the Sheriff's Department have an ongoing battle over the hearts and minds of the town, with the public pretty much split. So anything that is slightly controversial, you can bet there's a fair amount of finger pointing."

"Okay. I'm sort of used to that, on a much grander scale," Lucas answered back. "Shit, we never know who to trust, so we don't trust anyone."

"That would probably work well in this case, too."

Devon made a quick swerve to avoid a small car with blackened windows from hitting them. They had merged onto the freeway and took the overpass headed to 280 North.

"You okay, honey?" Nick asked as he leaned forward and put his hand on her shoulder.

"I'm fine. That asshole just doesn't know how to drive is all."

Lucas knew she was hauling ass to get them up to Sonoma County as soon as possible, while they had some chance to do some searching in the woods. But he wanted to get there without an incident, and he could tell Devon wasn't used to driving fast.

"So you were saying there's a pissing match going on. Is anybody focused on finding Marcy?"

"Oh yes, nothing like a murder to get the community all worked up. You know Cloverdale is a small town. That's part of the problem. Everyone knows everyone else's business."

"Right now, I'm thinking that's a good thing," said Lucas.

"See, I made the mistake of calling the Cloverdale P.D. But your cabin is in the County, Sheriff's jurisdiction."

"So who did you tell about the trap door?"

"I told the Cloverdale P.D."

"Okay. So who's taking lead here on the search?"

"That's what gets kind of interesting. We got some worried about stumbling onto a pot farm and getting shot."

"Shit. We got terrorists with a training camp and they're worried about pot?"

"Nope. They're not worried about the pot. They're worried about the gangs who guard the pot."

Lucas checked the passing lights as they swung their way onto the five-lane 280 Freeway. There was practically no traffic. He tried to think about where she would go. Could she have gotten herself safely out of the house and was hiding in the forest? Or, did they capture her as she was forced out, take her some place else? Marcy had told him about the neighbor and the young boys. Lucas didn't think they even knew how to drive.

"Someone's helping them. We just have to find out who that is," said Lucas. "The one in Tennessee? They had a whole house filled with paper money. Floor to ceiling. They've been making so much money selling drugs, they have plenty to buy political favors. They did it in Nashville. Those guys run the prison there. They could do far worse in a little town of less than ten thousand people, no problem."

During the two-hour drive, Lucas and Nick discussed all the scenarios they could think of. If Marcy was on her own, it would only be a matter of time before she'd find a way to contact one of them. Eventually, she would. If she could stay hidden.

But if she was being held by yet another group, or worse, being transported to one of the larger training camps up in Oregon, they were screwed. That would involve a plan taking up hundreds of man hours and probably the FBI, just like when they had a large scale drug bust. The jurisdictions fell all over themselves for the percentage rights to the drug spoilage, but they had to play nice with the Bureau.

Lucas wasn't prepared for the site of his little piece of Heaven, looking more like a burned out building in Bagdad or Mosul. Smoke still filtered up to the darkening sky. Perimeter lights had been set up, juiced to one large engine unit from downtown Cloverdale. Blue and red lights flashed, the vehicles fanning out like at a drive-in movie. Lucas walked like a zombie through all the noise of the radios, the generator and sound of the water pumps occasionally kicking in as a four man crew continued looking for hot spots.

The fire investigator introduced himself. He was one of the only men who wore a yellow jacket, but did not wear a hat.

"How did it start?" Lucas asked.

"They found something as an accelerant. I think you had lighter fluid or cleaning supplies under the sink, like most people? We think they poured it, ignited it and left."

"Can I?" Lucas asked, pointing the charred spines of the once-beautiful cabin.

"Sure, just walk the perimeter. There are still hot spots inside, so don't step there."

"No problem." Lucas and Nick began waling around the edge of the debris field.

"We cut the power of course. Your propane tank exploded," the inspector said as he followed behind them pointing out the high-lights of the destruction, like he was giving them a tour of an art gallery. "Any idea why someone would want to torch this place?"

"No clue," Lucas answered him. "But it was broken into and vandalized not more than a week ago. Kind of a teenage thrill thing, we thought at the time. This goes along those same lines."

"What did they take?"

"As far as we can tell, nothing."

"I'm told you never met these people?" the inspector asked Lucas.

"That's right."

"The woman who is missing, Marcy Gelland, saw them," offered Nick. I did see the break in, helped with the cleanup, and Lucas is right, it did look more like some kids having fun at his family's expense."

"And what makes you think it was kids, like the kids from next door?"

"Because they shredded some girlie magazines, right, Nick?" Lucas turned to Nick, who confirmed it.

"They peed on them, too."

"So all they did was destroy? They didn't take anything?"

"Not a damned thing." Lucas made his way over to here the bedroom closet would have been, swiped the charred detritus to the side with his shoe. The hatch cover was burned all the way through. Partially burned pieces of furniture and flooring had dropped down into the five foot space. Lucas remembered his grandfather telling him it was the safest place to hide if anything dangerous happened to them. He remembered playing in it when he was a child. It earned him a fair share of scoldings.

Lucas jumped into the space and searched the walls with his penlight flashlight. Someone had written "Boathouse." He looked up to the inspector. "There a lake with a boathouse around here?"

"Over toward the camp there's a man-made lake and I think a small shed protecting a pile of stacked canoes," answered the inspector.

"Wonder how the hell she knew about that," said Lucas. "Where is this lake?"

The inspector gave him a hand up. "If she came over from the compound next door, she would have run right past it."

"Wonder how the hell she got out while the house was burning," muttered Nick.

"I have no idea. But I hope to God she did. Let's go."

At the fire scene, Marcy had managed to scramble out through the flames, the smoke giving her cover. She hid in the scrub behind the cabin, undetected. A green van picked up the boys, who had obviously been waiting for it. The van barreled off down the road before any of the emergency vehicles arrived. The driver's door was marked with some sort of official insignia she couldn't read.

She wondered if other men were still at the complex and would soon be looking for her. She needed to make it to the boathouse so, if need be, she could wait it out until she was safe. Until someone she trusted showed up.

Seeing the coast clear, she ran as fast as she could until she got to the old red structure, pried open the locked wooden door and let herself in. She stayed in there while emergency crews were working in the distance. She wasn't going to go out there in her sooty clothes and be arrested for being an arsonist. The only people she would reveal herself to were Lucas, Nick or Devon.

None of the fire crew or investigators even came close to looking at the boathouse, so she began to feel safe. She worked to stop from falling asleep in the warm space but was having difficulty.

She was tired, dirty, and her lungs were filled with soot. She desperately needed a drink of water.

Marcy scrambled out the back of the structure, stooped down, lay against the dock landing on her belly, and splashed water on her face, taking long sips of water to quench her thirst. She quietly returned to the relative safety of the wooden structure.

Finally, the number of flashing lights diminished, and several vehicles left the scene. In spite of her efforts not to, she leaned against the doors of the little structure, and fell into a deep sleep.

Hours later, she was jarred awake when she heard a noise. Through the slim crack between the doors, she saw four figures jogging straight toward her. She braced herself, waiting until they stepped into the moonlight and out of the shadow of the forest, her hand firmly gripping the knife handle. If it came to it, she'd go out fighting. She was ready for the final showdown.

CHAPTER 40

Lucas considered the message might be a trap, but his heart couldn't afford to wait any longer. If something had happened to Marcy, if she was injured or being held, or worse, the sooner he could find her the better. Devon held back to the shadows, just in case, while the three men approached the door.

As he got to within twenty feet of the outside of the building the red doors burst open and Marcy came running out, jumping into his arms.

"God, you're safe, Marcy. Thank God," he whispered as he held her shaking body. He felt her break down, as sobbing overtook her.

"Shhhh, shh. You're safe. We got you. Nothing's going to happen to you anymore." He was rocking her from side to side. Nick put his arms around both of them. Within seconds Devon was there as well.

"Are you okay? Are you hurt in any way?" Lucas asked as he set her down. He brushed the hair from her face, blackened from the fire. He noticed a patch of her hair had been singed, but other than that, she looked pretty damned good.

"I'm fine," she beamed back up to him, tears making white lines down her cheeks. "I was hoping you'd see my message." She glanced over at the inspector.

"This is—"Lucas turned to the investigator with an apology.

"Russ Butler, ma'am. I work for the Cloverdale fire district."

Marcy nodded and allowed Devon to grab her, but her eyes came back to Lucas.

"So glad you're okay. What an ordeal. You held up like a champ, Marcy," said Devon.

The long looks Marcy was giving him as she spoke with Devon and Nick speared his heart.

"Come here," he finally said as he opened his arms. She nearly collapsed into him. She was mumbling words he couldn't make out. "It's all over, Marcy. Nothing is going to happen to you. I'm here now."

It took nearly an hour to finish with the Sheriff's Department. Lucas was still combing through the rubble for anything left untouched by the fire and was coming up completely empty. The house was gone, completely gone, but it had done its job and protected her from harm, just like his grandfather had instructed those many years ago. Little did he know that some day those safety instructions would save the life of the woman he loved.

He had a new appreciation for how fragile life was. He also knew that he wouldn't be able to put anything in front of his feelings for Marcy, and for her safety again. They needed to have a talk. He hoped she felt the same.

On the trip back to Bennett Valley, she leaned into him as they sat in the darkness behind Devon and Nick up front. His arm was draped around her shoulder as she snuggled into him. It had never felt so good to have someone need his protection.

His fingers traced up and down her upper arm. Marcy brought her right palm to his face as she lifted herself to look him in the eyes. "Thank you, Lucas. Thank you for everything."

"No, sweetheart. You are the hero of the day." He bent down to brush his lips against hers. "Not sure what I would have done if anything had happened to you, baby."

"You were there. You told me what to do. You gave me the courage I needed, Lucas. I would not have been able to survive without your help. I—"

He covered her mouth with his and allowed her wild scent to completely overtake him. Her lips needed him. He was trying to be gentle at first, but her need slammed up against his chest and he was soon consumed in the flames of her desire again. Her breathing became deep, their tongues mingling. He heard her faint moan which caused him to hitch his own breath.

"Sweetheart, love you, sweetheart," he whispered between kisses.

She grabbed his hand and kissed the center of his palm, then looked up at him with her twinkling brown eyes and placed his hand against her breast, and squeezed.

He chuckled. "Honey, if you don't think I'm getting the message, you're not as smart as I thought."

He knew Nick and Devon were aware of their fooling around in the back seat when he saw Devon take Nick's hand and they shared a smile.

Marcy slipped his hand under her bra and he felt the pillows of her flesh, warm and fragrant, waiting for him to enjoy. His pants were getting tight. He squirmed in the seat as she ran her fingers over the bulge in his jeans and she squeezed his package.

"We need that shower in a hurry, sweetheart," he whispered.

"I need you, Lucas. Your ass is mine until I tell you it's okay to go back to work."

"Yes, ma'am. The Navy doesn't own my body. You do."

"Glad to hear it, sailor. I have plans for you."

"I can't wait."

They arrived at the winery. Nick handed Lucas his backpack and winked. "Guest house is all ready for you guys. I think Devon and I are going to sleep in tomorrow," he said as Devon wrapped her arms around her husband. "Depending on when we all surface, we'll have food should you be in need of some nourishment."

"Thanks, man," Lucas said. "Thanks for everything." He gave Nick a quick hug, hugged Devon, giving her a peck on the cheek, and took Marcy's hand, squeezed it, and led her around the back to the guest house.

He could see shadows inside the main house as lights were turned off, including the bright patio light that threatened their privacy. With the crickets chirping in the background, a light cool breeze running off the rustling grapevines all around them, he placed his hand to Marcy's neck, letting his fingers lace through her hair, tilted her head back and looked down on her glowing face. Her eyes smiled back at him. "Seeing your dirty face is one of the most beautiful things I've ever seen, Marcy."

She drew her arms up around his neck. "Lucas, I need you to undress me."

"Of course," he said, thrilled. "Wouldn't want to—whoa," he said as she quickly unbuckled his belt and shoved her hands into his pants.

"I bet I get you naked before you even get started," she whispered through half-lidded eyes.

"Not a chance." But he got snagged getting her pants off. The feel of the lace of her panties against her smooth rear end put him in a trance he wanted to savor.

He kicked off his shoes and his pants fell to his ankles. He stepped out of them, kneeling in front of her as she pulled his shirt off his back from his waist up over his head.

"See, you're slow," she teased, removing her own shirt and bra, her breasts in full view.

He reached up and squeezed, watching her arch her back with the pleasure of his touch. He dropped his hands to his thighs, his erection pointing to the stars above.

"I'm going to go real slow Marcy. I'm taking my time. I'm gonna make you beg me to stop."

"Another promise you won't be able to keep. There's no way I'll ever stop. You'll have to peel me off your body a week from now."

He stood, taking her hand and leading her into the little cottage.

The room was lightly scented with a fresh vanilla aroma. She followed him to the tiled shower. After turning on the warm water, he soaped her arms and neck as she pressed her backside against the wall, watching his face as he smoothed gel all over her body. His fingers kneaded down her spine, starting just under her hairline, and one by one, working his way down to the crack in her butt. With both hands, he pressed her forward against his groin, squeezing her cheeks, lifting her as she pushed against his hardness. She raised one thigh over his hip and rubbed the lips of her sex over his cock.

She gave him a long lingering smile. "My turn."

She placed her palms on his shoulders, moving him to sit on the tiled bench seat. His fingers found her opening, but he massaged all around it as she arched back, took some gel and rubbed her palms over his chest, his neck, his shoulders, and then lower stroking his cock and squeezing his balls. She stepped aside and let the water sluice off him, and then she placed her knees on each side of the bench and lifted her lithe body up over him. In one long fluid movement, her breasts leaving a hot trail down his chest, she angled her pelvis and came down on his shaft.

She began a slow rhythm up and down, raising and lowering her body on him, writhing like his private dancer. He buried his head in her chest, bit her nipples, helped her move up and down on him by palming her butt cheeks, and supporting her body's weight. She ground down against him, kissed his temple, hugged his face to her chest, massaging his temples with her probing fingers. Into his ear she whispered, "I want you to come in my mouth."

"Yes, baby," was all he could say.

She began to lift off him, and he grabbed her hips and ground her down on him again. "Please, Lucas. I want you in my mouth," she whispered again.

This time he allowed her to slide off him as she kneeled before him on the slower floor. The water was starting to get cold, so she arched her upper torso and turned the valve off. As the steamy water dripped around them, the drain gurgling, she placed her lips at the tip of his head, running her tongue over him, sucking him gently.

He moved his pelvis forward as she fully took him in her mouth. One hand found his balls and squeezed as she swallowed all of him deep. Back and forth, her movements were long, careful, and needy. He never wanted it to end. He felt himself get harder the more she worked on him. She registered her pleasure with little whimpers, coaxing him up and down. Several strokes later, he was bursting inside her mouth as she sucked against his pulsations.

He was near completion. Her fingers formed a ring at the base of his cock and one last time she squeezed the full length of him, then sucked his tip. Rolling back on her haunches her sultry smile teased him further.

"Let's rinse off and try something else," he said to her. His fingers had already found her opening before she could stand.

He turned her around and pressed himself, still hard, into the soft valley between her butt cheeks. She turned on the water as he continued to rub against her soft flesh, stimulating him further.

He pulled her to him, spreading her cheeks, finding her opening and helping himself inside her. Marcy moaned, pressing the wall with her palms as he entered her, thrusting up deep. His thumb pressed against her clit from the front, and she jumped, spreading her knees and pushing him deeper still. He stroked in and out of her tight opening, making her little organ stiff, feeling her give way, start to let herself go.

The cold water was delicious. He bit her shoulder, the side of her neck as she melted into him, giving him full access to all of her. He felt her juices begin to flow as he pressed her clit again, holding firm while he impaled her deeper still. She stopped breathing, held her breath and then exhaled as her body began the rolling orgasm he knew had been waiting for him right at the edge.

She covered his hands with one of her own, the other against the wall, giving her traction as she helped his fingers press against her while she came.

The fluffy white bath sheet wrapped around both of them, hot and sticking to her thighs as they lay together in bed. Marcy was going to try to keep her promise, but more importantly, she wanted to keep up with this brave warrior. She needed to show him she had all the stamina he had, and perhaps a little more, if possible.

When she found his cock, he angled his pelvis, pressing against her, a smile affixed to his lips. The morning sunlight made the sheets whiter, and the scruffy beard on his chin and cheeks gleam golden in the new morning light.

He opened his eyes as she massaged him to a full erection. "Will it be like this every morning, Marcy?"

She nodded her head. "I promise."

He touched her cheek with his fingertips. "You happy?"

"Never happier."

Lucas inhaled, rolled on top of her, spreading her thighs with his knees. "Every morning, then," he whispered and bit her ear lobe. He kissed her ear, sending an erotic zing down her spine.

"Every morning. Night too. I'm in for it, the whole way," she heard herself say.

She was looking for some hesitation on his part, some indication she'd gone round the bend faster than he had. Was he uncomfortable with the intensity between them that had started nearly from the moment they met?

He was bending down, watching her.

"What? Something wrong, Lucas?"

"Not at all." He pressed his cock against her opening, waiting for her to make the next move.

Marcy watched his eyes change as she grabbed his cheeks and pulled him deep inside her. It began to build an intense session that left them both wrung out and gasping for air.

"I have something for you," he said when she woke up. He was sitting across the bedroom in an overstuffed chair, still deliciously naked.

"Well I thought you already brought something. And then something else, and then another one, and so on. So get over here and give it to me," she laughed back at him.

He jumped back into bed, his long warm body lying against hers. He held her hand up, kissed each finger, inserting them one by one into his mouth. When her fourth finger came out, it was wearing a ring. It was a beautiful dark ruby in an antique setting.

"Belonged to my mom. I want you to have it."

"It's beautiful, Lucas. Thank you." She kissed him, then examined the ring again.

"I asked you once, and you said yes. Marry me, Marcy. Say yes again."

"On one condition."

"Shoot."

"Ask me every day. Ask me to marry you over and over again. I promise, the answer will always be yes."

"Done deal."

"But Lucas, we still have the same problem."

"Problem? What problem?"

"You gotta get divorced first, my love."

The End

SEAL BROTHERHOOD SERIES

Accidental SEAL (Book 1)
Fallen SEAL Legacy (Book 2)
SEAL Under Covers (Book 3)
SEAL The Deal (Book 4)
Cruisin' For A SEAL (Book 5)
SEAL My Destiny (Book 6)
SEAL Of My Heart (Book 7)

BAD BOYS OF SEAL TEAM 3

SEAL's Promise (Book 1)
SEAL My Home (Book 2)
SEAL's Code (Book 3)

BAND OF BACHELORS

Lucas (Book 1)
Alex (Book 2)

TRUE BLUE SEALS

True Navy Blue (prequel to Zak)
Zak (Book 1)

NOVELLAS

SEAL Encounter
SEAL Endeavor
True Navy Blue (prequel to Zak)
Fredo's Secret
Nashville SEAL

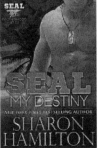

BAD BOYS
OF SEAL TEAM 3

BOOK 1

BOOK 2

BOOK 3

BAND OF BACHELORS

BOOK 1

BOOK 2

PREQUEL TO ZAK

BOOK 1

**TRUE BLUE
SEALS**

SEAL
NOVELLAS

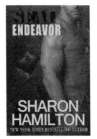

Golden Vampires
OF TUSCANY

BOOK 1   BOOK 2

THE GUARDIANS

BOOK 1   BOOK 2   BOOK 3

ABOUT THE AUTHOR

Sharon's award-winning spicy Navy SEAL stories in the SEAL Brotherhood series, have consistently made best sellers lists and review sites. Her characters follow a sometimes rocky road to redemption through passion and true love.

Her Golden Vampires of Tuscany are not like any vamps you've read before, since they don't go to ground and can walk around in the full light of the sun.

Her Guardian Angels struggle with the human charges they are sent to save, often escaping their vanilla world of Heaven for the brief human one. You won't find any of these beings in any Sunday school class.

She lives in Sonoma County, California with her husband, and two Dobermans. A lifelong organic gardener, when she's not writing, she's getting verra verra dirty in the mud, or wandering Farmer's Markets looking for new Heirloom varieties of vegetables and flowers.